LOSING A HERO

HOT HERO SERIES BOOK THREE

HANNAH BLAKE

Credits
Editing and proofread: Pam Gonzales @Love2readromance
Formatting: Author's Own
Cover: Author's Own

✳ Created with Vellum

For Karen and Angela. You both deserve a lifetime of happy ever afters.

PROLOGUE

Gabe

"You're not like any other guy I've ever met, Gabe," she says simply as she stacks up another line of cocaine.

"Some might say that's a good thing," I reply, wondering when her doing drugs became an acceptable part of our Saturday nights.

"You got a £20?"

"No. You need to stop shovelling that shit up your nose."

"And you need to stop being such a bore."

"You don't need it, we could just order takeout and watch a movie like old times," I almost plead with her.

She opens her purse, emptying the contents of it on the coffee table and scrambles around to find a bank note. When she finds one, I watch her roll it and sniff the neat line of white powder up in one go.

"I'm sorry," she says, looking up at me, and I notice the pupils of her usually pretty blue eyes have shrunk to little pinpoints. Her sparkly eyes were one of the things that first attracted me to her, that and her smile. Both of which I didn't see much of anymore.

The smiles, a tight, frowning line, and the sparkles have dulled over time, like a torch slowly running out of battery.

"I didn't mean to say you're a bore," she explains, her expression softening. "Things have been really hectic with the new series coming out. I've missed you. It gets lonely on set every day."

"You didn't look lonely in those photos of you and Chad," I point out.

"Awww, is my boy jealous? You're even sexier when you're jealous."

"I'm not jealous, I trust you. I'm just pissed you were out partying with Chad, when you could have been at home with me."

"Okay, I get it. I'm a screw up. But I'm here now," she soothes, running her freshly painted fingertips up her leg. She pauses when she reaches the edge of her black silk dressing gown, and seductively pushes the fabric upwards to reveal the top of her thigh. My eyes trace the newly revealed crease down to her needy pussy, and my cock twitches in my pants at the sight.

She sniffs to inhale the last few white specks of powder from her nose, and wipes it clean with her hand before looking back at me with her come-to-bed-with-me pout.

Usually, I would be straight over there, undressing her and taking what's mine, but that's just it. She doesn't feel like mine anymore. I glance around the room at the life we've built together, a world of lies. We were faking it. Both clinging onto something that was dead and gone, and for the first time when she attempted to make everything right by fucking me, I didn't want her. I didn't want any of this shit anymore. I need more, I need something real.

"I'm done, Ange. I think we both know this isn't working."

"Of course it's working, stop overthinking things and get over here. I need you."

"No, you don't. You don't need anything anymore, except drugs, alcohol and parties."

"Jesus, baby, I know I haven't been around much lately, but it doesn't mean I don't need you. You're probably the only real thing in my life nowadays."

"It's too late. I'm sick of constantly picking up the pieces of your fucked-up life."

"What are you trying to say, Gabe? You've fallen out of love with me?"

I take in her sulky pout, but notice there's more anger in her tone than upset. She's equally as over me as I am her, she just doesn't want to admit it.

"I'm done, Angela."

"You can't just break up with me." I smile as her voice goes high pitched, like me breaking up with her is the most unreasonable thing to ever happen. To a woman who is surrounded by people who are paid to say yes to her, it probably is.

"Why not?" I ask, my voice as calm as I feel. For me, this relationship ended a long time ago, and I've made peace with my decision to walk away. Angela wasn't the sweet girl I'd hung out with in college. She was a crazy successful actress, and a secret drug addict. The lifestyle suited her, I'd given up believing she wanted something different. She had gone her way, and I'd gone mine, but somehow, we'd kept the relationship going. Maybe for the sex, or for the loyalty I felt to look out for her. But after nights of arguments or worrying about where she was, what she was doing and who she was doing it with, I've realised it's no longer worth it. There's nothing left between us anymore.

"Because I'm pregnant," she replies with a sickening smile on her face that knocks me to my stomach.

Her words shake me to the core, and she relaxes back into the sofa, knowing that she's got me.

CHAPTER 1

Evelyn

I wriggle my fingers a little before settling them back around his and take in the sight of our hands intertwined. Trying to imagine this was my everyday normal, I snuggle deeper into him and watch his perfect face as he sleeps. My body is relaxed and my mind at ease because for a weekend, a whole beautiful weekend, my husband is home. It wasn't the life I thought we'd have. Him joining the army had come out of nowhere and knocked every plan I had for us out into space. But I've learned that plans don't matter in the long run, not when you're with the one you love. Suddenly everything that mattered becomes unimportant in comparison to what your other half wants or needs.

Leaving me wasn't what Marshall had wanted, but I understood that as hard as it is, the army is in his blood. It's become his life, more than either of us could have ever imagined, and with every piece of me, I will keep fighting as hard as I can to not resent his choice.

His dark eyelashes flicker, and I'm met with the bluest of blue eyes looking back at me.

"Come here, you," he says, and I snuggle into him so our torsos are touching. "Closer," he whispers, his voice gravelly from just waking up.

"Like this?" I tease, throwing my leg over his and pressing my most private part up against his thigh.

He arches an eyebrow at me playfully before ordering again, "No, even closer." He pulls my whole body on top of his in one easy move so I'm staring down at him, my boobs squished against his naked chest, and my nipples swell instantly in response to the touch. "You'll never get close enough, Mrs. Embers. It doesn't matter if you're this close," he squeezes my ass cheeks, pushing my groin down into him, "or a thousand miles away. You're always in here. Don't ever forget it." He takes my fingertips and presses them to his lips, kissing them before placing them over his heavily beating heart.

"Where are you?" he asks in the same way he always has."

"Right here," I reply.

"Right where?" he whispers on a smile.

"In your heart."

"In my fucking DNA," he says, sliding a steady hand over my naked cheeks and up to my hips before pulling me onto him.

It's the first weekend he's been home in months, and the thousandth time he's pulled me onto him since he walked through the door last night. Every kiss, every touch, making up for all the lost time. His fingers work my body relentlessly, over and over, sending me into a blissful state of ecstasy.

This is more than making love.

This is home.

I rotate my hips, and his buck up in pleasure as his lips take my mouth again in the sexiest of kisses, our tongues licking and sucking every possible inch of each other's mouths. We don't break for air, him thrusting hard underneath me, and me pushing back in sync to let him hit my deepest spot every single time. When the pressure, the desire, the need becomes too much, I let go, and he moans out my name into my mouth.

"Evie," his muffled sound echoes through my core. As we ride out our orgasms, our lips finally part, and he pulls me back down towards his thick toned chest. "I love you, Evie. I love you so much," he pants out breathlessly.

"I love you too, Marshall. I've missed you," I admit, and the powerful blissful feeling of actually having him here, holding me in his arms, overwhelms me.

"Don't. Please don't cry, Evie."

I can't respond, the thick lump in my throat silences me, and instead, I close my eyes and rest my head against his chest, inhaling the heavenly smell of him.

"Try not to think about it," his gravelly voice almost pleads. He's asking the impossible, and he knows it. We are both aware that we are on borrowed time, and when Monday comes, he will disappear again. This time to the place I've been dreading most of all. Afghanistan. I knew as soon as the twin towers in America were attacked, that he'd be called upon. A sinking feeling had hit me straight in the gut when I'd saw the news on CNN, and it hadn't really gone away ever since.

"I'm trying," I reply, honestly. "Are you gonna let me go long enough to make you breakfast, at least?" I smile at him, lifting the mood.

"Now, there's an offer you know I won't refuse," he replies.

As I head to the kitchen to make his favourite sausage and egg on toast, I can't help but smile as I think back to the wedding vows we made, just a few months ago.

"Evelyn Embers, I loved you before I even knew what it meant to love someone. You are my other half and mean the world to me. Without you, I can't breathe. Be my wife, and I promise that I will spend the rest of our future making you happy, protecting you and loving you like, I always have."

I had simply nodded my head, unable to find my voice or stop the tears from rolling down my cheeks.

"Yes," I replied. *"Yes, Yes, Yes!"* He had squeezed my hand tightly in excitement. I remember taking a deep breath, and slowly exhaling in

an attempt to dislodge the lump in my throat, so I could say what I wanted to say to him.

"Marshall Embers, I promise to love you every day of my life. You make me smile every time I am near you. I can't wait to share all of my firsts with you. You are my best friend. I will try to be a good wife to you, even if I don't really know what that means yet. I will even cook for you! Most of all, I will be loyal to you, and let you follow your heart wherever it takes you because I believe in you and everything you stand for so. What do you say?"

"Yes. I say yes to all of it. Even the goddamn cooking!"

Serving up the food with extra ketchup, just the way he likes it, I add a cup of tea to the tray, and carefully carry it upstairs to him.

"Breakfast in bed." He smiles smugly as I enter the room. "What in the world did I do to deserve you, Evie?"

I climb onto the bed next to him, tucking my legs back under the cotton sheets and make contact once again. Whenever he's home, our bodies are always connected like that, neither of us can get enough of the other.

We grow quiet as we eat, and I revel in the normality of the morning. This start to the day, is everything I want in life. Him being here, us together, I need this. I try my hardest to savour every minute knowing that he'll soon be gone, and this memory will be locked safely into my mind's treasury box with all of the others. In my dreams, I'd dream of him, and on those lonely mornings when I wake up alone, it would be this moment, him dropping crumbs on the bed and wiping ketchup from his chin, that will get me through the day without him.

"What have you got planned for us today? Please, tell me we're staying put?" he asks, interrupting my thoughts.

"Not quite." I smile. "We're going to see your family, of course."

"Ugh." He lets out a heavy groan, and I scowl at him.

"Don't be like that, everyone's missed you."

"It's not my family I mind seeing, but I know what that means."

"I did say we'd pop into my parents too, but we don't have to stay long," I reassure him. A familiar sinking feeling furling in my stomach at the mention of my parents. In the four months that had passed since we got married, my relationship with my parents has become increasingly strained. They still can't get over the fact that I married him as soon as I'd turned eighteen.

I am still mad at them for not letting us marry when I'd first asked them, just after prom night, when he'd proposed.

My mind darts back to the stupid discussion we'd had with both sets of parents around the table.

Pulling out my carefully folded piece of paper, I'd been shaking like a leaf when I announced that I wanted to share something with everyone. I'd read it out confidently, determined not to let my nerves get the better of me.

REASONS *I* WANT *to marry Marshall.*

1. *I love him.*

IT WAS an obvious place to start, but nevertheless it was the truth, and it felt like a good jumping off point. My dad had just glared at me, so I'd made sure I added, "Not in the high school sweetheart kind of way. In the proper way, the same way my parents love each other.

HE'D VISIBLY WINCED at my words, and his stern expression told me he'd already rebuked the idea that Marshall and I could ever have something as serious as what he had with mum.

2. *I can't imagine a life without him.*

. . .

"It has always only ever been Marshall for me. I think everyone knows that. I have loved him since before I even understood it, and I will never, could never, imagine a life without him."

3. "We get the picture, Evelyn." My dad had interrupted. "But it's not all that easy. You're both only sixteen years old."

"Let her finish, dad," Marshall had commanded, his eyes shining with pride and giving me the strength to continue against both of our parents' wishes.

3. I don't want to waste any time.

We are not like other couples. Marshall will be going into the army soon, and our time together will be limited. We don't have any to waste. I don't want him out in some foreign country with just a girlfriend. I want him to be able to say he has a wife back home. People will respect our relationship a lot more if we are married, and we deserve to be taken seriously."

It was the truth, but they hadn't cared, and so we'd waited patiently for two whole years, until we were old enough to marry without their consent. My relationship with my mum had never quite been the same since that day. She wasn't used to saying no to me, but then, I wasn't used to asking for anything from them. Dad's firm and resounding 'no' was like a thick wedge driving us further apart. By the time my wedding had came around, he was barely speaking to me at all. He walked me down the aisle, but the only look in his eye when we reached Marshall, was disappointment. He'd explained the night before, for the thousandth time, that I was throwing my life away, and that even at eighteen, I was far too young to know what I wanted for the rest of my life. Mum was a little more understanding, but remained dutiful to my father, and agreed that he had a point. She was stuck in the middle, and for the first time, the three musketeers, as we called ourselves, were divided. Dad hadn't even let Marshall stay at the house, and I resented him for trying to keep us separate.

"Have you seen much of them since I've been gone, Evie?" Marshall asks with interest.

"Not really, things have been much the same. No worse." I shrug.

"But no better either," he adds, understanding the complex relationship I now have with my parents. He lived with the consequences every bit as much as I did.

Luckily, his parents had been completely supportive of us. During the final year in high school, they'd let me stay over every weekend, so we hadn't been completely starved of time to be intimate.

Having our own place was something we had both dreamed of, and his parents had bought the house for us as a wedding gift. They said they were investing in a property anyway, but we all knew they were doing this for us, and we loved them dearly for it.

They wouldn't accept any rent from us, and their generosity allowed us to buy a few things to make it homely. Marshall earned a fair wage as a soldier. Enough to afford us a comfortable life. I had fallen lucky with my job at Betty's Blooms.

Tanya, my manager, had taken me on straight after my apprenticeship finished, and I loved working alongside her. The wages weren't great, but I got to work with flowers every day and had an endless supply of fresh cut orchids for my dining table.

"Time to get up," I announce, kissing him one more time before jumping back up off the bed and wriggling into my skinny jeans.

He groans as he goes about his business, but follows my lead, and reluctantly begins to get dressed. I catch sight of his naked back and thick shoulder muscles as he reaches up to lift a red t-shirt over his head.

Damn, my man is sexy. Every single muscle is defined to the maximum, and I feel overwhelmed with pride at his strength. I'll bet he's the best soldier the British Army has ever had.

"You keep staring at me like that, and we will be straight back in bed, Evie."

I bite my lip and feign in embarrassment at being caught drooling over him. "You're my husband, remember? That means I get to stare at you as often as like.

Marshall

HER HUSBAND. She said it so naturally, and I fucking loved hearing it. I didn't think I had forgotten how much I love her, but when we are together, our connection blows my mind. I'm proud that she's coping without me, I always knew she was a strong woman. It's one of the things I love most about her. She's held it all together so well while I've been gone, and has turned our house into a home. "Are you happy, Evie?" I ask, my concerns escaping my thoughts.

"Of course. You're here. I'm the luckiest girl in the world," she replies. I don't ask out loud, I don't want to damper her mood, but I can't help thinking, *what about when I'm gone.* The thought of her being lonely or unhappy kills me. That's why I'd asked Candice to keep an eye out for her. My big sister was finally good for something other than teasing the crap out of me.

"You seen much of Candy?" I ask.

"Yeah, she's been popping in all the time after work. We just had takeout together the other day."

"I wondered why my ears are burning," I joke.

"You do realise we have a lot more to talk about than just you, right?"

"Nah, I'll bet one hundred quids I'm all you two speak about, especially Candice. I'll bet she's all jealous that I'm off travelling, when she's always been a bit of an explorer."

"She's just fine right here, thank you. Don't you dare be encouraging her to leave me behind too, or I might just have to sign up for the army myself."

"Don't even joke about that," I warn her. There was no way in hell

I'd ever let her put herself in danger. It had been one of my reasons for signing up. To keep her safe. To keep us all safe, my family, my country, I wanted to do everything I can to protect them all.

"Don't worry, I'm not planning on going anywhere," she reassures me.

"Good, I wouldn't let you even if you were."

We head downstairs and outside, before jumping into Evie's white Kia. I have to fold my knees up to my elbows to be able to fit inside, but it was all she needed, as she was usually the only one using it.

She giggles at the sight of me all squished up behind the wheel, and I arch an eyebrow at her playfully, turning her giggle into a full-blown laugh.

"Is my sister home this weekend?"

"Yeah, she said she will be in. She's missed you too, even if she'd never admit it."

"I can't wait to see everyone. When I'm away it feels like forever, but then when I'm back, it's like I never left."

"That's because it's home," she says simply in her sweet soft voice that follows me wherever I go.

She gazes out of the window, daydreaming for most of the short drive through Bourton-on-the-Water, to my parents' house. I wave as we pass the postman, the same postman that has delivered mail to my family for as long as I can remember. I swear, time stands still in this place. It doesn't take long to reach my childhood home and as soon as we do, I see my Mum and Dad waiting outside, pottering in the garden. Both pretending to be busy, and both clearly excited and waiting for me to arrive. Mum throws herself at me, as I wangle my way out of the stupid tiny car. She barely reaches my chest, and I tower over her, something my dad's always teased her about.

"You've grown!" she exclaims.

Mum it's only been a few months. I think you'll find you've always been that short." She slaps me and then hugs me again, and we all laugh.

"I've missed you, son," my dad greets me with a brief man hug, pounding a fist into my back as he pulls me in.

"You, too Dad, has Mum been causing you grief while I've been gone?"

"Of course, son. That's what she does best."

"Hey you two," Mum warns us playfully. "No homemade sconces for either of you, if you carry on."

"Did somebody say homemade scones?" Candice appears in the doorway and runs over to greet Evelyn, before turning her attention to me.

"Still on for that spin class?" I hear her ask my wife, who nods in reply before my sis turns her attention to me.

"Brother."

"Sister," I reply, and we both grin at our weird, but familiar, greeting towards each other.

"Let's go inside. I want to hear all about everything," my mum says, ushering everyone inside where there's a colossal pile of freshly baked scones, jams, cream and her best teapot full of piping hot tea.

We spend a good few hours with my family, catching up on the months we'd lost. Dad's high cholesterol still bothering Mum. Although it's clearly not worrying him, as he shovels down copious amounts of clotted cream. I leave feeling happy that Evie is as much part of the family as Candice and I, and my parents have clearly taken her under their wing. It's relieving to know she has people looking out for her when I'm not around.

The drive to Evie's parent's place doesn't take long, but it feels like forever as the tension builds between us all the way there. It's a very different greeting when we reach her childhood home. She tentatively knocks on the door and awaits one of her parents to answer. Of course, it's her Mum that does, and she smiles an awkward smile, first to me, then to Evie.

"Marshall's home for the weekend, so we thought we'd pop in and see you both."

"Great, come on in," she says. "Your dad will be pleased."

It was a lie, and all three of us knew it. We follow her inside and are seated in the living room, surrounded by photos of Evie as a toddler. I guess they found it difficult to accept that one day she'd grow up. I sit quietly while Evie and her mum catch up, and the two women visibly appear to relax more once they've got chatting. Evie's left her bouncing chestnut locks loose, and they are swaying and cascading over her shoulders as she talks. She's so fucking beautiful. Sometimes I forget how much so, and then I see her like this. Natural, no makeup, jeans and a plain black tank top. She knocks me off my feet. My hand falls to my wedding ring, and I give it a twist, thinking how lucky I am that she married me. She didn't even hesitate when I'd asked her that night at prom. Her hair had been swept up then, the pink corsage I'd given her, tied neatly around her wrist.

We'd gone outside to get some air, and I'd danced with her, the music just barely audible from the dance hall behind us.

"I want you to know that however far we travel apart, whatever bad stuff happens to us, I'm always gonna love you like this, Evie. You're the only girl for me." She'd leaned in closer, her scent of fruity bubble gum enveloping me. The words had come easily, without a single thought in my head. "Marry me."

"What did you just say?"

"You know exactly what I said, Evie. *Marry me*." I punched the words out slowly so the pronunciation was crystal clear. Her eyes had shined bright green as she beamed up at me.

"I can't marry you just like that." She clicked her fingers to make the point.

"So, you're saying no, then?" I had tried not to look as bruised as I felt.

"Are you serious right now, Marshy? Quit foolin' around." She threw a playful punch in my direction, which I caught her balled first in my palm. I wrapped my fingers around hers, pulling her close, so we were face to face, nose to nose, breathing each other's air.

"Evie, you're the best thing about my life, and the only girl I'll ever love. I want the world to know how serious we are, so that's why I'm asking you. Marry me." Her mouth had opened to reply, but nothing came out. She just looked at me blankly, and I noticed a tear slide down her cheek, and her eyes quickly fill with more. Just as I was about to ask if she's okay, she nodded her head at me.

"Yes?" I had grinned at her as a smile spread across her pretty features, her lips looking more kissable than ever. "Is that a yes I see?"

"Yes." She giggled. "Yes. I'll marry you. You know I'll marry you. Marshall. I'd marry you tomorrow. You're the only one I could ever give my forever to."

"Tomorrow, hey?"

"Tomorrow." She nodded before I covered her mouth with my own, our tongues sliding together in a needy kiss that confirmed she really would marry me tomorrow.

That had been the start of the two-year battle with her parents. A battle where there were no winners, only stress and irreparable cracks in relationships.

Her father enters the room, and the atmosphere becomes palpable. I stand and shake his hand, needing to try and make this better for Evie. It was hard to believe how close they had all been when we were growing up. Her parents even used to like me. They'd sit alongside my folks and cheer me on at football games, and invite me around for Sunday roast dinners. But that was before their only daughter had wanted to marry when she was barely out of high school.

"Marshall. Evelyn. It's good to see you both."

"It's good to see you too, Dad." She flashes him a warm but reserved smile. It's polite, but I notice it doesn't reach her eyes.

"I'll put the kettle on, and you can tell your dad all about your new job," her mum says, before disappearing into the kitchen, leaving the three of us sitting there.

"So, the job's going really well, Dad. Tanya, my boss, is great, and we've been really busy with all the summer weddings."

"I'm pleased you have found a decent job. Something to keep you busy is always good."

"But?" she replies, knowing her dad all too well.

"It's a bit late for but's, Evelyn. You know my thoughts on your… situation." She immediately tenses up at his response, and I brace myself, knowing this is one war I can't protect her from.

"What situation? You mean my marriage, Dad. Or my career, or just my whole fucking life?" she shouts, flying off the handle.

"Don't put words in my mouth, young lady. Have some respect for where you are and who you are speaking to."

Well, that does it. Evie jumps to her feet, once again ready to fight the battle that should have been left in the past.

"Respect. Don't tell me about respect, Dad. Did you have any? No! Where was your respect for me and my choices? I told you how much being married meant to me, how much being with Marshall meant to me."

Damn, I hate seeing her so emotional, and I can tell by the way her voice cracks that she's nearing tears. Her mum bursts through the door with a fresh tray of tea, in an attempt to diffuse another verbal bomb from exploding.

"Darling, you're married now. All's well that ends well, let's let bygones be bygones. You know how much I can't stand all this… This, confrontation."

"It's not that I won't leave it, Mum. It's the fact that Dad still disapproves of my marriage. Actually, scrap that. He casts shade on my whole bloody life. I don't deserve it. Marshall is a good, kind man, who loves me. He's been there for me through thick and thin. You both know that, and now, just because of his career choice, you both treat me like I'm…"

Her voice trails off, and my girl begins to cry. The sight and sound of it fucking kills me, the same way it did when she fell out with her best friend in the last year of high school. Except, they'd kissed and made up after just a few days. Somehow, I have a feeling it's going to be a much longer journey until she makes up with her parents.

Mrs. Embers turns to her husband and tries to soothe his obvious anger.

"Don't fuss over me, I'm fine. I just won't have my own daughter talk to me like that. I walked her down the aisle, gave her away, despite not wanting to, or thinking what's best for her, and all that's not enough. Now she wants me to give her my approval. You all want to pretend like this is going to have a happy ended? Go ahead, but you need to wake up and smell the coffee. She's eighteen years old, she's still a goddamn child, for all intents and purposes. She's given her whole life up for him. She'll never have a normal family. He will always be away on some mission. Which means that she will always be left on her own. Christmases alone. Birthdays alone. She's signed herself up for a life of misery, and you're just as bad for encouraging it from the very start."

He ends his tirade and turns his attention from his wife, back to the two of us. The full realisation of his words, and the fact that we are sitting right here, hits him. He isn't a bad man, bad tempered maybe, but I refrain from retaliating, as it would only cause more unnecessary upset for Evie.

"I'm going. We didn't come around for this, and we won't be coming back until you get some respect for me and my *situation*." She spits the word out angrily before storming out, and I pass Mrs. Embers a respectful half smile as I follow her.

She barely speaks on the ride back home and I leave her with her thoughts, squeezing her leg as I control the wheel with one hand. When we reach the house a few minutes later, I open her door to help her out and she buckles into heavy sobs. I take her into my arms and usher her inside where I can hold her properly.

"It won't always be like this," I murmur, trying to reassure her. "It'll get easier as time goes on. Once your dad sees that you're coping, and that your happy, he will soon come around."

CHAPTER 2

Evelyn

I wipe my tears away, determined not to let them wreck the little time we have together. It was my own stupid mistake for taking him over there. I should have known my stubborn dad would still be just as annoyed at me now, as he was the night before my wedding day.

"I told you we should have stayed in bed all day," he says, breaking the tension and causing me to smile, in spite of my tears.

"I really should have listened to you," I agree.

"Shall we start the day again?"

"Sure," I reply without any need for persuasion. My body is craving his touch, the only thing that could ever shift my black mood is one of his infamous cuddles. He takes my hand and leads me up the stairs, asking if I'm okay, but knowing I'm not.

We undress ourselves quickly and jump beneath the duvet stark naked, our skin instantly connecting, closely followed by our lips. Our love for each other seeps out of every pore as he runs his fingertips up the back of my neck and into my hair. He breaks our kiss, keeping his face close to mine, our lips almost touching.

But he doesn't kiss me, instead he whispers, "Chick flick?" A smile spreads across my face, he knows me better than I know myself at times.

"Perfection," I reply, and he grabs the remote from the side of the bed, flicking on the TV.

I snuggle into him, and we settle into watching my all-time favourite Twilight movie. We've watched it together countless times, but seeing Robert Patterson kiss Bella for the first time never gets old. He snuggles me up and all the anger towards my parents is calmed. We watch the whole movie, barely saying a word to each other, him mimicking some of the cheesy lines and making me giggle.

"I kinda wish you were a vampire." I sigh as the credits roll up.

"Coz' that's not weird at all," he jokes.

"I don't mean the pointy teeth, I mean the way he can just appear by her side whenever she needs him. You gotta admit that would be cool."

"It sure would," he replies, "are you hungry, I'm starving."

"Oh god, I'm so sorry. I'm a mess. I never get to cook for you, and now your home, and I'm making you watch chick movies and visit my parents' house. Let me fix you something up, whatever you fancy?"

"Stay where you are. I never get to look after you, either. How about you carry on with your Twilight binge, and I'll grab us something to eat."

"You're going to cook?"

"Don't sound so surprised, I have skills, you know?"

"Skills?"

"Okay, maybe that was exaggerating, but I can certainly manage a basic meal." He shrugs, pulling his boxer shorts on and grabbing his t-shirt from the floor.

"Basic sounds perfect," I reply, rolling over and messing with the remote until the next movie begins. I settle in and can hear him rustling about in the kitchen as I relax in bed. How the hell did I get so lucky?

He returns a short time later with a stack of bacon and an egg on toast, accompanied by a bottle of wine and a tube of our favourite barbecue flavoured Pringles.

"Wow, it's the perfect feast," I say as he puts the plates down on the bed. "My breath is going to smell so bad, you won't even want to kiss me after this," I warn him.

"I doubt that," he replies, shuffling back into bed beside me. He can't stand my addiction to chick flicks, but I love the fact that he puts up with them, knowing how happy they make me. By the time we are finished the bed and both of us are covered in crumbs, and neither of us care. This is us; messy, carefree and comfortable. We don't make love that night, we just fall asleep with the TV on, cuddled up to each other. Much of the next morning is spent the same way.

"We gotta move out of this bed." I laugh. "It really is a dump."

"Okay, I have something planned. You stay here and clean up a bit. I'll be back in half an hour."

"Where are you going?" I ask him, feeling disappointed that he wants to go somewhere without me when we have such little time together.

"You'll see later, it's a surprise."

"I love you, husband," I tell him, reaching up to kiss him goodbye. The word sounds so good and refreshing when I say it. I'm not sure the novelty will ever wear off.

He plants a soft kiss on my head, taking my chin in his hand and tilting my face up to meet his loving gaze.

"I love you too, wife." Following up the statement with another kiss, this one hotter and heavier, his lips crushing mine. "I won't be long, get yourself dressed," he instructs before disappearing, and I hear him close the front door behind him a few minutes later.

I'm reluctant to leave the comfort of my bed, not caring one bit about the crumbs and mess. I'd take this any day over lying here alone. The sheets smell like him, a thick masculine scent creeping up into the air as I shake off the duvet and begin to strip down the bedding.

After throwing my dressing gown around myself, I wrap every-thing into a huge bundle and take it downstairs, shoving it into the

washer and switching on the cycle. I grab a glass of water and dart
back up to the shower. Gathering my hair up on top of my head and
switching on the water, I let the water warm for a few minutes before
stepping into the bathtub. Our bathroom is tiny, so there's no space
for a real shower, just a hose over the bath taps, but it's enough. Our
home isn't fancy, big or glamorous, but it's ours, and I wouldn't
change it for the world.

Lathering my body in coconut body wash and rinsing it off again, I
allow myself to daydream about what my surprise might be. Marshall
has always loved treating me right. All the way through high school he
was always springing things on me.

We had even less money then, but he made sure that whatever
pocket money he did get, was spent on me. While the other lads were
all spending money buying cigarettes from kids in older year groups,
Marshall was busy buying me my favourite milkshakes to sip after
class. He would always be there, walking me home, watching movies
with me on weekends.

He was like my shadow, maybe that's why I feel so close to him
now. So, connected, even when he's sometimes miles away. I guess
that's how you know you've found your soul mate.

Switching off the power and wrapping myself in a bath towel, I pat
myself dry and tip toe over to the bedroom. We don't have a wardrobe
yet, just a set of drawers with our clothes neatly folded inside. Mine in
the top three and his in the bottom. It's gorgeous and sunny outside,
so I choose a cute white crop top with a denim pinafore dress.

MY PHONE BLEEPS with a message from him as I'm getting dressed.
*Stop trying to guess *annoyed face emoji**
I flip him my reply before shuffling into my trainers.
*I'm not *angel face emoji**
Another message quickly follows.
*Liar *laughing face emoji**

· · ·

It brings a smile to my face, and I finish up getting ready by letting my hair down and brushing it out. Just as I'm stuffing my keys, phone and lip balm into my leather rucksack, I hear Marshall letting himself back in downstairs.

"You ready, princess," he calls up to me.

I grab my bag and run to meet him, shouting back, "Ready."

He's waiting at the bottom of the stairs with a silly grin on his face and a huge wicker basket full of goodies.

"A picnic! I knew it, I love picnics!" I throw my arms around his neck and squeeze him tight.

"I know you do," he murmurs, squeezing me back and starts to walk towards the front door. I follow him out into the fresh warm air, and take the basket as he locks up behind us.

"Where did you get this thing?" I ask, lifting the basket slightly.

"My mum's. It's ancient, I think it was my grandma's, grandma's."

"It's gorgeous."

"I knew you'd like it, I spotted it in the kitchen yesterday and asked if we could borrow it."

"Which means you've been planning our picnic since yesterday, how did I not guess?"

"Maybe you don't know me as well as you think you do, wifey. I have plenty of hidden secrets, you know?"

"Yeah right." I roll my eyes, and we both laugh at the ridiculous notion.

There was nothing mysterious about my Marshall. It is one of the things I love most about him. He's as transparent as a sheet of glass, straight talking and always gives me his most honest opinion.

He takes the basket from me, and I don't need to ask where we're going. We follow the river, which is fuller than usual from the rain last week, and round the corner towards the cemetery.

It's not that we are a pair of gothic zombie worshippers, but this has always been our place. We quietly pass the tombstones, and follow the path around to the back of the church. Our willow tree looks just as pretty as ever, with the summer sun shining down on its bright green leaves. Marshall squeezes my hand, and we set about laying our checked picnic rug over the grass.

"It's good to be home." He sighs happily as we sit down on the rug a few minutes later.

"Definitely, this place never changes," I reply. Glancing around as memories of our teenage years flood back to me.

Marshall must be thinking the same thing as he asks, "Want to kiss like the first time?"

He doesn't need to ask twice, I climb over the picnic goodies and straddle him. Wrapping my fingers up in his short blonde hair, I kiss him like there's no tomorrow. His own kiss matches mine perfectly, taking me right back to the first time we had kissed right next to this spot, hidden under the branches of the willow tree. No one ever came here, except for on Sundays, but we'd sneak under the branches, and hide as if the whole world could see us. We were only eleven at the time. It was young, but we'd felt ready. The kiss had been awkward at first, neither of us had known what we were doing, but the strange feeling of his tongue in my mouth had made me feel closer to Marshall, and grown up in a way I hadn't before.

It had been some years later when we'd returned to the very same spot, and I'd lost my virginity to him. Over the years we always seemed to wind back up here, barefoot on the grass, just the two of us. It was quiet and peaceful, a world away from anyone and everyone, and being back here always brought about a feeling of serenity. I always knew I would marry Marshall, but being back here with him often felt like a dream rather than my reality.

His hands wrap around my waist as he kisses me, and I take in the sweet sensation of his mouth on mine. When we eventually break for air, he snuggles me into his chest, so I'm leaning back against him, and we tuck into our picnic.

"So, tell me everything. How have you really been getting on without me?" he asks as I bite into a cheese sandwich.

"I've been doing surprisingly okay. I miss you, of course, but I've been keeping really busy. I joined a new spin class."

"Now that's something I'd like to see," he says in a smug smile.

"Are you implying that I'm not in good shape, Mr. Embers?" I chastise him while holding a cream cake up to his mouth.

"Never." He smiles, taking a huge bite and making a mess over his face. He licks it up from around his mouth, and I finish up the tiny bit that's left.

"You've clearly been working out, your arms are huge," I comment, taking in his huge biceps that are tightly wrapped around me.

"Yeah, it's been pretty intense," he replies.

"Are you happy though, do you like it?"

"Evelyn, I love it. When I'm training, or out on the front line, it's like I'm alive. I just know it's what I am supposed to be doing, like a sixth sense or something."

My heart feels light but heavy all at the same time. Happy for him, that he gets to do a job that he loves so much and is so passionate about. Sad for me because it means I have to give more of him up than I want to. But this was the life I had chosen, against everybody's best advice, except from Marshall's of course. That's because he is the only one who understands our connection, the unbreakable bond that combines husband and wife, weaving a thread so intricately between them, that nothing life throws at them could ever untangle it.

"Tell me about your new job. I want to hear everything," he demands, pouring me a glass of sparkling white wine.

"It's really great, I actually love it. Tanya is so nice…"

"Who's Tanya?" he asks, cutting me off mid-sentence.

"She's my boss, remember? I did tell you about her. Anyway, she says that even though it's only temporary for now, if I keep working hard there's no reason why she won't offer me a permanent job, once summer is over."

"That's cool, can you see yourself working there long term? I mean, is that what you want to do?"

"At first, I wasn't sure whether I'd like it, but now, I have really fallen in love with it. The shop is always so busy, it takes my mind off missing you. Plus, I'm actually getting good at arranging the flowers. Tanya says I have a real eye for design."

"I'll bet, you've always been into arty shit like that. Remember your life drawing stage?"

I deplete into a fit of giggles at the memory of me making him hold still while I attempted to sketch him, sitting in my living room. He'd been carefully draped across the sofa, and was sitting stark naked when my mum had walked in on us. Her face had been an absolute picture and she turned so red she was almost purple. She'd shouted at me and screamed at Marshall to get out.

When he'd respectfully explained that he couldn't go yet, as he had no clothes on. It had been the death of both of us, and I'd laughed until tears were rolling down my cheeks.

It was still just as funny now, and from the way Marshall's laughing, I can tell he recalls the memory just as vividly.

As my laughter eventually subsides, I sigh happily and sag against him.

He lowers his head and speaks softly into my ear, "I love the way you laugh."

Something in the way his voice is low and gentle makes me turn around to face him, and when I do, I'm met with huge blue eyes full of lust and want.

"I love the way you look at me like that," I fire back, staring into them, wanting to lose myself in them completely. Needing him to take over my body, the same way he had all those summers ago when he'd taken me for the first time. It didn't feel any different. Even now that we're married my skin still prickles with goose bumps under the warm sensation of his touch. He brushes a strand of my hair away from my cheek, wrapping it around my ear so nothing is blocking his path to me.

"I love the way you kiss me." The sentence barely gets a chance to escape his lips before mine crash onto his and take his mouth for my own. Every touch, each teasing lick making up for all the months of not kissing him. His hands slide up my back expertly working my muscles, and I groan as they reach up to my shoulders. He massages them deeply, his fingers bringing every inch of my skin to life, and his tongue explores my mouth in hot, purposeful kisses.

"Come on," I manage to say as we break for air, and he doesn't say anything. There's no need for words, as he jumps to his feet and holds back the branches of our huge willow tree. We step underneath the draping branches just like we used to do as kids. Except this time, we're both definitely adults, and there is nothing childish about the look in his eyes right now.

"Hold on," he instructs me, before disappearing back outside, and reappearing a few moments later with our picnic blanket. He spreads it out on the ground, rids himself of his jeans before turning his attention back to me and I almost melt under his loaded stare.

Our bodies crash into each other's in a frenzied kiss, and in seconds I am straddling him on the ground. He's sitting upright, and I fit into his lap perfectly. His hands get to work on my back again, this time working their way up the inside of my dress, which is now hitched up around my waist. They travel all the way up my spine until he takes hold of my head and kisses me with everything he has.

I moan into his mouth to let him know it's not enough. It will never be enough, with Marshall I will always want more. I craved him whenever he is away from me, and when he was with me, my body demands it.

Releasing his grip, his hands fall to my waist, and he begins working my hips, rotating them slowly. My excitement building as I imagine how good he will feel when he is inside me.

Only the thin cotton of my knickers stands between us, and his fingers slip under the seam a few moments later, stimulating every part of me until each nerve is tingling with desire. My hips roll of their own accord, and he stretches the newly wet cotton to one side, working me until I'm almost at a breaking point.

"Marshall," I pant out.

My hands frantically release him from his boxer shorts, and his hardness stands to attention between us. I begin working him with my hands, pumping him up and down until he loses control of our kiss and lifts me up, lowering me onto him. I cry out, losing myself completely in the sheer pleasure of feeling the man I love rocking me back and forth, taking me for his own enjoyment, and in turn, giving me my own.

We ride out or orgasm in perfect sync with each other, and I can only let out a breathless happy sigh when we slow our pace, and he says, "I love you, Mrs. Embers."

There is no need to reply, he knows I feel exactly the same way.

CHAPTER 3

*A*fter cleaning up, packing away the picnic and heading home, we spend the rest of the day locked away from the world. I leave my phone on the kitchen table and don't even bother to check it all evening. Marshall does the same. The world can wait.

We watch a film of his choice this time, Hulk, and I jump right out of my skin at all the scary parts. He teases me for being such a girl, and I revel in every second of it. We cook pizza and pasta together and leave the dishes for some other time. Tonight's not about cleaning, or anything else that distracts me from being with my man.

As usual, when we are together, the time flies by, and before we know it, it's the middle of the night. I wake to the soft murmur of my name on his lips.

"Evie, you fell asleep, baby."

I jump up, instantly mad at myself for wasting precious time we could have spent together.

"I'm sorry, I must have been… "

"Exhausted," he says, lifting me up and carrying me up the stairs in his huge solid arms. "Come on, let's get you to bed."

"What time is it?" I ask, still feeling groggy from being woken up.

"Almost three." I groan loudly and he pulls me in a little tighter.

"We only have a couple of hours, I don't want to waste them."

"We won't, I promise, but I'm tired too. Let's get some sleep."

We reach the bedroom, and he places me down on the bed before climbing in next to me and snuggling me up tight. I kiss him sleepily, and I don't sleep much after that. He crashes out within just a few minutes, and I lie awake, watching him breathe. He looks so peaceful, his blonde locks swept back off his smooth forehead and his full lips slightly parted. Unashamedly, I stretch across and grab my iPad from the top of my cosmetics drawers, taking a quick picture of him. He flinches a little, but doesn't wake up, and I quickly set the iPad aside and snuggle back into him.

I must eventually doze off as I wake to the sound of Marshall getting dressed. I've barely opened my eyes when he says, "We gotta go, wifey. We're running late."

Not ready to face the day, especially when I know what's coming, I roll back over and groan loudly.

"No, seriously. My flight leaves in two hours, and we've not even left yet."

"Shit, shit… shit," I mumble, jumping up and grabbing my trusted Victoria Secret jogging bottoms. I throw on a vest top and mismatched hoodie in the rush.

A few minutes later we're on our way to the airport. Marshall drives, he's better at dodging traffic and more ruthless than me on the roads. Despite his expert manoeuvring of the gridlocked motorway, we still only reach the airport just in time.

"Jesus, you've got twenty minutes to clear security and catch your flight."

"Easy." He grins, throwing his arms around me.

"Go." I push him away. "There's no time."

"Evie," he says as he pulls me back in and plants one last kiss on my lips.

"I know, I love you, too," I reply as he runs to the security gate.

"I love you more," he mouths back at me, before disappearing through bag checks and running towards the gate.

"Impossible," I say to myself quietly. I watch his rucksack and the back of his head until it's vanished completely, and I glance around suddenly feeling a little self-conscious. A heavy sigh escapes my lips and I pull the cuffs of my hoodie over my hands and wrap my arms around myself. *He's gone.*

The huge void hits me when I climb back into the empty car where we'd just sat, and I grab my phone as it beeps from the glove box.

MISS YOU ALREADY, *I'll write u* *red rose emoji*

I PRESS the buttons into the phone quickly, wanting him to get my reply before his plane takes off.

SAME. *Be careful* *two kiss emoji's*

SOME IMPATIENT IDIOT beeps at me, wanting to take my parking space. It's probably for the best, as it makes me pull off quickly rather than having a little cry, which is what I feel like doing.

Knowing the day would hit me hard, I try to keep busy, and once I've cleaned the whole house top to bottom, I change into my gym clothes and head to the gym to take all my frustration out on the treadmill. Sticking my headphones in, I blast the music out and lose myself in it. I set the pace to high and run until I can't think about anything other than catching my breath, and by the time my thirty minutes are up, I feel much better than when it began.

The day feels long without him, and the next day, even longer still. At least I have my job with Tanya to keep me busy, so I'm not completely lost. The days all blur into one, and finding ways to not miss Marshall becomes my new hobby of choice. I have my hair done, my nails done and then redone, I work late, wake early and fill every minute with anything I can to convince myself I'm not waiting around for him.

A full week passes before my first letter arrives, and I tear open the envelope devouring the words as quickly as possible before rereading it to take in what it actually says.

EVELYN,

Stop worrying about me. I know you will be, but you don't need to.

Serge says a few of us will be able to come home for Christmas, so keep your fingers crossed! It's tough out here, I might not be able to write as many letters for a while, but I'll call you when I can. Make sure you reach out to your parents, they will come around eventually, and you will need them at some point.

You're in my every thought.

Love you,

Marshall

TOUGH. I focus on the single word and wonder what it hides which is how bad things really are in Afghan and what part my husband is playing out there. The rest of his handwriting all blurs into one as tears fill up in my eyes. The emotions of the last few weeks without him come spilling out. Until now, my biggest fear had been the feeling of loneliness without him. Now, I have a whole fresh reason to worry, and instinctively, I have a really nasty gut feeling about things.

Of course, I completely ignore the advice he gave me before he left and flick on the news, curling up on the sofa and locking my eyes to the screen. Coverage of the war on Afghan has faded from the main tv channels, but CNN is still reporting on recent updates. The war on terror that had seemed so far away and removed from my life up until today, suddenly got real.

I watched the images of soldiers flashing up on the screen, a war-torn country in the background. It's hard to imagine my Marshall out there, amongst the chaos, but that's my reality now.

Instead of doing what I feel like doing, holing myself at home so I can watch CNN as much as I want to and wait for my next letter from him to arrive, I decide that I have to try to find a sense of normality for myself, while he is away.

It's a difficult transition to have him there one minute and gone the next. When he's home, it's as though I'm a unicorn riding a rainbow, and when he's gone, I'm standing under a massive storm cloud getting rained on.

I hadn't counted on it being so difficult and it's hard to imagine my life is going to be like this for a long time to come. Even with the massive crash in my mood now that he's gone, it's worth every inch of it.

The letter plays on my mind for the rest of the afternoon, and I'm in a constant state of anticipation, waiting for the next one to arrive. For the next few days I check the post as soon as I get home, and am disappointed to receive nothing from him. His mobile number does nothing when I ring it, he's obviously had no signal for a while. Days turn into weeks, and it's the longest time I've ever gone without hearing anything from him.

I don't visit my parents, I'm still angry at them for trying to cause a divide between Marshall and I. It should be them that reaches out to me after their shitty behaviour, not the other way around.

Tanya keeps to her promise, offering me a full-time job at Betty's Blooms. I absolutely love working alongside her, and before I know it, a couple of months have passed by when I finally hear from Marshall. I want to be mad at him, I had planned to give him a piece of my mind when I finally got the chance to speak to him. Instead, when I see his name flash up on my phone, I pick it up with trembling hands and can barely say anything at all.

"Evie, it's me, how are you?"

It's me. Like I didn't know who it was. Like I hadn't been imaging the gravelly tone of his voice since the last time we spoke.

"Evie, are you there?"

Swallowing the lump in my throat, I have to physically force myself to speak from underneath the tidal wave of relief that's washed over me.

"I'm here. I'm okay, are you okay?"

"I'm good. It's rough at the minute, there's hardly any, signal so I don't know when I'll be able to call you back."

"I've missed you."

"Jesus, Evie, I've missed you so fucking much. You're all that's keeping me going. The thought of you in my arms keeps me from going bat shit crazy without you."

His words come tumbling out quickly, and a smile passes my lips as I realise just how badly he's missed me.

"I love you, the months will fly by."

"What have you been up to? Tell me something normal, I need to hear it."

My mind is blank, and I want to somehow dive into the telephone line and be with him.

"Tanya's given me a job, so I'm technically a professional florist now!"

"That's awesome, Evie. I guess we both got what we wanted."

"I guess we did," I agree, half-heartedly. I try my best to push negative thoughts to one side and stay positive. It was unhealthy to let my mind wander to what could have been. If he hadn't chosen the army and…

Screw the devil in my head for thinking it, but what if he had just chosen me. I hated the self-doubt that reared its ugly head when I sometimes pictured his life away from me and hated myself for questioning, *wasn't I enough.*

"You visit your parents?"

Damn him for not beating around the bush and always shooting straight to the point. That's what happens when you know someone so well, all the small talk is laid aside over the years, and everything becomes so much more direct.

"No, I'll call them later."

"Make sure you do, they'll be worrying knowing you're on your own, and I can't stand the thought of it either."

"Candice has popped in a few times, and I'm working, so I haven't really been on my own. I can look after myself. Marshall, this is me you're talking to."

"I don't doubt it for a second, but Christmas will be less awkward if you reach out now."

"Okay, okay, I get it. I'll call them. Are you sure you'll be home for Christmas?"

"Sergeant seems to think so. There's no reason why I shouldn't be."

"I'm so excited to see you. You want me to cook dinner?"

"Of course, invite everyone, I'll help wash up if you give me extra desserts."

"What kind of dessert?"

"Fuck, Evie, you know exactly what fucking dessert I like. You know how long it's been since I had you?"

"A couple of months?"

"It feels like goddam years. My balls are aching for you."

"Save everything up for when I see you. I might just wrap myself in a red bow, and give you me for Christmas."

"Sweet fucking Jesus, Evie, I gotta go. Probably for the best, before my cock explodes."

I laugh in response and love the way that in just a few short savoured minutes he has me laughing. That was my Marshall.

"Look to the stars, Evie. I'll call you again as soon as I can."

"I'll leave the curtains open, I love you."

"I love you."

The call ended with those three simple words, given so easily by both of us. Like it was as common as saying "hello" or "goodbye," and for us, it was. An obvious turn of phrase like saying, "it's raining outside," or "see you soon." It was a fact that each of us stated without even having to think about it, and it had been that way for as long as I can remember.

Me loving him, him loving me. As sure as the sun rises and falls each day, that's how confident we were that what we shared could withstand any test, including being apart.

This is just one chapter in our marriage, I remind myself. Not the book.

* * *

THAT NIGHT I sleep with my curtains wide open. Watching and waiting for falling stars was our favourite thing to do, and it brought me comfort to think of him doing the exact same thing all those thousands of miles away. It had started as a joke in the first few years of high school when we'd had to study Shakespeare.

Marshall had been desperate to play Macbeth, but everyone had bullied him into playing Romeo because they said we were Star Crossed Lovers. It had sounded so romantic to me back then, it still did now. I remember my Mum trying to explain it to me and getting upset when I realised it meant that our relationship was doomed from the start. A victim of pressure from outside forces meddling and ruining what we had.

The kids at school hadn't known that, they'd thought it meant we were kissing and 'doing bits.' And they were right. Somehow the teachers caught wind of it and joined in with the teasing.

"Come on, you two," they'd say, "put each other down and get to class. I'm sure you star crossed lovers will find a way back to each other at break."

We didn't mind the teasing, and it's ironic that along the way, we have faced major obstacles getting in our way. My parents being the main one, and Marshall joining the army, close second.

I lie awake for hours staring at the window hoping to see a shooting star. I didn't expect to sleep, but it soothes me to focus on the night sky, rather than staring at my phone screen all night. If I take it to bed, I never get any rest, and through the night my anxiety seems to grow until I'm in a constant state of turmoil. Tossing, wriggling the duvet off and on again before checking my phone a million times just in case he's sent me a text, or something worse, like he gets hurt.

I must find sleep easily, as I don't wake until the twinkling sound of my alarm beeping from my dressing gown pocket, in the bathroom. I dash across and rummage around for it, desperate to shut it up and get back to the warmth of my bed.

I'm disturbed by a heavy knock at the door. The abruptness of the two heavy thuds fills me with an unexpected feeling of dread, and I slip into my dressing gown, knotting it around myself as I run downstairs. It's early, and I'm not expecting anybody, so I cautiously unclip the lock, letting the door open a little. I peek through the gap to see two soldiers dressed in full uniform and close the door again, refusing to hear what my heart knows they're about to tell me.

Another knock.

"Miss, we really need to speak with you today."

Silence.

Okay, Evie positive vibes. Remember, this is your Marshy, he wouldn't just leave you. I unclip the lock again and open the door to find an officer dressed in a smart blue uniform and a guy in jeans who has to be a priest, as his white collar is peeping out of his shirt.

Fuck. My throat feels like it's shrinking fast, like hardly any air is reaching my lungs, and I can barely breathe as I'm hit by a tight feeling in my chest.

"May we come in, Miss."

I step backwards, allowing them access, and they advise me to sit down, which I ignore. "Can you please confirm you are Evelyn Embers?"

"Yes. That's me. What's this all about?" I ask, praying they reply with anything other than what I think they're about to say

"The Secretary of the Army regrets to inform you that your husband was killed in action yesterday in Korengal Valley. He was involved in a small arms fire."

"A what? How do you know for sure it's Marsha…?" My voice trails off as I'm wracked with choking heavy sobs.

"An officer was able to identify him at the scene, Miss."

"What scene? It can't have been Marshall, I just spoke with him yesterday."

"Things can change very quickly on the frontline, Miss."

An inner strength over takes my body, and I march towards the stone-faced officer screaming at him now. "Tell me what happened, I have to know, why aren't you telling me the full story?"

He just looks at me blankly and somewhere a deep, harsh reality kicks me in the gut, and I calm down enough to ask, "Did he suffer? Was he in pain?"

"There is an ongoing investigation, Miss. Once the investigation is complete, you will have full access to the report."

"What the fuck does that even mean? This can't be happening." I break down, falling to my knees and feeling as if I've been winded, my mind racing over time. Mostly I'm angry, he said he'd never leave me, and now he's just gone, in the worst possible way.

A hand is placed on my shoulder. "We're sorry for your loss, Mrs. Embers. Is there anyone you would like us to contact for you? You shouldn't be on your own at a time like this." I shake my head without even looking up. '*On my own.*' That's all I am now, nothing matters without my Marshy.

"We will leave you to digest things and have the report sent to you as soon as it is ready."

The door clicks shut and it's over, my worst nightmare just became my reality, and it hurts worse than I ever thought it could.

CHAPTER 4

I couldn't take it in. Not today, not at the funeral and not now, a full three months later. Every time my phone pings I expect it to be a message from him, telling me that he's coming home soon.

His voice echoes around every room of our house to the point where I can't stand to be in it any longer. I've tried filling my days with things to do, or crying in bed for hours on end. It doesn't matter how I try to handle losing my husband, the hurt infiltrates every fibre of my being. I feel as though I'm gone too. An empty aching soul walking around in my old body, but no longer me anymore.

"You could have taken more time off, Evie. You didn't need to come in so soon after."

"I wanted to. I need to be busy," I reassure Tanya as I arrange a simple autumnal bouquet.

"Okay, but you'll tell me, won't you? If you feel like it's too soon, you will say it? Because, you really don't look well at all."

"I'm fine. I'll tell you if I'm struggling," I confirm before promptly spinning around and chucking up in the nearest flower bucket I can grab.

"Oh my god, see, you're not fine. That's the third time you've been sick this week."

I wipe my mouth on my sleeve, and refocus my vision as she disappears to bring me a glass of water.

"Honestly, I'm coping. I must be coming down with something."

"Do you want to go home for the afternoon?"

"No. It'll pass soon. I just need a minute." My stomach churns again as I say it, and I run to the bathroom, just in case I'm sick again.

When I walk back around to the front of the shop a few minutes later, Tanya is waiting for me like a tiger, ready to pounce on its prey.

"That's it. I'm not taking no for an answer." She folds her arms across herself and glares at me. "You're going home and you're going to do a pregnancy test too."

"A what? Tanya, have you lost your mind?"

"No. I am afraid you might have. Evie, you've been sick most mornings, and have barely eaten a stitch all week. You're not yourself, and no one else seems to want to tell you straight, but I will. You can't go on like this, girl," she rants. "You're a hot mess, and I understand you want to pretend like your whole world didn't just get turned upside down, but guess what? It did. And people are here for you, I'm here for you. But you have to begin to face reality."

Tears spring in my eyes and threaten to spill down my cheeks, but it doesn't stop her verbal onslaught.

"He's gone, Evie. He's not coming back, and I know it hurts like hell, but you will get through this. Take some time, take a test, just to rule it out, if anything. Marshall was home just a few months ago, and these things happen, Evie."

I almost feel the colour draining from my face and down to somewhere deep in the pit of my stomach. I want to be mad at her for just blurting everything out, but instead, I'm struck with the realisation that she's right.

"Okay, you win. I'll take the afternoon, but I'll be back in tomorrow, I need to..."

"Yeah, yeah, keep busy I get it," she cuts me off, taking my pinafore from me, as I pull it over my head. "Go home. I'll call you tonight."

"Tanya."

"Hm?"

"Thank you." It's all I can manage to say with a voice choked by my tears and my mind racing with possibilities.

Leaving Betty's Blooms, I wipe my eyes on the sleeve of my cream fluffy jumper, not caring about the mascara stains it leaves behind. I purchase a test from the pharmacy on the way home and practically run the rest of the way. It was a ridiculous notion that Tanya would even suggest I could be pregnant, but then again he was home not so long ago, right before.

Fuck. There it was again, that damn titanic feeling. Not when it hits the iceberg, the part where it plunges to the bottom of the ocean, never to be seen again. That was the only way to describe the sensation in my stomach that hit me every time I think of losing him.

In no time at all, I'm sitting on the loo in my bathroom and running the taps to try and coax a wee out. The tiniest trickle comes eventually, and I place the stick on the side of the sink, turn off the taps and nervously pace the landing.

After a minute I can't bear the suspense any longer, and I grab the stick frantically scanning for a line. There's nothing. I chuck it at the wall in frustration. Of course there's nothing, damn Tanya for suggesting there could be, and damn Marshall for leaving me.

Catching my reflection in the mirror, I swipe my fist across the shelf, sending our toothbrush pot flying, along with everything else. More tears come, and I succumb to my grief, falling to my knees and sobbing for longer than I should do.

We'd always wanted kids, we'd joked about their names, whose eyes they would have. It was another loss I'd encountered before even having a chance to experience it.

When I finally pull myself together and pick up the bits and pieces, arranging them neatly back on the shelf, I pick up the stick to chuck it away. As I do, a thin pink line catches my eye.

My eyes glaze over from staring at it that hard, and my body tenses completely. I'm in lockdown, unsure of how to feel or what reaction I'm supposed to have.

"Pregnant," I barely whisper the word into the air. "I'm pregnant!" I say again, this time in a high-pitched squeal, and suddenly I feel him.

He's here, around me, for the first time since he's gone, I really feel him, and it makes me happy and sad all at the same time.

"You're here," I whisper to the empty house. "We are going to have a baby, Marshall. Our own little miracle." I don't feel the stab of heartache I expect. Instead, I feel calm and strangely at peace. When I wander into our bedroom, still staring at the stick, I trip over a trainer and fall to the ground.

"Shit," I cuss out loud, I'm not hurt, but my knee instantly burns from the bang.

I pull myself up off the floor and lean my back against the bed to rub my knee, something on the floor catches my eye. Crawling over to the chest of drawers, I stretch my arm and fish around to try and grab the shiny plastic underneath. When I catch hold of it and pull it into view, I'm caught off guard realising that it's a keychain Marshall and I had made on Prom Night.

Clutching it to my chest, I take a deep breath before studying the tiny photo again. Marshall has his two fingers up behind my head and a huge silly grin on his face. I'm sticking my tongue out cheekily, and for a blissful minute I exist only in the photo. A smile reaches my lips and winds its way down, wrapping itself around my heart and warming it.

He'd pulled me into the photo booth and kissed me until I felt dizzy. Then right after the camera snapped, he'd tickled me until I couldn't breathe. It was one of my favourite things about my husband, his playful side. Although I rarely got to see it after he signed up for the army.

The news hits me like a hurricane, creating an unexpected storm in my life, and I have no idea what to do with it. One minute I want to run down the street yelling, "I'm pregnant," from the rooftops, and the next I want to hide away and keep the news all to myself.

Despite our fall outs, I decide that the person I most want to tell is my mum, so I drive over to my parents' place.

Both cars are parked on the driveway, so I know they're both in. Before I can wonder whether I'm making a mistake in telling them, my mum spots me through the window. Within seconds she's opening the front door and ushering me inside.

"Evie, honey, we missed you. How have you been?"

"Fine," comes my automated response.

The single word I have delivered over and over again since my husband was taken from me. It masks a world of pain, and most of the time, it is all I can manage.

"Oh, darling. You don't look fine."

"Thanks, Mum," I joke, a hint of a smile creeping up on me, and she rolls her eyes at me.

"You know I didn't mean it like that."

"Your dad will be pleased you've popped in. He's been asking about you. Why haven't you been picking up our calls, Evie? We want to be there for you."

"That's why I'm here, I have some news."

"News? What kind of news?"

My hand brushes my stomach instinctively, and before the words can escape my lips she snaps, "Oh no, Evie don't say it."

"I'm pregnant, Mum. I'm having Marshall's baby."

The crestfallen look on her face says it all. As though I've just told her I've been diagnosed with a terminal illness.

"Don't," I angrily spit the word at her. "Don't look at me like that. There's nothing you or anyone else can do to take this away from me. This is what I… what *we* both wanted. If you can't support me, then I'll do this on my own," I rant.

"Like hell you will," my dad's voice booms after me. "You're our only daughter, Evie. I know it's been a tough few years for us, but we are your family. Come and sit down, let's talk about this like adults, you're not the only one with news."

I look to Mum wondering whether one of them is ill. What news could they have, and I wonder whether they would have even told me if I hadn't just turned up on their doorstep.

Following them into the living room, as though reading my thoughts, my mum says, "We were going to contact you once the details were more final. It's your dad's business, love. He's expanding."

"As in taking on more staff? Are you really that busy?"

My dad's restaurants have always been popular but never enough that he could consider an early retirement. We were comfortable, but not rich by any means.

My dad attempts to make things clearer to me. "While we were away,"

"In Greece?" I cut him off, and he frowns at me before continuing.

"Yes, your mother and I visited some of the smaller islands this time, and we spotted an investment."

"An investment. In Greece?" I ask. This time he looks like he's going to spontaneously combust if I interrupt him again.

My mum interjects, "Hear your father out, Evelyn."

The use of my full name has me sitting still and listening like a moody teenager who's just been put in her place.

"I think it's a real opportunity. It's a beautiful small town up in the hills. Tourists are up in the area by six percent." *Wow, he's really researched this.* "The place is an absolute bargain. We'd be crazy not to snap it up, and you know how your Mum and I..."

"Have dreamt of this for like ever," I state, excitedly. Despite our disagreement about my marriage, I couldn't help but feel happy for them and the opportunity. "So, you were just going to up and leave me?"

"Of course not," my mum exclaims. "Evelyn, we're here for you for as long as you need us, you know that. Just because we don't agree with your choices, it doesn't mean we ever stopped loving you.

"Evelyn," my father says, in his serious tone. "You remember that you were once in the dream, too." My mind flashes back to my childhood, me skipping around the kitchen with my dad. Begging him to let me go, and play instead of trying to teach me how to cook up another of his Greek delights.

"I think this was your dream, Dad, but I'm happy for you, both of you."

"Evelyn, you're pregnant. That changes everything," my mum says, in a small voice.

"It doesn't have to. You can still go. I'll be fine here, I'll have my baby soon enough."

"Evelyn, you're still grieving. You don't have to answer right away, but I think you should seriously consider coming with us. I always dreamt you'd help me get the business off the ground. It would be the three of us again. We could really create something special, it will only take a few months to get things up and running, and it could be just the distraction you need."

"The four of us, Dad. It would be the four of us."

"We know this might seem sudden, but your dad's right, Evelyn. This could be a great opportunity for you and your baby. Let us look after you. Think of all the walks on the beach in the sunny weather. It would be amazing to have you with us, and you know we would never go without you. Especially not when you're carrying our grandchild," she adds, seeming more accepting of the idea now that my dad's taken the news in stride.

"I need to think about it. Will you give me some time?"

"Take as long as you need. We'll be going out there again in around two weeks' time."

"Okay, I'll let you know." I smile, feeling relieved that my parents had somehow become human again, rather than the enemy they'd turned into during the last few years.

It's only in the car on my way home that I realise, the one person I'm desperate to tell, isn't here.

Letting myself back into our empty living room, my decision is easily made. There's nothing here for me. Marshall isn't here anymore. I have to find a way to move on. Tanya was right, I can't go on like this. And it was only temporary.

A few months, my dad had said. Could I really do this? The thought made me anxious, slightly nauseous and just the tiny little bit excited.

It was the first time since he's been gone that the black storm cloud following me around, cleared for a moment, and I want to embrace it. I don't want everything to be dark anymore, I'm ready to let some light in.

CHAPTER 5

Three Years Later

*T*he initial few months had turned into three full years, and by the time we returned to The Cotswolds, my son, Marshall, was no longer a baby. He was a demanding, fun loving, beautiful little boy. I kiss his head of fluffy hair as we make our way back to our house in Bourton-on-the-Water.

"You ready to go home, Marshall?"

He smiles at me, flashing a neat little row of baby teeth and shouts, "Ready," as he throws his arms up above his head.

Greece was all he had known for the first years of his life, and I'm anxious to see what he thinks of life here in The Cotswolds. It was equally as quiet as the tiny island we'd just left, but certainly a lot less sunny.

Letting myself into my place was like taking a huge leap back in time, and I gasp at the sight of everything still in the same place I left it. I imagine this is what it feels like to step inside a photograph, surreal and disorientating.

Marshall wraps his tired arms around my neck, bringing me back to reality, and I squish him a little tighter whispering, "Welcome home, baby."

It feels good to be just the two of us for the first time, and I text my parents, letting them know we have arrived safely. They aren't happy about me coming back before them, but it feels right. We need this. Marshall needs to know where he belongs.

"Me tired," he moans, and I suddenly realise the enormity of the task ahead.

"We're going to need to get you a bedroom, but for tonight, you wanna sleep with Mummy?"

He nods, and I carry him upstairs to bed. He's almost asleep in my arms by the time I've undressed him. Stripping him down to his vest and underpants, I let him crash out. It's been a long day for a little boy, and he has been good as gold on his first ever plane ride.

"Shrawberries, Mummy?"

I giggle to myself, he never forgets a single thing.

"Yes, baby, tomorrow we will go and pick some strawberries."

"Pwomise?" he asks through tired eyes.

"I promise. Now get some sleep, little bear."

Damn my mum for her stories of England. I'll bet she didn't include anything practical, like buying a bed or groceries. There are a million things we need to do tomorrow, and thanks to her, Marshall is set for a day of strawberry picking and puddle jumping. I just hope his new life can live up to his slightly unrealistic expectations.

With Marshall curled up and fast asleep, I open up the drawers and take a look at all of his daddy's belongings still neatly folded and unchanged. Lifting out a t-shirt, I scrunch it to my nose and inhale, but the scent of him has gone. Three years is a long time, but seeing all our things together takes me back to my world of pain in a heartbeat.

Reminding myself they are just things, I begin lifting them into a neat pile next to the bed. When I'm finished, I feel a sense of accomplishment at the sight of the clear space in the drawers and the bunch of clothes ready to be packed away. I've already decided to donate all of Marshall's things to charity. It's what he would have wanted.

As determined as I am to keep moving forward, it's still hard to be here, and I wasn't prepared for all the emotions I would feel walking back into my old life. Having little Marshall with me makes every-thing bearable, and as tiny as he is, he's a tower of strength without even knowing it.

Undressing and throwing on some pyjamas, I brush my teeth before climbing into bed next to him. I scan the gap between the open curtains that is letting the light in, and I don't jump up to close them. Instead, I snuggle into my boy, staring into the night sky, hoping that somewhere, somehow, Marshall is with us.

* * *

WE WAKE and eat breakfast at a local coffee shop, as there's nothing in the cupboards at home. I treat Marshall to waffles and syrup, which he gets absolutely everywhere. My old car seems tiny now that there's a car seat in the back, and I feel a little overwhelmed at the thought of finding a job to save for a bigger one. I've managed to save all of my earnings from waitressing over in Greece, and my parents had been generous, giving me some money to help me get on my feet. The restaurant had been a real team effort, and I had enjoyed my shifts waiting tables and working the bar in the evenings, as much as my mum had enjoyed looking after Marshall.

We head towards the motorway to drive to the strawberry farm where my mum used to take me when I was younger. On the way, Marshall spots a huge strawberry on a sign for a new strawberry farm that can only have recently opened, as it wasn't there when I'd left for Greece.

"Shrawberries!" he yells, excitedly.

"Okay, yes, Strawberries, you wanna go pick some?"

"Yeah, pwease, Mummy," he replies, and I catch sight of him in my rear-view mirror looking as excited as ever.

I guess it would save us some time if we pull in here, since *we still have loads to do this afternoon.*

We turn in at the farm, and it's a long drive down a tree lined path to reach the car park. It's huge here, and when I pull Marshall out of his car seat and set him down in his wellies, it feels like we're a world away from anywhere. It's quiet, as it's still early, there's only a few other cars here. We make our way over to the stack of punnets. There's nobody manning the stand, just a sign saying, 'Help yourself, £2 per punnet.'

"You want to carry this one, Marshall, and Mummy will fill this one up?"

He takes the punnet from me and toddles off towards the massive rows of strawberries.

"Wait for Mummy, Marshall. We have to stay together remember."

He pays me no attention whatsoever, bends down to grab a juicy strawberry and pops it in his mouth before I can stop him.

"Marshall, we're supposed to wash them first, baby."

He grins up at me with red juices flooding his mouth and chin, and I can't help but laugh. Fumbling in my pocket, I reach for my phone.

"Let's take a picture of you. Ready?"

"Cheeeese," he says, through gritted teeth and wide grin. He's always been a little poser.

"Gorgeous. Okay, let's fill up our punnets. We want as many nice ones as we can get."

Marshall sets to work picking strawberries, eating a lot more than he puts in the punnet. I trip over, and in a split-second, Marshall runs off. I scoop up my bag and dash after him but typically, my cheeky little son thinks the whole thing's one big game. The more I chase him, the faster he tries to run, and the wobblier his chubby little legs become. Predicting exactly what's going to happen, I cup my hands around my mouth and shout out, "Marshall, slow down. Come back to Mummy," but there's no point.

As if watching a movie in slow motion, Marshall stumbles over his own wellies and falls face first into the mud.

I run over to him, his face covered with mud and tears, and I fall to my knees, pulling him into my lap.

"It's okay, baby. Mummy's got you."

He cries and scrunches up his hand, which is bleeding, and I give it a Mummy-make-it-better kiss before carrying him back towards the car. As we haven't been grocery shopping yet, I don't have any of Marshall's usual supplies with us, so I search around for a toilet to rinse his hand off.

Carrying him past the entrance where we got the punnets from, we make our way up towards the huge farmhouse at the back of the farm.

There must be some facilities here somewhere.

I'm growing impatient now as Marshall's crying is getting louder and his hand appears to still be bleeding.

"Okay, it's okay," I reassure him.

A young girl with dark, wavy hair approaches us with a sweet face that is full of concern. I'm guessing she's around six, maybe seven judging by her height. "Is he okay?" She asks. "I saw him fall down?"

"Yes, he's going to be fine, I just need somewhere to clean him up."

"Oh sure, we just opened so the toilets haven't been delivered yet. Come with me, he can have one of my plasters. Would you like that little boy, a plaster to make you feel better?"

I don't know if it's because he needs to break for air, or the shock of the high-pitched girly voice talking to him, but he stops crying. "Pwaster," he snuffles through his tears and snotty nose.

"I have a sweet, too. If your mummy says you're allowed one, sweets always make me feel better when I have a boo boo."

"You live here, at the farm?" I ask curiously, wondering where the polite little girl's parents are.

"I do, Miss… "

"Evelyn, I'm Evelyn, and this is Marshall. Maybe I shouldn't come inside. I don't think your mum would like it if a stranger wandered into your house, especially when we're this muddy."

"Oh, don't worry about that, we're always muddy in my house, and my mum's not here. It's just my dad, and he won't mind at all. He won't even be back until later, he's out on the tractor."

"Okay, well, if you're sure," I say, following her up to the back door of the house, and she pushes the door open for us. I cautiously follow her inside, glancing around at the beautiful traditional country kitchen in awe.

"You're sure your daddy won't mind us being here?"

"Of course not," she says, shoving a kitchen chair against the cupboards and climbing up to reach a box from the top shelf. "Here ya go," she continues, "everything you need is in here. It's a proper first aid kit. We got it last time I fell from my treehouse. That's why it has bandages, too. See," she asks, holding up a reel of stretchy bandages, as I take the box from her.

"Wow, you are certainly very organised. I hope you're careful when you're climbing in the future. That must have been a nasty fall."

"It was, I had a scab on my knee for three whole weeks afterwards," she discloses, matter of factly. "But you won't," she adds, bending down to try and make eye contact with a sulky Marshall. "You'll be better in no time," she reassures him.

He glances up at her and quietly says, "Me want sweets."

Usually I would chastise him for being so forward, but the little girl's head has already disappeared inside one of the bottom cupboards.

"You been making some friends, Poppy?"

Poppy almost hits her head on the way out of the cupboard and seems nearly as shocked as me at the appearance of the man, I'm guessing is her dad. My voice disappears as he steps forward, filling the room with his masculine presence.

He's topless, in low slung jeans that hang from his hips and reveal a deeply tanned set of abs. His chest is jewelled with beads of sweat, and his hazel eyes are locked on mine, clearly waiting for an explanation of who I am and what I'm doing standing in his kitchen.

"I... I…"

"This is Evelyn, Dad," Poppy announces, and I hold my hand out to shake his, which instantly feels ridiculously formal and awkward.

"Evelyn," he says slowly, my full name rolling off his tongue like hot butter.

His eyes continue burning into mine, searching for a reaction from me. I have no doubt that he's toying with me. The way he stares down at my hand and then back up at me, and the small smile on his lips before he accepts my hand shake, confirms it.

"Pleasure to meet you, Evelyn. Make yourself at home." He grins, and I shrink on the spot.

Damn it, what was I thinking following Poppy in here? What must I look like caked in mud and squashed strawberries?

It's not like I haven't seen a shirtless man before, I've practically spent the last three years on the beach surrounded by them. But none of them had a body like that, and none of them were standing so close to me.

"Thanks, we were just leaving," I say awkwardly, lifting Marshall from the countertop and back onto my hip. "I mean, we were getting a plaster for my son, Marshall. He fell… We both did, as you can see. Your daughter has been so kind to us, and she was just letting us clean up Marshall's cut a little, and now we've done that, so we're going. Thank you very much for letting us use your kitchen, Mr., Mr…"

"Gabe. My name is Gabe," he says with a relaxed smile that oozes confidence.

His teeth are pearly white, framed with full lips and a dark stubbled chin. His shoulders are broad, and every muscle is defined, from his biceps, right down to his naked wrist.

"Okay. Well, thanks again, Gabe, and it was lovely to meet you Poppy."

"Here you go, Marshall. Suck on this, and it will help you feel better. Come back and see us again soon," she says, handing him a chocolate milky bar.

"Thanks, Poppy. Bye," I say over my shoulder, already rushing out of the door, embarrassed that I just barged in and used the kitchen of some kind of cowboy god without even meeting him first.

"Shrawberries," Marshall says as I rush him back past the fruit fields, towards the car.

"Yeah, I think we're giving up on the strawberries, bab." I smile to myself as I strap him in and glance up to see cowboy god running down the path towards me.

"Wait," he shouts after me.

I open the car door pretending not to hear him, something about his self-confidence, borderline cockiness, mixed with his naked upper half makes me want to drive away from this place as quickly as possible and never look back.

"You forgot your strawberries." He smiles, handing me our half empty punnet of fruit.

"Thanks, you didn't have to…"

"It's my pleasure. Just a shame I won't get to watch you eat them," he murmurs as I climb into the car.

Was he flirting with me, or mocking me? I take one last look at his wicked grin and simply reply, "Bye, Gabe," before driving out of there without a single glance in my rear-view mirror.

Gabe

"Bye, Evelyn." I laugh, watching her drive out of sight. Kicking a cloud of earth up to replicate scoring a goal, I smile inwardly. "You've still got it, kid."

It had been a hell of a long time since I had a woman in my kitchen, and despite her desperately trying to avoid eye contact, I saw the effect I had on her. Sensed it when I shook her hand. It felt good to know I can still make a woman weak at the knees, when I wanted to, and she was one hell of a woman. All covered in mud like that, and being all caring and shit. If those two kids hadn't of been there, it would have been my shower she was using, not my fucking first aid box.

"Dad, you didn't have to scare her away, she was only getting a plaster," my little sass ball greets me, hand on hip as I approach the back door.

"You think I'm scary, Pops?"

"Not to me," she shrugs, and I pull her into a headlock, ruffling her hair as we walk back inside.

"You think you could mess with me, kid. Think you could take your old man down?"

"Easy."

"Oh, easy, huh? Okay, I'll give you ten seconds head start. That's ten whole seconds to take me down, but after that, you better run, little princess."

"Deal," she says, shaking my hand with our usual handshake before kicking me straight in the nuts as hard as she fucking can.

"Arrrgh," I yelp out, falling to the ground and grabbing my wounded parts. "What the…" I stop myself from yelling out the collection of cuss words running through my mind.

"Where in the world did you learn to do that, sweetie?"

"Rosie had a sleepover with Emily and her sister, Laura, has a boyfriend. Laura said if he lies to her again, she's going to finish him off for good. Emily asked what she means and Rosie told me that Laura said if you ever want to take a man down, you just gotta kick him in the private's as hard as you can."

"Wow, you girls really talk about a lot of grown up stuff." I wince as she stops for breath, and I fight to catch mine.

"Did I hurt you, Dad?"

She kneels down to check if I'm okay, and I put my mouth close to her little ears whispering, "Your ten seconds are up, little lady."

She lets out a deafening squeal and runs off upstairs laughing, as I struggle to get to my feet and chase her.

When I reach her bedroom, I see two small feet poking out from the bottom of her curtains. I creep over and whip back the pink fabric.

"Gotcha."

She squeals again, and I tickle her ribs until she yells, "Stop Dad, stop," and I collapse next to her on the bed.

"I think you won that one, Poppy. You're turning into a little ninja. Now, we still have a heap of work to do before the rain comes. Know anyone around here who can drive a tractor?"

She grins up at me, and her huge eyes flash with excitement.

"Really, Dad? You're really going to teach me how to drive the tractor?"

"I mean, unless you don't want to learn?"

As expected, she jumps up off the bed, and is already half way down the stairs when she shouts out, "Of course I want to learn. Thanks, Dad. I won't let you down, I've been dreaming of this day since I was a baby."

"Is that right?" I murmur to no one in particular, smiling at her melodrama.

She is her mother's daughter, for sure. My jaw locks at the thought of that godforsaken woman and everything she's put my child through. I grit my teeth at the thought of it and grab my plaid shirt from the end of the banister, throwing it on as I follow Poppy out to the tractor. I climb in and stretch a hand out for her to grab onto.

"Okay, Pops, let's do this. Climb on and don't touch anything until I say. Got it?"

"Got it," she confirms, climbing up onto my knee.

"On three, you're gonna steer us left as soon as we move off. Count with me, one, two…"

"Three," she shouts excitedly as I release the parking brake and bring my foot up off the clutch, wrapping an arm around her.

"That's it, Pops. Nice and easy, you got this."

"Am I doing it, Dad? Am I driving?"

"Like a true farmer, princess."

"It's actually really easy," she says, taking one hand off the wheel to move it around as she talks.

"Woah, let's keep both hands on the wheel for now. Okay?"

"Okay." She wraps both hands around the wheel, and I sit back, keeping my arms wrapped tightly around her waist.

"Where do you wanna take us?"

"All the way to the end of the farm, to my favourite part, of course."

"Of course," I repeat, I should have known she'd have wanted to go up to the lake. She had been fascinated with the geese living there ever since we moved here a few months ago. "I need to plough that top field, anyway."

She's quiet, and I wonder what she's thinking as we make our way over our seven acres of land up to the small lake.

"Are you happy here, Poppy?"

"I'd stay here forever, if I could, Dad. It's my favourite place in the whole wide world."

"Me too," I reply. It was true. Giving up my life in the city and stepping back from my world of paparazzi chaos had been a huge risk, but I knew as soon as I got here, moving was the right decision.

Maple Valley was the perfect retreat from my previous whirlwind existence, and every inch of fresh air I've inhaled since being here has made me feel more alive than I have in years. For Poppy, I hope this place can become a source of stability to her, she desperately needs it. Most six-year-old kids have only moved once, if at all, during their few short years. My Poppy has managed a total of thirteen moves, fourteen if you include coming here, three continents, countless countries, endless strangers coming and going from her life like trucks in a service station.

She had already seen far too much of the world, and I hadn't protected her when I should have. Most kids need saving from spiders or grizzly bears hiding under the bed late at night. Not Poppy. The only baddie in her life is the one nobody can save her from. Angela.

She was perfection incarnate, beautiful and shiny like the designer shoes she wore, until she was drunk. Then it all got nasty, and that meant, I'd spent the last six years of my life a slave to the vicious cycle of Angela's drug and alcohol addiction.

I'd followed her everywhere, from busy cities to secluded coasts. The best penthouse hotel suites down to the dirty floors of backstage toilet blocks. She was a huge star, and to the outside world she was the definition of a perfect mother. The working woman who had it all. But to Poppy and I, she was a train wreck, and I refuse to derail with her.

This time when she'd checked into rehab, I hadn't been to visit, nor begged her to turn her life around for the sake of our daughter. If Poppy wasn't the motivation she needed to change, then there really was no hope.

She'll have been checked out for around two months by now, and I haven't heard from her. It guts me that she hasn't made the effort to visit Poppy, but I refuse to bend to her mind games. She knows where we are. I only hope that when she's ready, she will come and see Poppy, and let her know how much she loves her. For me, my daughter had been my drug of choice ever since the doctor placed her in my arms, right after she was born. At the time, I honestly thought we could be a real family.

I should have known better.

Angela had always had her priorities wrong. When we'd gotten together, right out of college, we were both as career driven as each other. Our success had come with a hefty cost to both of us.

Angela lost her integrity, and I lost the woman I'd fallen in love with. She was smart, witty and absolutely stunning, but once she acquired a taste for cocaine, her wit became an endless stream of cruel jokes, which I was the butt of.

She was using her pussy rather than her brains to get where she wanted to be, and when she got there, she was no longer beautiful. Not to me, anyway.

I glance around at my new land as Poppy steers us through the fields. Nothing but rows of strawberries and empty fields of green grass surrounded by maple trees that put a welcome and visible wall up between us and the rest of the world.

"Dad," she asks as we reach the lake. Can you help me down, I really want to check on Sunshine and Rainbow? I promised them I'd come back."

"Sunshine and Rainbow?"

"My geese, Dad. I told you this last week. I knew you weren't listening. Remember, I said we can leave them here for now, but if it gets too cold in winter, we might need to bring them inside."

"Poppy, you are not keeping geese as pets." I sigh easing off the clutch and bringing the tractor to a stop not far from the lake, before I carefully lift Poppy off my knee and onto the ground.

"Be careful not to fall in," I shout after her, before jumping down myself.

I begin to take a look at the seat, which I think needs adjusting and Poppy lets out an almighty scream.

"Daddy, Dad, come quickly," she yells.

I haul ass towards her as quickly as possible, thinking she's got her foot stuck or she's fallen in somehow. When I reach her, she starts shushing me and giving me a stern scowl at the noise I'm making by running towards her.

"Shhh, look, it's Sunshine, she's had babies. Look how cute they are. Be quiet, or you'll scare them," she whispers.

Sure enough, as I reach Poppy, I can see six little fluffy goslings and a fierce looking Rainbow, as she calls him, looking like he's protecting them.

"Poppy, lookout, honey. I don't think the male likes you being so close to the babies. He's wild, remember? He might bite you."

"Dad," she says all dramatic and despairing. "He's not wild. I told you, he's my pet."

"I'm just saying, be careful," I warn and offer her my hand to pull her up from the damp spot she's kneeling in.

"Oh no, Dad, there's another one, look behind the long grass. I think he's hurt."

"Don't," I say firmly as she goes to pick the wounded little creature up. "Let me do it, just in case."

She doesn't look happy at my intervention, but Rainbow is also looking less that happy at our intrusion. I place myself strategically between the angry male goose and my fearless daughter, before picking up the injured gosling.

"Looks like his little leg is broken."

"He's not going to make it, is he?" She asks, looking like she's about to cry.

God, I hate that look. Wet eyes and a sulky pout, I never could stand to see her upset.

"I'm sure he'll be fine," I lie, placing him back down.

"No, don't leave him there. We have to take him to the house and help him get better."

"Poppy, there's no way we are keeping a wild goose inside our house."

"We're not, we're just looking after him until he gets better. Then we will reunite him with his parents, and they can be a family again."

"I swear, you watch too much tv some days. The goose will be fine. Now, let's get back before the rain sets in. Look, it's clouding over already," I point out, in an attempt to distract her.

"You go." She folds her arms across her chest and glares at me. "If the goose is staying here, then I am staying here with it."

"Poppy, this is crazy. Get in the tractor, we're going home."

"I won't do it, Dad. I won't leave him. If he died then some of that would be my fault, and I couldn't live with myself. I just couldn't. Please don't make me leave him out here all alone. In the cold," she adds for impact purposes, as it's not even particularly cold.

Don't do it. Don't give in to her. This is a goose, Gabe. You do not want a fucking goose in your house.

"Okay, fine. But just for a few days, until he's better."

"Thanks, Dad. You're the best." She smiles, and all of the sadness on her pretty little face disappears.

We ride back to the house, and I drive this time, with Poppy on my knee, and the wild little goose on hers.

CHAPTER 6

Evelyn

"There." I dust my hands off against each other, climbing down from the step ladder and glancing around the room. "What do you think, Marshall? Do you like your new big boy bedroom?"

"Rocket ship," he yells, running around the room and mimicking the huge rocket I've painted across his bedroom wall.

"That's right, and watch this, if we turn off the lights…" I pause and flick off the light switch, letting the room fall into darkness and watch my boys face, as the glow up stars I've scattered across his ceiling, light up and take his breath away.

"I can see the stars, Mummy."

"That's right, baby. They're all shining for you." A lump in my throat appears and turns into tears as he stands in awe of his new room and bursts into a beautiful rendition of 'Twinkle Twinkle Little Star.' I lift my fingers and twinkle them along with him, it was another moment I wished his daddy was here, and another moment I'd cherish for as long as I could.

I wanted him to always stay this way, little and unaware of everything he'd missed out on. Until now, he had only had me, and I had been enough. But tomorrow was a big day for both of us.

Starting pre-school was a huge leap forward. A new beginning for Marshall, and perhaps a new beginning for me.

Greece had been a welcome change, a diversion from the huge gaping hole in my heart, but now that I'm home, I can really begin to heal. Although, as I lay in bed alone, with Marshall in his new room next door, I question whether a broken heart can ever fully mend and be made whole again, or whether there will always be a piece of me that is missing, without him.

I wake hours before Marshall full of nervous energy and anxious about the day ahead. Slipping into my yoga leggings and vest, I tiptoe past his bedroom and downstairs to the living room, positioning myself in the centre of our rug. The next thirty mins is spent in a complete state of blissful solitude.

Practicing yoga had become my calm, and it was something I had loved about Greece. Sneaking out bright and early, leaving Marshall with my parents to have a few minutes quiet time on the beach to practice had been one of my favourite parts of the day. It was something I wanted to continue now that I'm back, even if it is a little hard to get up and out of bed when it's still dark outside.

After yoga, it's coffee and five minutes of tv before I go back upstairs and wake Marshall.

"Wake up, sleepy head," I say as I open the curtains in his bedroom.

"Mummy," he bolts upright and throws his arms in the air. I sit beside him for a minute and have a cuddle.

"It's time to get ready for big boy school, are you excited."

"Yes, I'm going to make wots of fwends."

"That's right. And you're going to have lots of fun, too. They'll be toys to play with and Legos to build. But first, you're going to need some breakfast."

Once we've eaten our toast soldiers and dippy egg, I dress him in a new little green tracksuit with a blue dinosaur on the front. He picked it out himself from the supermarket, and it looks so cute on him.

We walk to the nursery as it's not far from the house, and when the times comes to hand him over to the teacher, he is one of the first to go and sit in the circle. It's like leaving a limb behind, and I have to physically force myself to leave him there.

I expected him to cling to my leg and bawl his eyes out when it was time for me to go. Is it weird that I am a little disappointed he didn't? Instead, he waved and sat listening to the teacher as if he'd been going to school for weeks. He was ready for this, but it didn't mean I was.

Once I've been home and changed into jeans, a nude cami top and matching blazer, I make my way to Betty's Blooms. It was a day I'd had planned in my head for a long time, and I knew exactly what I needed to do, but asking for my old job back was a huge deal.

It had been three years since I'd seen or spoken to Tanya. She was one of my best friends, and I'd just walked out on her. On everyone. My old life was a distant memory, and I didn't expect to just walk back into it, picking up where I left off.

That said, I need a job and to stand on my own two feet. I know I can work at one of Dad's restaurants, but I'd much rather spend my time doing something I love.

Standing outside the door, I shake my hands out to try to dispel some of my nerves, and before I have chance to work out what I want to say, Tanya comes racing towards me from behind the glass. Bursting through the door, she greets me with a look of utter shock on her face.

"Oh my god!" she yells, "Evie! I can't believe it's really you. I saw you through the window and thought, am I seeing things? I feel like I need to pinch you to make sure you're real."

"Please don't." I laugh, and she throws her arms around me before taking a step back to eye me up and down again.

"What are you doing here? How long are you staying? It's just so good to see you, it's been so long. Come in and let's catch up."

I notice she flips the shop sign to 'closed' as we step inside.

"You don't have to close. It's fine, we can catch up while you work."

"Evie, it's been three bloody years, of course I'm closing the shop. I want to know every single thing. Shit, the last time I saw you." She glances to my stomach, not wanting to put her foot in it.

"I was pregnant," I confirm. "My son, Marshall is three now. He just started pre-school, today."

"Here?"

"Yeah, I figured I couldn't stay in Greece forever. There's only so much seafood a girl can eat before she needs a Sunday roast."

"Now, that's the truth." She smiles. "Fuck, Evie, I've really missed you. Where are you staying, with your parents?"

"No, they aren't due back until tomorrow, I'm at home."

She visibly winces at my reply, and I find myself reassuring her, "It's been fine. Marshall has his own bedroom now, and it actually feels good to be back where I belong."

"So, you're sticking around then?"

"That's the plan," I confirm. "I want to get Marshall settled into pre-school, and for him to grow up the same way me and his dad did. I'm hoping being here, around all our friends and family, hanging out where we used to hang out, will give him a stronger sense of self, as he gets older."

Her smile changes to a look of complete confusion.

"Marshall?"

"My son," I say, before realising the enormity of what I'm saying.

Tanya says nothing in response and throws her arms around me, hugging me for the longest time before saying, "I'm so happy for you, Evie. And the name is just perfect, I can't wait to meet him. Does he look like…"

"He's the image of him."

"Is it hard?"

"Sometimes. Some of the things he says, and he has this certain smile that he does, and all I can see is his dad's face. But in a way, it's a comfort too. Like there's a little piece of him always with me."

"I guess you'll be needing a job then?"

Meeting her eyes, I read her thoughts, and my cheeks burn with excitement.

"You're kidding?"

"Actually, I'm deadly serious. Our apprentice just quit to take a gap year with her new man, and I have three corporate events, two funerals and a swanky London hotel wants us for wedding, too."

"A swanky hotel in London? Tanya, that's amazing!"

"I know, it's been none stop, but honestly, I'm barely coping. Your timing is on point… That is, if you want your old job back?"

"Oh my god, Tan, of course I do. That's why I came over here. Obviously, to let you know I was back, but I was going to ask for my old job back, even if you only had a few hours a week to spare."

"A few hours a week?" She glances around the place looking exasperated and making me giggle. "More like all the hours a week you got! But seriously, no pressure. Whatever hours you want, they are yours."

"You've made my day, possibly my year. I was so worried about finding a job, and I didn't even know if Betty's Blooms, or you, would still be here when I got back."

"Oh, we're not going anywhere."

"Good, because as long as Marshall's in nursery, I'll be here helping you."

"When can you start?"

"Well, I have a couple of hours now if you'll have me."

"Girl, you know you're part of the furniture."

I grab a pinafore and slip it over my head, and Tanya grins, making her way over to the door and flipping the sign to 'open.'

"I'm so damn happy you're here. We've got so much to catch up on. Although I feel kind of pasty with you standing next to me, looking all Mediterranean."

"That's what three years in Greece does for you. It's the thing I'm going to miss most, too. There's something magical about waking up to the sunshine every morning."

"It sounds like a dream."

"It almost feels like one now that I'm back at home."

"How's things with your mum and dad now?"

"They've really stepped up to the plate. Both of them have really looked out for me, and they're obsessed with Marshall. They're flying back this weekend, but I honestly think they are only coming home for us. They were so at home out there."

"At least you'll have a babysitter on tap."

I laugh at her remark and raise an eyebrow.

"What for? I haven't left Marshall since I had him. Except to work at the restaurant, and that was mostly when he was asleep."

"Oh no." She shakes her head at me. "That's just not good enough, Evelyn Embers. Don't think I won't tell you straight just because it's been a minute since you were last here." I throw her a look that feigns annoyance, not expecting her to understand how much I hate leaving Marshall, even for short periods of time.

Tayna continues, "What? Don't look at me like that. Wait 'til you meet him, you wouldn't wanna leave him either.

You're twenty-four years old, you've still got your whole life ahead of you, and you've not had a night out in three years?" She throws me a look of something between disappointment and disgust before continuing, "Your parents are back this weekend, right?"

"Yeah."

"Okay, Saturday night. How about it? You, me and some cocktails?"

My gut reaction is no way. Going out wasn't my thing, or at least, it wasn't anymore. But her enthusiasm is infectious. I'd missed her company, and Marshall would be happy to have a sleepover with his Nanny.

By the time I'm done over analysing, I've run out of reasons to say no, so I find myself saying, "Sounds good, let's do it."

"Eek! I'm excited, I haven't been out in so long. Since the last girl left, I've been putting in so many hours here, you wouldn't believe it. Does everyone know your back? Candice might be up for a night out, too?"

A knot forms in my stomach at the mention of her name.

"I haven't spoken to her," I admit.

"What, since you've been back? She will be so happy to see you."

"I wouldn't be so sure about that," I murmur. "It's been a long time since I spoke to her. After Marshall, everything was such a blur, and when my parents put the offer out there about the restaurant, I just upped and left."

"Are you saying, she didn't even know where you'd gone?"

"No one did. I meant to stay in touch with them. I sent a few messages at first and a photo when Marshall was born. After that, I guess it was easier to just shut everything out. I didn't know I'd be out there so long. The time just passed by, and now I don't know how to reach out."

My wrongdoings come pouring out of me like a busted water pipe, and it feels good to confide in my old friend.

"Oh, Evie, don't beat yourself up. I'm sure Marshall's family will understand once you explain it to them."

"I wish it was that straight forward but even I can't make sense of why it's so hard to face them. How do you explain to someone that you've kept their Grandson and Nephew from them, for all that time?

I'm honestly dreading seeing them again. The pain in their eyes is like looking in a fucking mirror, and I'm not sure I'll ever be ready for it."

"Okay, it's a mess, I'll admit, but I think it's about what you do next that matters. You can't change what's happened and you don't have to explain. You just have to concentrate on doing the right thing now."

"I guess." I shrug, fighting the urge to get emotional.

The truth is, I have no idea how Marshall's family will react when they see me, but it's another step, another reality I need to face in order to be able to move forward. Keeping Marshall from them was selfish and unexplainably horrible, and I hate me for it even more than they will. It had been easier not to think about them, or him, or anyone other than my little boy. We'd existed in a safe, some days happy bubble for the longest time, and coming home was like taking a giant pin and bursting it.

Gabe

"A<small>RE</small> you sure you've packed your toothbrush?"

"Yes, Dad. I've got everything. Stop worrying, it's not like I haven't slept out before."

"Staying at your nan's is different, Pops. I want you to…"

"Remember to say please and thank you, don't stay up too late and no fizzy pop, I know, Dad.

"And I want you to…" She glares at me, raising her eyebrows at me. "Check on Frosty, make sure to feed him twice a day and keep him somewhere warm. I got it."

"It's Fluffy, Dad, her name's Fluffy."

I can't help laughing a little at the disgust on her face that I got the little birds name wrong. Or the fact that he's still here three weeks after finding him.

"Okay, let's go," I say, grabbing my keys off the side table and heading into town to drop her off at Rosie's for the night.

It was another step towards her growing up, and the thought of that scared the crap out of me, but I had to let her go a little. She had stayed in so many different places while living with her Mum that this was probably nothing to her, but it didn't make it any less daunting to me.

Rosie's dad seemed like a nice guy, and I'd chatted with her mum a few times at school, but she's my baby. I think I'll still be worrying like this when she's eighteen years old.

I drop her off and head to Jak's bar to meet with my old boss. He's been nagging at me ever since I left London to, at least, have a beer with him, but knowing Harry, they'll be more to it than that.

He's already waiting for me when I get there, wearing a full suit, and his briefcase is popped open on the table.

"Harry," I greet him as I walk towards him.

"Gabe," he replies with a friendly nod. He smirks on sight of my checked shirt and jeans.

"Don't," I warn him.

"What? Country life clearly suits you," he mocks.

"What brings you all the way from the city?" I ask, getting straight down to business.

"You do. Let me buy you a beer, and we can talk."

"I'll get them," I say, not letting him have the upper hand and ordering two scotch on the rocks.

In not planning on this being a long meeting, I can tell from Harry's suit that he's here on business rather than pleasure.

"I'll get straight to it. We've been offered a stint at New York Fashion Week. I can get us front row at every show and into every fucking after party. All you have to do," he leans forward, locking his fists together under his chin, "is name your price."

I scoff and shake my head before replying, "Not happening. I told you, I'm on a break."

"A break? We are talking hundreds of thousands of pounds. You don't just walk away from deals this big, Gabe."

"I already have." I smile. "Look around you, Harry," I say, glancing around the room. "We're in the middle of nowhere, and I happen to fucking love it here. I don't care if it's a hundred thousand pounds. Ain't nothin' gonna bring me back to the city."

"Damn it," he groans, downing his whiskey and slamming it back down on the table. His frustration has me laughing again, which only appears to piss him off more.

"What's the matter with you, H? Can't you just send Ben, or go yourself?"

He doesn't answer.

"They've asked for me, haven't they?"

A grin spreads across my face, and he looks like he wants to punch it straight off my lips.

"Yes, they've asked for you. Something about wanting a more classic approach, and apparently everyone else on the team is too commercial. Whatever the hell that means."

I'm falling apart with laughter now.

"I knew it. What did I tell you last Christmas? Old is the new, new."

"Great, you were right, now can you please call Angela, tell her to take care of her goddamn shit for a change and get your ass back to the city?"

"And what shit exactly is it that your referring to, Harry. If by shit you mean my daughter than you better pick that briefcase up and get the fuck outta here before I crush your face with it. You got me?"

The colour drains right out of his face.

"Of course I don't mean your daughter. Jesus, man, what the hell is wrong with you? I'm on your side, remember? We're partners, or we were, until you just dropped your life and became some sort of hillbilly."

"Out of respect for all the years we've worked together, I'm gonna pretend that you didn't just say that. In fact, I'm gonna pretend we didn't have this meeting at all. Get out of my shit, Harry, and tell the firm that my break just became fucking permanent."

Downing my shot, I slam my glass back down on the table and give him a look that lets him know I'm serious about this. He doesn't say anything in response, and I watch him leave and hope to god it's the last time I ever see him.

Making money was all Harry had ever cared about, it's why we worked so well together over the years.

Right out of college we had our drive in common, except his end goal was always making money. Mine had started with taking good pictures, and was really just a hobby that became an obsession.

My career took a twist when I'd made a shit ton of money for a photo of The Royals on their honeymoon. It helped that the Princess was topless, of course, but to me, it was money for nothing, and I became hooked.

My career had always been easy, as when I began seeing Angela. She was up and coming, and nobody knew about our relationship. So we made money selling shots of her that were private and inti-mate. The photo's drove Angela's career forward, and I gained respect as a credible photographer. Ever since, I've photographed countless models and celebrities and flown all over the world. Which worked well as Angela's career was unpredictable, and after we broke up, she would up and relocate with Poppy at the drop of a hat.

It was a weird arrangement that I would travel with them after we had split, but it kept Pops safe, and that was my number one priority.

Downing another scotch, the bar is starting to fill up, and the music has been cranked up to Saturday night level. I order another beer, still seething from my exchange with Harry, but what I'm really annoyed about is the truth in his comment that Angela should get back here and sort out her shit.

She was surely out of rehab by now, and it wasn't like her to just not show up. Usually we heard something. As far as I know I'm still her emergency contact, so if she'd relapsed, I would have got a late-night call from the hospital.

Poppy pretended she didn't mind. She never talked about her, which I know is because she doesn't want to upset me by bringing her up. She shouldn't have to even think the way she does, a whole world of stress and worrying brought on her by her own mum.

The thought has me feeling furious, and I order another couple of beers. It's been a long time since I've drank this much alcohol, and the heat of liquor hitting the back of my throat feels really fucking good.

I feel a pair of eyes burning into my cheek. When I look up, I see her. Kitchen intruder, glaring at me all judgemental like.

She's in skin tight jeans that outline the curve of her hips perfectly, and the high waist accentuates her hourglass figure. Her black top matches her high heels, and she's classy but sexy as shit all at the same time. She's easily as hot as any of the hundreds of models I've photographed. Except, she somehow has no idea of her effect on any of the men in here, who have clearly all noticed her, too.

As soon as my eyes lock on hers she looks away, but I wait, and sure enough, she eventually looks back, with that same look of distaste. As though she's never seen a guy drink alcohol before.

She doesn't acknowledge me in any way, or tell her friend I'm here, which surprisingly disappoints me. Instead, she struts right over to the bar next to me and completely disregards me, ordering a drink for herself and her friend. I watch her take the first sip, her lips curling as the sharp taste hits her palette. I can tell she doesn't drink much from her reaction.

"Stalking and trespassing. Wow, you're really quite the criminal, Evelyn."

I can tell that I've caught her attention by remembering her name, and she smiles in spite of herself, falling right into my seductive trap.

"I am not a stalker, or a trespasser, for that matter. My criminal record is squeaky clean, I wonder if you can say the same?"

"Ouch," I say, pretending to wince from her comeback.

"I'm merely pointing out the facts. First you're in my house, then you're in my bar…"

"I'm sorry, what? Your bar? Oh my god, I can't…" She laughs at my cocky disposition.

"Aren't you going to introduce me to your friend?"

"Tanya, this is…"

Did she really forget my name? Or is she toying with me?

"Gabe." I nod at her friend, thinking how much they are like chalk and cheese, and it only highlights again how delicious this standoffish woman is.

Since Angela, I had been off women with a capital O, but the way this one is pretending I have no effect on her whatsoever makes me want to rip the strap right off her skimpy top and take her tits with my mouth right here on this fucking bar top. Instead, I simply order her and her friend another drink and slide them towards her.

"We seem to have gotten off on the wrong foot, so how about we start again. I'm Gabe, I just bought a strawberry farm, which I'm still wrapping my head around and most importantly, I'm single, if you're looking for a playmate?"

I was teasing her again, but her friend snaps up my offer before she has a chance to reply.

"She's not interested. She's…"

"A dance then?" I suggest, taking her hand and pulling her onto the dance floor. I spin her around and position my hands on her killer hips, which I notice, although only slightly, are starting to sway in time with the music. Falling into rhythm with her, I push up against her so my own hips are right beneath hers, and her ass is so close to my cock it's threatening to swell.

"What are you doing?" she yells over the music.

"Dancing," I shout back, twisting her hips around so she's facing me.

"No, I mean…"

"Don't question it," I say, cutting her off. "Just enjoy it."

For a minute I don't know if she's going to slap me, but she doesn't. Instead, she laughs and dances with me. It's been a while since I was on a dance floor, or even in a bar, for that matter, but she has moves like a cheerleader and every sway accentuates her gorgeous shape.

"I don't dance, Gabe," she yells.

"You look like your dancing to me," I say, and the smile that's on her lips reaches her eyes, making them shine and telling me that all those other smiles were fake. I feel like I just hit the jackpot unlocking the real one, and she beams at me through long fluttery lashes.

"You're gorgeous," I shout as she breaks from my grip for the first time, but continues dancing.

My body instantly misses the contact, and I dance closer to her, my body seeking out hers.

"What?" she shouts, unable to hear me over the music.

I catch her hand and wrap it around my neck bringing my face close to hers. "I said you're gorgeous."

She looks right at me this time, and I can't read her thoughts.

"So are you," she says simply, before her dark eyes cloud over, replacing that sparkle with a dull ache. "I got to go," she mumbles, running towards the door, closely followed by her friend, and I get the feeling I shouldn't follow, but I do.

I find them outside, she's crying, and her friend has an arm around her, trying to calm her down. Intrigued by what has upset her, I don't let my presence be known. Lighting up a cigarette, I smoke it quietly and listen in to their conversation.

"Did you see me dancing, Tan? I haven't danced like that since…" She breaks down into tears again and her friend whispers something to her before she says, "I just keep asking myself, is it always going to be like this?"

I wonder what the hell she is talking about and light another cigarette, striding over and offering it to her.

"I don't smoke," she says, looking embarrassed and wiping her tears.

"You don't dance either. Seems like you're breaking a lot of habits tonight, huh?"

This time her friend smiles at me and Evelyn reaches up and takes the cigarette, inhaling a long drag before coughing her guts up. "Wow." I laugh, "You really don't smoke."

She scowls at me and takes another drag in an attempt to prove me wrong. Although, I notice it's a much smaller one this time, and she still coughs afterwards.

She looks up towards me with tears still in her eyes, and my fingers twitch to wipe them away. Maybe it's because she's younger than me, but I have an overwhelming need to look after this woman and make sure she's okay.

Damn it, what the fuck is wrong with me, looking after woman never did me any good before.

"Let me walk you girls home?"

"Then you'll know where I live," she points out.

"Then we'll be on an even playing field," I reply.

She gives a small smile, and I pull her to her bare feet. Slipping her shoes back on, and leading the way to her house. We walk side by side, all three of us not saying much, and we pass her friends place on the way.

"Will you be okay from here?" She eyeballs me suspiciously.

"Yeah, I'm good. Thanks for tonight, Tanya."

"Anytime, call me."

"I'll call you," Evelyn says, and her friend let's herself into what must be an apartment above a florist shop.

"She always so protective of you?" I ask out of curiosity.

"She's one of my best friends." She shrugs. "You didn't have to walk us home."

"It's nothing."

"For what it's worth, whatever it is that's got you all shook up like that, it's not worth your tears."

"You have no idea," she whispers and even in my intoxicated state I sense not to push her any further. "Thanks again for the other day, your daughter is so lovely."

"She can be, she can also be a little ball of fire."

"Marshall is exactly the same. One minute he's all butter that wouldn't melt, the next he's the cheekiest little monkey."

"They keep you on your toes, that's for sure. Was his finger okay?"

"He was fine, all forgotten about once we were home. This is me," she adds, coming to a stop outside a small white house with a huge basket full of flowers hanging next to the door.

"Nice." All I can think about is her being alone in there and how much I want to taste her on my tongue, but the fresh air has me sober enough to realise I'm a single dad with a ton of baggage and she's… complicated.

"Goodnight, Gabe." She smiles. Not the one that reaches her eyes, but the small kind that she gives to strangers. I want the other one, but I have a feeling I'm not going to get it. Not tonight, anyway.

Lifting my fingertip to her temple, I trace the outline of her face down to her cheek, and she allows me to.

"Goodnight, Evelyn," I murmur looking straight into her eyes, searching for a sign that I am having the same effect on her as she is having on me, but all I see is pain.

Instinctively and without thinking I step towards her; my finger still touching her cheek and take her lips for my own. She doesn't push me away. I'm surprised when her lips part, allowing me entrance, and I wrap my fingers up in her loose waves, tugging slightly as I suppress the urge to lift her up and wrap her legs around my waist.

Her kiss is exactly what I expected, soft and shy. Gentle, yet demanding. I can tell that she's curious of me and of how far I would take things, if she let me.

All of the way.

Her tender kiss, leaves me desperate for more and I only pull away when I taste a warm salty tear fall into my mouth.

"I can't do this," she says, before hurriedly opening her front door and disappearing inside, leaving me standing here wondering what the hell just happened.

I don't just kiss women I hardly know, and I definitely don't dance and walk people home. I might have once, but not anymore. I don't know what this woman has, but it's got me completely wrapped up in her.

"Damn it," I say, walking back towards Jak's to look for a taxi.

In another lifetime I would have had that woman screaming out my name within minutes.

Now I'm just the guy with problems that would only make whatever she has going on, a hundred times worse. No one wants to be that guy.

CHAPTER 7

Evelyn

*A*s soon as I arrive at work Tanya has that tell-me-everything look on her face that instantly lifts my mood and makes me giggle.

"Who the hell was that?"

"Cowboy god." I smile. "I met him the other day at the new strawberry farm down the road. I think he owns it."

"He's gorgeous."

"Yeah, he thinks so, too." I laugh, rolling my eyes.

"You didn't tell me you'd met some-one."

"I haven't. Marshall fell over, and his little girl said we could use his kitchen to get him cleaned up."

"He has a daughter," she ponders over this new piece of information. "And a wife?"

"No, it's just him and his daughter. Besides, he wouldn't have danced with me like that if he had a wife," I point out.

"You two had some serious moves, as I recall. You looked great together."

"Not happening." I stop her before she goes on a tangent, I already thrashed out in my head last night.

"I'm married, remember," I say, flashing her my wedding ring that's hanging from a thin gold chain around my neck.

"For what it's worth, I think you should never say never."

I shrug her off and get stuck into the spring gift bag arrangements we are working on.

"He was really cute though," she continues. "Did you two get talking when he walked you home?"

"Mmm," I mumble, non-committedly.

"I knew it. Something happened, didn't it? You like him, don't you? I just knew it from the way you let him walk us home."

I throw her a shut-up-and-don't-go-there look, which she ignores and continues to pry.

"Okay, I kissed him. Now, can we please drop this?"

"You dance with cowboy god and kiss him, and now you don't want to talk about it. I mean, come on, your killing me here. You know how much I love a happy ever after."

"Happy ever after? Tanya, I was more than a little worse for wear. He was clearly drunk, too. I'll probably never see him again, and even if I did... Nothing. Would. Happen."

"Because."

"Because reality. Kids. Baggage. Not to mention the fact that I'm still technically married."

"Pretty sure Marshall wouldn't have wanted you to be on your own forever," she points out. The truth in her words is like a bee sting to bare flesh.

"I'm not on my own, I have Marshall."

"You know exactly what I'm getting at." She rolls her eyes dramatically.

Thankfully we're interrupted by a customer, and we don't speak about the kiss again, but it doesn't stop me thinking about it for the rest of my shift.

It wasn't so much the way his kiss felt, but the way I felt when he kissed me. It hadn't felt bad, or wrong, or like I was cheating on Marshall.

In that moment, I felt like I was alive in a way that I hadn't for so long. I hadn't noticed the way my body ached to be held, until Gabe's fingers had twisted my hair and his unassuming kiss had taken over my every thought. Now I have been reminded of how my body responded to a man's touch, and it's awakened something in me that I wasn't prepared for.

Cowboy god probably kissed women like that all the time, and I'm pretty sure, he has no idea how much of a game changer last night was for me. It's opened a can of worms, and no matter how hard I try, I can't stuff them back into the can.

Was I ready to move on? Had I dishonoured Marshall, disrespected our marriage? Am I ready to start dating, and if so, is it fair to date someone knowing that it's never going to go anywhere because my heart already belongs to someone else?

Thinking of Marshall is overwhelming and reminds me that there's something I've been putting off since returning to The Cotswolds. Curling a lilac ribbon around the final spring arrangement, I catch Tanya watching me, trying to figure out all the answers to the questions I can't even answer myself.

"Do you mind if I leave early today, there's someone I need to see before Marshall finishes nursery."

"Is it cowboy god?"

"No." I laugh, rolling my eyes and shaking my head. "No, it isn't."

"Okay, thanks for today, Evie. This would have taken me for ever, and look at these things, they are so pretty. Did I mention how glad I am that you're back?"

"A few times." I smile as she admires my work. "Honestly, it doesn't even feel like work. It's more like a form of therapy. I'll see you tomorrow."

"See you in the morning. Don't forget we have that bride coming in first thing."

"I'll be here," I shout back on my way out of the door. Marshall finishes soon, so I don't have much time, but I have to do this. I need to put things right.

I follow the river along from Betty's Blooms and towards Marshall's parents' house. Just seeing it standing there makes my heart stand still, and I gasp to catch my breath while figuring out what I'll say to them. How will I explain why I had to leave, and tell them all about their grandson?

Suddenly, I regret not reaching out to them more, all I'd given them is a few photos. Knowing them the way I do, their forgiveness wasn't going to be easily earned. I remind myself, this isn't about me, this is about Marshall knowing his grandparents, so I step forward and stop myself as I notice someone pulling up outside. A huge black fancy car and a young man in a suit steps out, lifting his little boy out of the backseat and carrying him inside.

My eyes are glued to the scene as he puts the key in the lock and lets himself in through the front door. My feet are locked to their spot, long after the man and boy disappear inside. I study the house and notice other changes too, a new front door and expensive solar panels on the roof that Mr. Embers would never have splashed out on. A knot forms in my stomach and squeezes tightly as I realise, they have gone.

How could I have been so foolish? I'd expected everything to stay the same, like I could just waltz back into a postcard three years later and pick up where I left off. But this wasn't a pretty postcard picture, this was real life, and just like my life had changed, clearly everyone else's has, also.

With an hour to spare before it's time to collect Marshall, I wander around aimlessly and try to plan my next move. Everything has been so easy since I came home, I'm not about to let one hurdle get the better of me. I just need a plan of how to track them down.

As I take a turn down the windy backstreets of Bourton-on-the-Water, I come to another place that takes my breath away. The churchyard. I haven't been here since I was last here with Marshall, it was where we had picnicked and the very spot where Marshall was conceived.

Walking towards it, I reach and touch the branches, parting them before climbing underneath, the curtain of leaves and sitting underneath the way we had when we were kids. It breaks my heart and makes me smile all at the same time.

For a while I just sit and soak in the memories of us and all the firsts we'd shared underneath this very tree, and by the time I collect Marshall, I feel calm and at one with myself.

Remembering who I am wasn't easy when all I've been for so long is a mum, but with my job at the florist and the house starting to take shape, pieces of me are beginning to reconnect.

I run a finger over my lips, recalling the feel of Gabe's kiss and the trace of a smile settles there. To him I was just like any other woman, and it felt good to be myself and not just someone's widow.

Marshall bursts out of nursery and chatters all the way home. When we arrive, I'm so busy keeping up with his chatter and juggling all of the sparkly artwork he's brought home to notice the huge bunch of peonies sitting on my doorstep.

"Look, Mummy, we got fwowers." I pick them up and read the label.

Dance with me again this Saturday?

"Yes, we did, baby. You think they're pretty?"

"Pretty like Mummy," he replies, and I cuddle him before we step inside.

The place is an organised mess, and I place the last few items that are folded neatly on the sofa into the box marked 'charity.'

"Would you like to go for a bike ride, Marshall?" It was a stupid question as he just recently got his balance bike, and riding it was his new favourite hobby.

"Yes, pwease, Mummy."

"Perfect, let's have our snack, and then we will ride all the way to town like a big boy."

* * *

IT'S NOT FAR to the charity shop, but every step feels as though my trainers have bricks in them. I've dragged my feet with this for long enough, and I know in my head it's time for this, but the knowledge doesn't make it any easier on my heart.

"Here we go, little man. That was a fantastic job, you rode all the way here."

"Can we ride back?"

"Of course, we can. We just need to hand over this box, and then we can go again. You want to look around the shop for a minute?"

He nods his head, and we step inside. We could have drove here, it would have been much easier, as the box full of Marshall's belongings was heavy, and my arms ached from carrying it. It was almost as though by walking, I got to hold onto a piece of him for a little bit longer.

I hand the box to the elderly man working there, and as I turn to leave, Marshall runs over to me.

"Mummy look, it's a sholdwer like Daddy."

He's waving a little teddy dressed in army uniform at me, and I reel in shock.

"His father was a soldier?" the gentleman asks.

"He was," I reply. "He served in Afghanistan."

The elderly gentleman bows his head.

"Wernburg, Germany, 1945. I've had that little teddy bear ever since, but my grandchildren are all grown up now. Take it for your son, and thank you for your kind donation," he offers.

"Thank you so much. He will be sure to look after it."

We leave the shop and Marshall rides his bike home again with his new teddy popping its head out of my handbag.

CHAPTER 8

Gabe

*R*eading the letter again I crumple it and toss it at the wall, gritting my teeth in frustration. Full custody. She hadn't fucking seen Poppy in almost a year, and now she wants to take her from me. Angela never fails to surprise me, but even for her this was a low blow. I don't think any judge in their right mind would grant full custody to a woman with her track record of drugs, and alcohol addiction, coupled with the fact that she's barely been in Poppy's life. However, money talks, and money was the one thing she did have going for her.

If she wants a battle, she's fucking got one. There's not a chance in hell that she's about to disrupt my daughter's life again when it's only just become settled. Surely, a judge will take into consideration the fact that she has started full time school for the first time in years and is making new friends.

As crazy as the situations had gotten over the years, we had always managed to sort things out between us. Usually by me giving into her and agreeing to fly thousands of miles to be with Poppy while she works, if you can even call it that.

How the hell can 'The Crowne Plaza' qualify as a home address? But it doesn't matter how ridiculous her petition is, I'm going to fight fire with fire and hire a decent attorney to finish this thing quickly and with as little impact on Poppy as possible.

As I dig out some new strawberry rows, I wonder how long she has been in London and why she hadn't bothered to come and see our daughter.

By the time I've showered and changed I'm running late. Great. Now Evelyn's bound to think I'm screwing her around. That's if she even shows up. It has been a hell of a long time since I had arranged to meet up with a woman, and the timing is way off, as I need to focus everything I have on making sure Poppy is safe.

But the way she sees right through me and that sadness in her eyes that disappeared when she danced with me has been playing on my mind ever since. I don't know what I have to offer, or where this thing can go. All I know is that I have to see her again.

Jumping into my truck, I speed out onto the main road. I figure I can leave the truck in the village and pick it up tomorrow. Driving will be a hell of a lot quicker than trying to grab a cab on a Saturday night. I'm lucky my dad has agreed to stay home with Poppy, so I can have the night to myself, and I am feeling confident in casual jeans with a black polo shirt.

Walking into the bar, I'm disappointed to find that she hasn't shown up. I order a scotch on the rocks and sip it slowly, might as well have one for the road. My eyes scan the crowd over the rim of my glass, and when I finish the last drop, I admit defeat and head back out to my car.

I notice her across the car park, walking away from the bar. Her hair looks slightly different in a ponytail, but her curves are on full display in tight black leather pants.

"You running out on me?" I shout after her.

She turns to meet my gaze with a look of surprise.

"No… Well, kind of," she admits.

"You came all the way here to stand me up?"

"No, of course not. I was coming to meet you, but then I got here…"

"And what, you got here, saw me sitting at the bar and thought, nah, he's just not for me. Is it the hair?" I ask, running my fingers through my locks pretending to be self-conscious.

It only appears for a minute, but I see it, that brief sparkle in her eye is definitely there before it changes to something more serious.

"It's not the hair." She smiles. "I actually like your hair. But I came to thank you for all the flowers, and to ask you to stop sending them, as I… This can never go anywhere."

"Right, well… Now that you've got that off your chest, do you want to get out of here?"

"Did you just hear what I said?"

"Yes. You said you liked my hair," I say, and she pouts at me in frustration. "I'm kidding, I heard the other bit, too, and if I'm honest, you're probably right. This probably will never go anywhere because I'm not some fun guy who dances in bars on Saturday night. I'm a single dad about to head into a messy custody battle with my ex. I'm the kind of guy that a woman like you should run a thousand miles away from."

"So, then, why are you sending me flowers?"

I pull her in close to me, and kiss her with the same intensity I did the first time I met her. "Because you kiss like that," I whisper, pulling away. "So, now we've agreed that this is never going to happen. Do you want to get out of here? If it's the last time we see each other, we might as well have some fun, right?"

"Right," she says quietly.

"My truck is right over here. Hop in, there's somewhere I want to take you."

She looks at me like I'm a little crazy, but doesn't argue, stepping into my passenger seat when I open the door for her.

"Where are you taking me?"

"You'll see. Where's Marshall tonight?"

"With his Nanna and Grandad. He's staying over," she offers.

Is she telling me that so I know she has all night to spare?

"Where's Poppy?"

"She's at home, with my dad, probably putting her pet goose to bed or something."

"Pet goose?"

"Don't ask."

"Isn't this the way to your place?"

"Yeah, I only moved here recently, so I don't know the area yet," I admit.

She looks across at me with slight confusion on her pretty face.

"Don't worry, there's something I want to show you. I haven't taken anyone there yet, and I could do with a woman's opinion."

She watches the maple trees flying by us, as I drive past the house and out towards the lake.

Stepping out of the truck and walking around to open her door, I hold her hand for her to jump out. The touch of her skin has me wanting to devour her, and I take the liberty of keeping hold of it.

"This way, it's not far."

"I can hardly see anything, it's pitch black out here."

I squeeze her hand a little tighter. "Just trust me, it's not far at all."

I guide her through the trees to the clearing I've made and reveal my best kept secret. The tree house I've created for Poppy is almost complete and even in the dark it looks epic, if I may say so myself.

Weeks of hammering and sawing had finally paid off, and I can't wait to reveal it to her soon, but I want this space to be a place where she can be all girly and shit.

Angela is one of the most glamorous women I know, and when she was around Poppy, she was always spraying her with perfume and letting her use her lipsticks. Not that she'd ever admit it, but I think Pops misses that part of herself, and although she laughs when I let her paint my nails, we both know it's not the same.

Evelyn let's out a loud gasp in sight of the treehouse.

"Did you do this, Gabe?"

"Yeah, it's a surprise for Poppy, but I want to make sure it's perfect before I show her."

"It's amazing, I've never seen anything like it before."

"Think you can climb this thing in your heels," I ask, taking hold of the bottom rung of the ladder.

"Not without breaking my neck," she says, before sliding off her ankle boots.

"Will you catch me if I fall?"

"Of course," I answer without hesitation.

In another world I'd catch her, hold onto her and make her mine. She is so effortlessly sexy, and I watch her ass as she climbs the ladder, suppressing the urge to take a bite out of it as it moves past my face.

I follow her up the ladder, and we step inside the treehouse.

"Oh my god, Gabe this is so beautiful. I can't believe you created this, it's so perfect."

She glances upwards, taking in the glass rooftop that clearly displays all of the stars above us. We are so far out into the country-side that the air is clear, and in the dark of night, they are easily visi-ble, and she stares up at them in awe. I trace the line from her slightly parted lips, down to her throat and gulp at the thought of kissing her again.

"Do you think it's girly enough?" I ask, wondering what she makes of my efforts to make this place into everything Poppy could dream of.

"It's stunning. She's a lucky little girl. I can't believe you made all this by hand."

"You ready to see the best part?"

"There's more?"

"Close your eyes."

She hesitates, second-guessing me but closes her eyes after a few seconds, and I flick the switch that lights the whole place up with white fairy lights.

"You can open them now."

She flickers her eyes open, and her mouth widens at the sight of the lights. Her expression is my confirmation that the treehouse is definitely girly enough.

"Gabe, this is so pretty. It's perfect."

"Pretty and perfect. I could say the same about your ass in those pants. Now, can we have that dance you were coming to meet me for?"

Her eyes darken. "That's not why I was coming to meet you."

I wrap my arm around her waist, just above the soft curve of her hips and say softly, "Let's just pretend it was."

As though my touch invades her thoughts, she doesn't object any further, and I begin to sway my hips gently. She falls in sync with my movements, resting her head on my chest and I pull her in tighter.

Her body reacts to my every move, and she rocks her hips gently in time with me as I wrap my fingers around hers, locking our hands together. Closing my eyes, I inhale a deep breath and let myself imagine a world where this gorgeous woman was mine.

I'm aching to kiss her, but I don't want to be the reason her eyes fill with sadness again. Instead, I want to find out how it got there in the first place.

Evelyn

"WHY DID you run the other day when I kissed you, Evelyn?" he asks in a soft murmur as we come to a stop outside and sit on the edge of the decking, our legs swinging in the air.

"I was scared."

"Do I scare you?"

"No, well… Maybe a little."

"You know, it's funny. The first time I saw you, in my kitchen, Poppy told me off for scaring you away."

"She did?" I ask, smiling at the thought of his bossy daughter putting him in his place.

"Weird, right?"

"Can I ask you something, Gabe?"

"Sure."

"How old are you?"

"How old do you think I am?"

"I don't know, mid-twenties?"

"No you don't, you know I'm older than that," he replies, arching an eyebrow at me.

"Late twenties?" she guesses again.

"I'm thirty-five… Which makes me too old for you, right?"

"I don't know, I'm twenty-four."

"But, since we already established this isn't going anywhere, I figure it doesn't matter." He reasons, letting the fact of the matter sit in the silent air around us, disappointing us both.

"What's your story, Gabe?" I ask, genuinely intrigued to find out how this ridiculously gorgeous man found himself living in the middle of nowhere, farming strawberries.

"Too long a story for one night." He shrugs, looking down to his feet and banging his boots together, awkwardly.

I don't know why, but sensing that he needs to talk, I am compelled to lean my head against his shoulder and reassure him that I have all night to listen.

"I was a kid when I met my ex, Angela. We both were." He sighs as if the story weighs heavy on him. "She was a drama student, and I was a paparazzo. I basically gave her, her career, and she became famous overnight."

"Your ex-girlfriend is famous?"

"My ex is Angela Farrow."

"As in the actress Angela Farrow."

He moans in acknowledgement, and I'm guessing the sound of her full name tugs on his heartstrings the same way mine are yanked and knotted whenever someone mentions Marshall.

"She's a really great actress," I offer, unsure of what to say to this new piece of information.

"Don't."

"Don't what?" I ask, biting my lip and tucking a loose string of hair behind my ear.

"You said that as though you're somehow insignificant in comparison. You're not. I don't know much about you, Evelyn, but I can see you care about your kid. So you've already got one up on Angela." He stares, wryly.

Poppy. I hadn't even considered her until now, and how she had been affected by having a parent so famous as Oscar Winning Angela Farrow. I glance up at Gabe, trying to read his thoughts, but his eyes are dark and clouded, and there are flecks of raw vulnerability there, that I hadn't noticed before.

"After she hit the big time, my career became mostly about following her around and photographing her to look like the caring mother she wasn't, as she was constantly photographed doing drugs and partying. She lost the plot…"

I glance up at him, and he reads my thoughts.

"Why didn't I leave? I ask myself that all the time, but I couldn't. Part of me felt somehow responsible, I'd helped her to get to where she was and should have done more to stop her before, she was out of control. And then Poppy. No matter what that woman does, Poppy dotes on her. I couldn't do that to her."

"So, you stayed."

"Yeah."

"You shouldn't ever feel guilty for staying. It seems to me like you stayed for the right reasons."

"That doesn't matter to Poppy. You know, all she wants is her mum's approval and Angela hasn't so much as wrote to her in months. Instead, all I got in the mail was a fucking custody battle."

"She's going for custody?" I ask, genuinely shocked that after everything Angela has put Gabe through, she would try to take Poppy from him.

"Full apparently. See what I said about you not needing to worry. A relationship with anyone other than a decent solicitor is the furthest thing from my mind.

His hurt is tangible in the space between us, and I tilt my chin up to find him facing me. This time it's me who kisses him without a single hesitation. My lips melting into his and stripping away all of his complication and baggage until he's just a man, kissing his woman, I mean *'a'* woman, and he lets me know how good he feels by kissing me back.

"Why do you always look like that after you kiss me?" he asks as we break for air.

"Like what?"

"I don't know. Scared. Sad. Mostly just sad."

Crap, this guy reads me like an open book.

"Because I am sad. I mean, not just when I'm kissing you," I add hurriedly upon seeing his change of expression. "Most of the time, actually," I admit. I'm kind of a nutcase. I get happy, then I get sad because I feel bad for being happy."

"Yep, definitely a nutcase." He nods with the hint of a smile that causes my own lips to curl upwards.

"I lost my husband," I confess, blurting it out quickly to get rid of the awkward words that were the cause of all the sadness he is talking about.

"I had no idea, I'm so…"

"He was a soldier," I volunteer. "He went to Afghan, and that was that."

He looks straight at me, but doesn't put an arm around me, as though accepting that no amount of comfort could begin to address what I have been through.

"Your son?"

"I found out I was pregnant not long after he passed away." A lump forms in my throat that almost prevents me from getting the words out. Realisation dawns on him that I've been on my own for the last three years.

"Did you love him?"

My forehead immediately bunches up, and I snap at him, taking offence to the question.

"Of course, I loved him, he was my husband."

"Not necessarily," he says, looking out to the skyline above the treetops. "People marry for a whole bunch of reasons."

"Not me. Marshall was my high-school sweetheart. Everybody called us star crossed lovers. We were forever."

"I don't know how you do it. Get up every day and just… Carry on."

"At first it's just auto-pilot," I say, surprising myself. This is the first time I've spoken so openly about losing Marshall. "After a while it got easier. Having Marshall helped. We both moved to Greece to help my parents open a restaurant out there, so we've lived by the beach for the last few years. We only came back to The Cotswolds a few weeks ago because Marshall needed to start school, and I needed to…"

"Face the past. I get it. I think you're amazing, by the way," his voice dripping with sincerity as he puts an arm around me. "Now, it's my turn to feel shitty."

"Sorry, I didn't mean to depress you."

"You didn't. I just realised that this really isn't going to happen. Wow. I didn't think it was possible to find anyone with as much baggage as me. You knocked it out of the park."

"Thanks for showing me this place, Gabe," I say, glancing around. "It really is like a fairy-tale."

"You know, the lights aren't the only special feature. Check this out."

He jumps up, making me jump too, in case he falls off the edge, but he doesn't flinch or acknowledge that we are around fifty feet off the floor.

"You won't believe this, are you up for a challenge?"

"It depends on the challenge," I answer, curious to know what tricks cowboy god has up his sleeve.

He grabs my hand, hauling me to my feet and leading me to the other side of the platform decking surrounding the treehouse.

"Oh no, no… no… no," I say, pulling away as I realise what he has in mind.

A fucking zipline. The highest, longest zipline I have ever seen, running all the way from our feet to somewhere I can't even see as it's pitch black.

"You can do this. If you can raise a kid, you gotta be able to do this," he says, matter of factly.

"This is completely not the same."

"Do you always say no to fun?"

I think on his question, his arched eyebrow challenging me, goading me until I find myself saying, "No. Just the type of fun where I might die."

"You think I'd let you die?"

"What if I fall?"

"You won't. Why would you let go, when you know if you let go, you'll die?"

"Are you crazy?"

"A little," he replies, hooking himself up to the zipline and disappearing before my very eyes before I can argue with him any further.

"Gabe," I call after him as I watch him sail down the line as if he is flying."

"You gotta try this," he screams at the top of his voice, and his gravelly tone echoes through the empty night sky.

"I told you, I'm not doing it," I yell back, cupping my hands around my mouth to make sure he hears me.

"You got this, Evelyn," comes his confident voice from somewhere below.

"Not happening," I shout, looking at the zipline, wondering why anyone in their right mind would ever choose to plunge from this high up into the depths of the forest. Especially at night.

Marshall would have been all over this, he always loved a challenge. Nothing ever scared or intimidated him, he was similar to Gabe in that way. And then it dawns on me, Gabe is right. I do say no to fun.

Since losing my husband, and especially since having Marshall, I said no to anything that had a remote risk attached to it. I have become a worrier. Always second guessing myself and thinking up the worst possible outcomes, shutting opportunities down before they have chance to be properly considered.

This is something the old Evie would have done in a heartbeat. My body starts tingling in anticipation, could I really be thinking about doing this?

"Your turn," comes Gabe's voice, echoing before it reaches me. "Or are you too chicken?"

Oh, he did not just call me that. Moving quickly, I grip the two handlebars and cling on to the zipline for my life. Dropping from the safety of the edge of the tree house and sailing through the black of night.

"Arrrrrgggghhh! I scream out as I fly through the air. "Gabe," I shout, wondering whereabouts he is.

"I'm right here, I got you," he calls back, and his shadow comes into view.

Before either of us can do anything about it, I slam into him with the force of my entire body, causing him to stumble and fall backwards. Landing on top of him, I deplete into fits of giggles, and he starts to laugh too.

"You definitely got me." I laugh, looking down at him from my new awkward position.

"That's it."

"What's it?"

"You've got this smile," he whispers, our noses almost touching. "You don't do it often, but when you do, shit it's fucking beautiful."

Taken aback, I lean forward and place my lips on his in a gentle kiss that soon turns into something more when his tongue finds mine.

"You know what I said earlier, about this never going to happen."

I moan in response, still reeling from the strength and warmth of his kiss.

"We might need to rethink that one."

I don't disagree with him. There's something about the way Gabe affects me that I can't say no to. When I'm with him, I become lost in him, and everything else seems so much easier than facing reality.

As we stand up, I try to follow the line of the zipline back up to the tree house, my vision blurring in the darkness.

"I can't believe you would let Poppy use that thing. It can't be safe, surely?"

"There's a net right underneath, Evelyn."

"There is?"

"Of course, Poppy's my world. Safety first, and then fun, right?" He grins.

I slap him lightly on the arm. "Why didn't you tell me," I hiss angrily.

"Because if you knew there was a net, you wouldn't have felt the way you did when you came hurtling down towards me.

"Oh yeah, and how was that?" I ask, playfully.

He steps into my personal space and brings his face closer to mine, causing me to look up at him.

"Alive," he murmurs, before kissing me all over again.

This time, he lifts me up, and my legs fall naturally around his hips as he slams my back into the zipline post.

"Gabe, I can't…" I breathe out, gasping for air when he finally pulls away.

"And I can't not see you again," he simply states.

"Race you to the top," I say, darting off towards the tree house ladder.

"Unless you're too chicken?"

He chases after me, catching me, and we kiss again against the ladder before having a few more goes on the zipline. We spend most of the night sat out on the decking, talking about all kind of things. By the time we run out of conversation, the sun is coming up, and both of us realise just how long we have been out here for.

"Looks like it might be home time," he suggests.

"Oh, shit, I need to get back to Marshall."

"I'll drive you, it's still early, you'll be back well before he is."

"I had such a great time, Gabe."

"Me too," he says, and we walk back to the car with an awkwardness between us.

As we reach the truck, he goes to open to door for me then pulls back, and instead, pins me against it. "I have to see you again."

"Gabe, I…"

"I know it's crazy, but I just fucking have to," he reasons. "Is Marshall staying out next weekend, too?"

"No," his eyes search mine for a solution.

"He is staying out the one after that, though. I guess we could do something," I volunteer.

"I'll meet you at the same time. Come to Jak's and dress up, I want to take you somewhere?"

"Like a date?" I ask, feeling slightly crushed. I'm ready for something, but what, I haven't figured out yet.

"Call it whatever the fuck you want, as long as you show up, I'm good."

"I grin at his exasperated tone, and his hungry lips smash into mine, taking my mouth for one last time before I really have to get home.

Climbing into the car beside him feels strange after spending the night together. In daylight he was every inch as gorgeous, and I cringe as he catches me glancing up at him.

His hair is unkempt and flops over his hazel eyes every now and again before he flips it out of the way with his hand. His dark stubble outlines a strong jawline, and as my eyes fall to his lips, my stomach tenses slightly.

He cranks up the radio, blasting out Bruno Mars, Just the Way You Are. He seems completely unaware that I'm sitting here as he pushes up his sleeves and sings along to the words.

He reaches over and squeezes my thigh when Bruno sings, 'And when you smile, the whole world stops and stares for a while,' and I can't help beaming at him.

The road disappears quickly, and we reach my place in just a few minutes.

"The weekend after next," he reminds me.

"Goodnight, Gabe." I smile back at him, getting out of the car.

"Good morning, Evelyn," he says back, and I watch as he reverses away from my doorstep and turns back to wink at me, before pulling off.

CHAPTER 9

Gabe

"$\mathcal{I}$f you hold still then it won't hurt as much," I explain as I wrestle Poppy's hair into a bobble.

"I am holding still, you just need to wrap it around. You're not doing it like I showed you, Dad."

"I am, wait… I think I've got it," I say through gritted teeth, as I snap the band off my finger and trap her hair into a ponytail.

"You did it! Thanks, Dad. Now for the ribbon," she says excitedly, holding up a long, thin piece of yellow ribbon.

"Um, you never mentioned a ribbon, Pops."

"It's easy, just tie it like a shoelace." She shrugs.

"A shoelace?" I question, taking the silky strand from her.

"All the girls have them, Dad. If I'm going to be the May Queen, I need to look as pretty as I can."

"Poppy, you don't need a ribbon or fancy dress to make yourself look pretty, you're already the most beautiful girl I have ever seen."

"Thanks, Dad. Now, the ribbon?" She quips, and I realise there's no getting out of this.

As I tie it in as neatly as I can, a sinking feeling pulls in my stomach. It should be Angela doing things like this with her, brushing her hair and picking out her dress. It is so unfair that she is stuck with my fumbly fingers. What could I know about looking pretty?

"I think you're ready," I say with pride, and she darts off to check in the mirror.

"This is great, Dad, You're getting better at this," she offers, wriggling with the bow to make each loop more equal.

The shrillest of high-pitched squeals pierces my ears, and I grin smugly as she runs back into the room.

"You like it then?"

"Oh, Dad, it's perfect," she declares, holding up the frilly yellow dress for me to admire. "Thank you, thank you," she yells before running towards me. I lower myself so she can throw her arms around my neck, and she squeezes me as tightly as she can in a hug so heartfelt it almost chokes me to fuckin' tears.

"Go and put it on then, you don't want to be late."

With that, she disappears, and I check my emails, firing off a bunch of responses to work that Harry must have sent my way. It's the last thing on my mind, and I have no plans of working with him again now, or in the future. It's been months since I so much as lifted up my camera, and I've missed it.

Before photography became my career, it was my life and the only hobby I'd ever known. The thought of shooting again makes me grab my smaller camera from the hall cupboard and throw it around my neck as we leave the house.

"You're taking your camera?" Poppy asks, raising an eyebrow at me suspiciously. Had it really been that long since she saw me with it?

"You think I'd miss out on a shot of you in your princess dress?"

"Queen, Dad. I'm the May *Queen*," she corrects me.

"Please accept my humble apology, your royal highness," I say, waving a hand in her direction.

"That's better," she replies, smoothing over the puffy layers of dress as we head into town.

"What does humble mean?" she asks and laughs when I arch an eyebrow at her.

"It means you know yourself, and always remember where you come from and who you truly are," I reason.

"Why would anyone forget who they are?" She looks completely flummoxed at the idea and holds out her hands in frustration.

Ask your dickhead of a Mum, I think to myself, before replying.

"Some people don't think roots are important, but roots are everything. It's like a tree, it can only grow big and tall if it has good strong roots in the first place."

"I'm going to be really big then, aren't I, Dad?"

"What makes you say that?"

"Because you're my roots, and you're really strong, and I could never forget anything about you."

Her sweet words punch me straight in the gut, knocking the damn wind right out of me.

"Then you're going to be some kind of giant." I smile, squeezing her leg as we pull up at the May Day Festival.

I had no idea that people still did things like this. I feel like we're Bill and Ted and have just arrived in a time machine rather than my truck.

The village is packed, and there's everything from vintage fairground games to candy floss stands and donkey rides.

"Over there, Dad. I can see the float," Poppy says, pulling me over towards her school class float.

Really, it's an old milk wagon covered in glittery fabric, but from the way Pops' eyes widen when she sees it, you would think the throne in the middle was made of solid gold.

"Oh, isn't it just gorgeous," she exclaims. "Look, there's Emily with Miss Davies."

I glance up to find Poppy's teacher grinning from my daughter to me, her face telling me I did a fucking good job with her outfit.

"Okay, you go and wait over there. I want you to see me as I come around the corner," Poppy instructs.

"I'll be there. Be careful when the wagon is moving. Don't be moving around up there, you could fall off."

"Don't worry, Dad, I'll be fine. Wave to me, okay?"

"Okay, have a good time, baby," I say, before letting her run over to Miss Davies, who hasn't taken her eyes off us.

She's almost half my age, but I don't miss that spark in her eyes when I nod over and acknowledge her. The blood from my head rushes straight to my cock for a minute, and my thoughts turn to Evelyn. It's been so long since I'd kissed a woman, it had been hard not to take things further, but I knew she wasn't ready. The last thing I want to do is scare her off.

Making my way over to wait for Poppy, a sweet voice saying my name causes me to glance up.

"Evelyn? Hi, what are you doing here?"

"Not winning that Paw Patrol teddy for Marshall," she replies, pointing to a cute Dalmatian wearing a fireman's helmet."

"Hey, Marshall. Want me to try to help?"

He eyes me cautiously, and I don't think he remembers me.

"We're goo…" Evelyn starts to say before her son cuts her off.

"Yeah, pwease," he says, his eyes still locked on me.

"Sure thing, buddy," I say, stepping closer towards them and picking up a beanbag. "If I get this on the first go, you're going on a date with me, before next Saturday. I can't wait until then."

"It's only a week away." She rolls her eyes.

"You remembered then?"

"Of course."

"And you weren't going to stand me up?"

"You'll have to wait and see."

"I'm an impatient guy." I shrug. "Ready, Marshall, here we go," I say, chucking the bean bag and knocking the coconut in the centre clean off its stand.

"Yay!" Marshall cheers, clapping his chubby little hands.

"Did you ever doubt me?" I tease him, and he says nothing,

cuddling the teddy when it's placed in his arms like it's the best thing in the world.

"Thanks, I was running out of 50p's." She smiles her full beautiful fucking smile.

"Tomorrow?"

"I can't."

"I think you can. Marshall will be at school," I point out.

"I have to work."

"Take a day off?"

"I'll see what I can do," she offers, non-committedly.

Her chocolate waves are loose over her creamy shoulders that are exposed by a strappy summer dress with flowers all over it. It clings to her every curve, her tits peeking out of the top like two sweet muffins I want to bite. Her legs are tanned and long, even in casual flat sandals, and the length of her dress is high enough on her thigh to make me ache for her. It's everything I can do not to lean forward and kiss her.

Instead, I stay to Marshall, "Doesn't your mummy look beautiful today?"

He regards her for a minute, and she squeezes his hand awkwardly struggling with the compliment.

"You sure look the part for a city boy," she returns, and I proudly jerk at my gilet.

"I never knew things like this existed," I admit.

"I've been coming to the May Day Festival since I was a little girl. There's something magical about the whole village getting together and watching the parade."

"I've been told to wait over there, for the Queen's arrival."

"Oh, Gabe, she's not?"

"She sure is."

"I bet she's so excited."

"She's beside herself. They should be coming around the corner any minute," I say, making my way over to where Poppy told me to wait for her. Evelyn walks alongside me, and scoops Marshall up on her hip, so he can see better.

"I can't see, Mummy," he complains, lifting his hands in the air.

"Wanna come up on my shoulders, Marshall?"

He looks a little unsure but nods his head, and I take him from Evelyn before she has a chance to argue, throwing him over my head, and onto my shoulders. His hands rest on my head and I hold his leg with one hand, grabbing Evelyn's hand with my free one and squeezing it tightly to reassure her.

As we round the corner, the parade of floats starts driving past us, and my daughter beams at me from her royal throne in the middle of her class float. Her eyes widen in surprise as she spots Marshall on my shoulders, and then fall to Evelyn who is standing beside me. Her hands fly up over her mouth dramatically, and she starts waving at all three of us like crazy before throwing me a final mischievous, knowing look as she passes by. She is already way too excited about this.

Over the last few months, thanks to her little sleepover club, Poppy has appointed herself as my dating guru. If it wasn't annoying as hell, it would actually be kind of cute.

"She looks amazing," Evelyn murmurs, waving back at Poppy.

"She's definitely got the whole royal vibe down." I grin. "What are you doing now," I ask, lifting Marshall over my head and placing him on the ground in front of me.

"Nothing." She shrugs. "Isn't that kind of the point of bank holidays?"

"Maybe around here," I reply, giving it some thought. "In London, bank holidays are just like any other day, but it seems like in The Cotswolds a day off really is a day off, right?"

"Exactly, Marshall and I are going to grab some lunch and spend the rest of the afternoon at the fete."

"Let me buy you lunch, and you can tell me everything about this doing nothing business."

"Dad!" Poppy interrupts us, bombing towards me like a yellow bundle of frilly stuff. "Did you see me; did you see me?" she yells before reaching me.

"You looked awesome, Pops."

"I love your dress," Evelyn says, smiling sweetly at Poppy who laps up the attention like a cat with a plate of milk.

"Thanks, my dad's designer friend made it. He sent it all the way from London, just for me."

"Wow," Evelyn replies, widening her eyes at me in a shit-that-must-have-cost-you-a-fortune look.

It did. I nod back and shrug to let her know I can afford it. She doesn't seem like the materialistic type in the slightest, but it can't hurt to let her know money's not an issue for me.

"Dad, Rosie's getting hot dogs for lunch. Can we get some, pleeeease."

She throws me the puppy eyes, and Evelyn chuckles when they have the desired effect on me.

"Well, I was going to ask Evelyn and Marshall if they wanted to join us for lunch. If that's okay with you, Pops, but I'm not sure…"

"Hot dogs sound good to me," Evelyn says, throwing me a 'no arguments' look before smiling at Poppy. "But you know what Marshall and I like on days like this?"

Poppy eyes her suspiciously, before Marshall spies the food wagon closes to us and shouts, "Candy fwoss!"

Everyone laughs, and when I lock eyes with Evelyn, I see a glimpse of that carefree woman I'm becoming obsessed with.

"You get the candy floss, Poppy and I will take care of the rest," I say, throwing her a wink that's just between the two of us before watching her turn away.

She walks with confidence, flipping her hair back over her shoulder as she reaches down to tell Marshall something.

I love how attached she is to him and how much he clearly adores her. The kind of bond every child should have with their parent. I know it well because I have it with my girl, there isn't anything I wouldn't do to put a smile on her cute little face.

"Dad," she says, my eyes still locked on Evelyn, following her to the queue and watching her count coins into Marshall's hand. "The hot dogs?" Poppy's eyes quiz me before she rolls them in despair. I swear this kid has been here before, her eyes burning into mine like she knows exactly what I'm thinking.

"Hot dogs." I nod, grinning at her and squeezing her hand when she slides it into mine.

She doesn't normally hold my hand, she's always been fiercely independent, and it feels good that she wants to show me off.

We meet a couple of her friends and their mums in the queue, and I notice Evelyn glances over when she sees the other mums chatting to me. I humour them for a few minutes before dismissing them and turn my attention back to Poppy. There's only one woman I'm interested in making small talk with, and she's making her way over to a spot of grass with two arms full of candy floss bags.

Evelyn

THE AFTERNOON with Gabe and Poppy had been an unexpected and refreshingly easy time. Despite my attempts to resist, he'd insisted we go on a date, and when I'd agreed to meet him after dropping Marshall off, I hadn't expected to feel like this.

I'd said yes before all the niggling thoughts of self-doubt crept in. Now they are like screaming sirens in my head, causing my palms to become clammy. I rub them over my denim clad thighs and pull my hair over my left shoulder, smoothing the ends with my fingers as his truck pulls up alongside mine.

What am I doing? Before I can try to make any sense of why I'm going on an official date with a man other than my husband, he runs a hand through his hair and throws me *that* smile. It's a definite thank-god-you-showed-up smile that incites a warm burn in my cheeks.

Donning a simple white polo shirt and loose navy cargo pants he pulls off the relaxed casual vibe with ease.

"Hi, it's been a while," he jokes.

"It's been less than twenty-four hours," I point out.

"It's been too long," he says with a low growl that makes him sound as though he wants to throw me across his bonnet there and then. My cheeks burn even hotter, and a tingle starts up in between my legs at the thought of it.

"You don't play hard to get, do you?"

"I don't play, at all," he says, opening the passenger door of his truck and helps me step inside.

I wonder what he means by his comment, as he strikes me as the type of guy who would take a different woman to bed every weekend. He could too, I muse as he walks around the truck and jumps into the seat beside me. I'll bet there isn't a woman in the world who could resist his effortless charm.

At the same time, he strikes me as honest and genuine. I admire that about him already, he's not afraid to say exactly what he's thinking and share things about himself.

"So, where are you taking me?"

"You'll see," is all he replies, before starting up the engine and pulling out onto the main road.

"Seriously," I ask as he cranks up the volume to 50 Cent and spits a rap verse from Candy Shop out.

"Lights on, or lights off, she like it from…" I reach forward and switch the channel before we reach the word 'behind.'

He laughs when 'In Those Jeans' plays out and starts up rapping again, this time gesturing to my ass and making me giggle along with him.

We're about half an hour from Bourton-on-the-Water when we begin to slow down, and Gabe drives into the car park of an Equestrian Centre.

"You ride?" I ask, wondering how a city boy like him would know anything about horses.

"A little, I had some lessons back in high school and took to it. It's been a while, but I know enough for what we're doing."

"Which is?"

"Come on," he says, stepping out of the truck, and I jump out to follow him.

A few minutes later when the farmhand brings two horses over, ready for us to ride, I start to panic. I've never rode before, and the two horses we've been given are bloody huge.

"Gabe, I think you're underestimating how hard it is to ride for someone that's not done it before."

His eyes shine green, lighting up at my comment, and an undeniable smirk hits his lips.

"What?" I ask, wondering if he is mocking me.

"Nothing, I just… I was hoping you hadn't. I like doing things for the first time with you."

"Oh, it'll defiantly be a first all right. First time I end up in the Accident and Emergency department on a date."

"You won't. I'll help you, it's easier than you think." He shrugs before confidently mounting the tall black stallion, leaving me staring up at the equally huge grey one standing next to me.

Here goes nothing. I wedge my foot into the stirrup and push as hard as I can to throw my other leg over the horse but go nowhere.

"You gotta really give it some welly," Gabe coaxes and this time when I try, I push up with everything I have.

In one slightly awkward and embarrassing movement, I find myself sat in the middle of the saddle, and I grin at Gabe in satisfaction.

"Follow the track around to the left and keep away from the roads," the farmhand instructs us. "You want me to come with you?" he offers, clearly on my account.

I want you to get me down off this thing and help me get my feet back on the ground again, my inside voice screams out. But I don't say anything because the truth is that even though I'm outside of my comfort zone, there's something exciting about having no idea about how this is going to go.

"No, we'll be fine. Thanks."

"No problem, call me if you need anything," he says to Gabe before turning to me. "Go easy up there," he warns and chuckling at me as he walks away.

"You've got this," Gabe reassures me, and I watch him click his heels against the horse's body, causing it to begin to walk.

I do the same, and my horse starts with a jump, and even though we are only moving at walking pace, I let out a scream before I can stop it escaping my lips.

"You scared, Evelyn?"

"Not at all," I lie, sarcasm evident in my tone as I gulp, and Gabe speeds up a little to walk alongside me.

"See," he says after a few minutes. "You're a natural."

"I don't know about that," I say jiggling about on the saddle as we make our way across the field, moving further away from the farm and into the open space. There's nothing around us for miles, and it feels like a complete escape from everything and everyone. That, I can do. I might suck at horse riding, but running away was something I've become an expert at.

"You look good up there, remember to relax and you will find the horse relaxes with you. Loosen your hands," he instructs me, and I do. "That's it, it's all in the body, use your body to control the movements rather than your hands. Here, watch this."

He let's go, holding both reins in one hand and gestures for me to do the same. When I do, he catches my free hand in his and wraps his fingers around mine. His hand swallows mine and feels firm and in control. The skin on skin contact fills me with something much more than desire, it fills me with hope.

We walk for a while, hand in hand before he pulls us to a stop and jumps down from his horse, tying it around the tree. His hands wrap around my waist to lift me from my horse, and when I touch the ground, he holds me there for a minute, regarding me. When he drops his hold on me, I realise how easy it was to let him touch me like that.

My heart calms from the fast, heavy beats it had pumped when his hands were my waist, and I follow him, stroking the horse's nose as he ties him up.

"Now, for the real fun, you ever been cloud watching, Evelyn?"

"Nope."

"You'll love it. Come and lie next to me," he lies down in the grass, and I feel awkward towering over him so I quickly lie down, too.

"See the racing car?"

I squint my eyes and tilt my chin a little but see nothing.

"All I see is clouds."

"That's because you're not really looking. If you just relax for a while, you'll see something."

"Okay," I say, turning to face him.

"Who taught you how to do this?" I ask, unable to relax as easily as he clearly can.

"My grandma. It's the only thing I remember about her?"

"I'm sorry. You must have been young when she passed?"

"Oh, she's not dead, I just haven't seen her. It's complicated." He shrugs.

"Families usually are." I sigh, thinking of my own messed up situation with Marshall's parents.

"I hope Marshall always stays in touch with his grandparents. It seems even more important now that his daddy's not around."

Gabe props himself up on his elbow and slides a hand over my waistline that creates a trail of butterflies swirling in its wake.

"You're amazing, you know? Always thinking of Marshall, he's going to be one kick ass little kid with you looking out for him like that."

"I hope so, he deserves it."

"It's a gift, you know? Loving him like that, not all mums have it."

His eyes cloud over with a heavy sadness that hits me straight in the gut, the amber in them dimming and leaving only a dull shade of emerald green.

"Angela?"

"Angela, my mum, my grandma, I'm plagued by women that are so fucking unlike you."

He looks away, tilting his face back to the sky, and I sense the conversation is too painful to continue. In an attempt to lighten the mood, I look away from him and back to the sky.

After a few moments of uncomfortable silence, I yell, "I see one. A face, right there. Do you see it?"

"That's not a face, it's an island," he says.

"Na ah, there's the nose, and see the mouth almost smiling at us?"

"That's clearly a palm tree, Jesus, Evelyn." He chuckles.

"It's mad how the same thing looks so different to both of us. I guess we're both right, it just depends how you see it."

"What do you see now?" he asks, propping himself up so he's leaning over me, blocking my view.

I take in his deep eyes that are burning into mine, switching from green to amber under my gaze. His strong jawline is dusted in dark stubble that frames his full, kissable lips.

"I see a man that wants to kiss me," I say softly.

"Look again."

"I see a man that wants to fuck me?" I say boldly, and he lets out a groan in frustration, trailing a finger from my shoulder to my finger tip.

Pulling us up to a sitting position, he brings his face so close to mind I can barely comprehend his question when he asks it again.

"Now what, Evelyn, now what do you see?"

"What do you want me to say?" I whisper as his arm works its way around my back and squeezes my waist tightly.

"Say exactly what you see," he whispers, his full lips almost brushing against mine.

"I just see that you want me."

He leans forward and brushes his lips softly against mine, parting them with his tongue. His hands roam my hips and work their way up to my shoulders as he kisses me with an intensity that leaves us both breathless.

"I think we both know that I want to do more than just fuck you," he says, arching an eyebrow at me all matter-of-fact-like.

CHAPTER 10

Gabe

*S*he'd hit the nail right on the fucking head. I just wanted her. There was no sense to it, no label. All I knew is that when I'm near her I felt ten years younger and more like the man I wanted to be.

Undoubtedly, I wanted to fuck her. Wanted to feel that sweet mouth wrapped around my cock so much that I ached for her whenever she wasn't with me.

For the next four days she'd called in sick to work, and I've spent every spare hour with her. Being around her is like my morning coffee, addictive and easy to say yes to. Similarly to coffee, she leaves a slow burn long after she's gone, and my feelings towards her have completely blindsided me.

We've drank endless coffees together, took long walks along the river and even picked out some things for Poppy's birthday. It wasn't like our kids hadn't met each other before, but now Saturday night is finally here, it feels like a huge deal having her and Marshall over.

Poppy is beside herself with excitement and is decorating the table with vases of flowers she's collected from around the farm. I toss some sauce into the stir fry and shake the wok around, careful not to spill any on my fresh shirt.

Having a date in your own home, with two kids is definitely an unusual situation, but I'm determined to own it.

"It smells delicious, Dad. Don't forget to do your hair." She grins at me with eyes full of mischief.

"What's wrong with my hair?" I ask, smoothing a hand over it.

"Nothing," she says, sashaying towards the living room before casually adding, "If you like the poufy look."

"My hair is poufy, what the heck is poufy?"

"It's okay, Dad. You just need to smooth it out a little. I'm sure Evelyn isn't dating you because of your hair."

"You are far too grown up for words, missy and who said we were dating?"

"You're cooking a meal in your fancy shirt, and you invited her over to eat with us. That's a date, Dad, just admit it."

"Okay, okay, but don't go telling anybody, this is between us, okay?"

"Pinkie promise," she replies, holding out her tiny pinkie for me to shake.

Lights shine in through the window, and I smooth over my hair again to make sure it's not 'poufy.'

"They're here," Poppy shouts, placing the last vase of flowers in the centre of the table.

A few minutes later, I open the door before she gets a chance to knock.

"Hey, you two, come in."

"Thanks," she replies, formally, highlighting that she feels as awkward as I do about sharing a meal with our kids.

We'd done it at the May Day Festival without a second thought, but this was different. This was me putting myself on the line and her doing the same.

I watch her eyes fall to my chest and then my hips, and wonder if she wants me as much as I want her. I highly fucking doubt it. She looks so good in snug fitting jeans and a loose cream jumper that hangs off her shoulder, leaving her sun kissed skin exposed and begging me to touch it.

"You look gorgeous," I whisper as she takes Marshall's coat off him and hands it to me. She coughs awkwardly and her cheeks burn pink at the compliment.

"Thanks," she replies softly before walking over to the table.

"Hi, Poppy. Wow, did you do all this?"

"Yeah, I wanted to make it look nice for us."

"You did a great job, it looks so pretty," she says, sitting Marshall down next to her at the table.

"Fwowers," he shouts, stretching forward to reach them, and Evelyn quickly moves the vase out of his way much to Poppy's relief.

We all sit down to dinner, and the conversation flows easy. I'm not expecting a call so when my phone rings just after serving dessert, I excuse myself and take the call in the living room.

The number is unknown but I recognise the voice straight away.

"Angela?"

"Don't put the phone down. I just want to see how you're getting on? Harry told me you've bought a farm."

"You're screwing Harry?"

"No, I am not fucking your partner. Jesus, Gabe, what the hell do you take me for?"

She says it as though it's beyond all realms of possibility when we both know that's the only way he'd have given her any information about me. Despite being pissed off that I left London, I'd thought his loyalties would lie with me. That's business for you, pussy over partner, every time.

"Did he give you the address?"

"Maybe," she teases down the line. "Why, do you want me to come and visit? I'm off the stuff now, you know? Ninety-nine days sober," she announces proudly.

"I got your letter; does it still stand."

"Unless you're willing to meet up and talk, I'm sure we could come to some kind of agreement."

"I don't care if you're sober for the next ten years, Angela. I'll never be that person you turned me into again."

"It's so easy to blame everyone else, isn't it, Gabe. You've always been good at that, maybe you should take a look at yourself to see why I went elsewhere."

"I know exactly why you went elsewhere, Angela, and I'm not saying I'm perfect by any means, but I was there for Poppy from the start. Where the fuck were you?" I hiss into the phone, moving towards the window so Poppy and the others can't hear me.

"You can't hold it against me forever, Gabe. I'm clean now, and I want my daughter back. I'll see you in court."

Fuck. I crunch the phone in my hand, almost breaking it, before tossing it on the sofa and pacing the room.

The sound of laughter from the kitchen punches through my dark thoughts, and I wander back in to find Evelyn with her head tilted back and Poppy tossing Smarties at her mouth.

Both their eyes widen as she manages to catch one.

"That's so cool, try it Dad."

"I can't, I'm too big."

"Kneel down," she commands, picking some more Smarties off the top of the chocolate cake.

"Yeah, kneewul down," Marshall joins in.

I kneel down, open my mouth and catch the sweet Poppy hurls at me on the very first attempt.

"Impressive." Evelyn nods with playful approval.

"Me twy, I wanna frow one," Marshall shouts and Poppy places it in his hand.

He cackles loudly when I manage to catch it.

"Gen, do it again."

"I think we need to tidy this place up," Evelyn interrupts. "Everything okay? We waited to eat, but it looked so good we had to dig in."

"I can see that." I chuckle at the sight of Marshall's face and hands completely covered in sticky chocolate cake.

"Why don't you two go and play, and leave me and Evelyn to clean this place up," I ask Poppy.

"Do you want to come and see my baby gosling, Marshall? She's really cute. His names Fluffy."

"Go see Fwuffy?" Marshall asks, looking up to Evelyn to make sure he is allowed to go.

"Of course, be careful on the stairs though, do one at a time."

"I'll help him, don't worry."

"Thank you, sweetheart," Evelyn says, wiping his hands down before lifting him out of his chair.

They disappear upstairs, and I turn to see Evelyn bending over the kitchen table, wiping the surface, her curvy ass pointing directly at me.

Before she realises her position, I'm on her. My hands roaming her ass and squeezing her hips, I let out a groan as she allows me to part her legs and rub my hand straight over her centre.

"Do you like to play, Evelyn?"

"Mmm," she moans, and my cock swells at the sound.

I take hold of her waist and lift her up onto the table, parting her legs to stand between them. When I kiss her, her hands fall to my chest and the touch has me desperate to feel her skin on mine.

"Do you have any idea what you do to me, woman?" I say on a low growl.

She lets me know she does by tracing her fingers down over my torso, all the way to my waistband. She hooks her fingers slightly inside and pulls me towards her, my arousal pressing hard against her pussy.

When she looks at me, I can see from the shine in her eyes that she knows exactly what she's doing to me. It's the first time she's hinted that she might be ready for something more than just kissing, and I kiss her with full force to let her know I've got so much more to give her than just kissing.

Fuck, if this woman wanted to play, we would play.

A heavy thud echoes through the ceiling, disturbing my primal need to take her over the kitchen table right here and now.

Adjusting my crotch, I reluctantly pull away from her.

"I'll go and check on them. How am I supposed to walk around with this?" I grin, pointing to the huge bulge in my pants.

She chuckles in response, a light, happy sound. The house was only ever me and Poppy. It was always just the two of us, and I liked it that way. But having Evelyn here was a welcome change, and she breathes a life into the house that I didn't realise was missing.

As I take the stairs, leaving her in the kitchen, I wonder how and when I'm going to tell her that I want more from her. I know I don't deserve it, not at my age. My dating days were long gone, but selfishly I don't care. Every time she smiles that fucking smile my gut screams at me to hold on to this woman and never let her go.

"What have you two been up to?" I ask, popping my head around the door to see Poppy's duvet wedged between her bed and her wardrobe doors.

"We made a den, can we sleep in it, please, Dad? Everyone always gets their friends to stay over, and mine never do."

"That's not true, you had Rosie to stay that time."

"That was my birthday, so it doesn't count."

"Let me see what Evelyn thinks, remember Marshall's still only little."

"I'll look after him, Dad. We're playing with my old zoo set, he really likes it."

"What do you think, Marshall? You wanna sleep in there with Pops?"

"Sweepover," he replies, his voice full of excitement.

"Okay, I'll think about it." I shrug, leaving them to play some more and heading back downstairs to find Evelyn drying the last of the dishes.

"You didn't have to do that," I say, walking over to her and placing my hands on her shoulders.

"It's nothing. Are the kids alright?"

"Oh, they're more than alright," I answer, smoothing her hair away from her neck so I can place a kiss on it.

"They want to sleepover. I said I'd ask you."

She turns around to face me, and I keep hold of her, gripping her waist with my hands.

"I guess that's good news, that they are getting on so well."

"Poppy gets on with everyone. I think she's just excited to have someone younger than me around to play with."

"I'll pop up and see them, and just make sure Marshall knows what's he's agreeing to."

"I think he knows alright, they made a den already."

She laughs, and that shining sparkle glitters in her eyes when they meet me.

"Never mind the kids, I want to know if you'll be okay with a sleepover, Evelyn?"

I feel her body stiffen under my touch, and it only makes me grip her waist tighter, pulling her body towards mine.

"Will you build me a den?" she teases.

"Girl, I'd build you a whole fucking castle, if you wanted me to."

"Then I'll stay," she says softly.

Evelyn

Tiptoeing into the bedroom after leaving them to play for a while, I hear Poppy singing to Marshall to help him go to sleep. Her voice is the sweetest, cutest thing I ever heard, and I pause for a minute outside the room to listen.

Marshall hasn't had many people put him to bed in his little life, and I'm surprised he hadn't cried for me or wanted to go home yet. I was half expecting him to run out of there at the mention of a sleep-over over. Instead, when I peek around the door, I find him curled up on a pile of pillows with Poppy's zoo animals arranged neatly around him.

"Mummy, I'm sweeping in the jungle with Poppy."

"Did you make this together?"

Poppy nods at me sleepily, and it's like looking at a childlike version of Gabe. She has his thick hair, only longer and the same hazel eyes that switch from green to yellow depending where the light hits them. Glancing around the room, I wonder what kind of woman could ever leave their daughter behind.

"I think Marshall was a bit scared, so we put the animals around him to keep him safe."

"That's so sweet of you, Poppy. Thank you for looking after him. You know, Marshall always has a story before bedtime, would you like me to read one to you both."

"I would like that so much; my Dad usually reads these ones to me, but I like any story."

"Marshall, what story would you like?"

"Ewaphant, pwease."

"Okay, turn out the lights please, Poppy, we will leave the lamp on if that's okay with you?"

She jumps up and switches the lights out, and I lie down next to Marshall. Poppy takes me by surprise by lying down beside me, and I'm reminded of how little she still is.

"This is the story of the elephant and the royal May Queen," I start, and she gasps with excitement and snuggles into me.

I make up a story, trying to fit something in for each of them, and by the time I'm finished Marshall is fast asleep.

"Are you going to be okay sleeping here?"

"I wish I could sleep in here every day," she whispers.

"It's a great den. Sweet dreams, Poppy."

"Thanks for the story, Evelyn. I hope you come back, I really like you," she says, not knowing the profound affect her heartfelt words have on me.

"I really like you, too," I whisper back.

Sensing someone there, my eyes dart to the doorway to find Gabe standing there watching us. I've no idea how long he's been standing there, but from the way he's smiling at me I sense it's been a while. He comes and offers me a hand, pulling me to my feet, and I watch him tuck Poppy in and kiss her goodnight. The familiarity and bond between them so obvious it elicits a thick lump in my throat and not for the first time, I wish that my son had the same routine with his daddy.

"I'm right downstairs if you need me, Pops," he reassures her, before catching my hand and squeezing it as we make our way back downstairs.

"Oh my god, what is this?" I ask, grinning at the sight of cushions and blankets all scattered across the floor and the log burner dancing with open flames.

"It's a blanket fort. Not exactly a castle, but I was improvising."

"It's perfect." I smile.

"So are you."

"No, Gabe, I'm really not. I've made my fair share of mistakes over the last few years," I admit, climbing across to prop myself up against the sofa beside him, amongst the cushions on the floor.

"I can't imagine you've ever messed up too badly," he says, his voice calm and soothing, like rubbing tiger balm over an aching muscle.

He's so straightforward, it makes it easy to lay all my flaws out on the table and feels good having someone to offload to.

"After I lost Marshall, I went off the radar. I didn't tell anyone where I was or when I was coming back. It was selfish, but I needed to focus on being a mum to Marshall and do what was best for both of us."

"It's not selfish to look after yourself, Evelyn. You were grieving, you did what you needed to do, and I'm sure the people that care about you will understand that."

"When I got back, I went to see Marshall's parents, to apologise and explain…"

"And?"

"They were gone, they've moved out and could be anywhere by now. I'll be able to find them, it just threw me a little. I guess I'd expected everyone else's lives to just stand still while I was gone."

"Life never stands still." He shrugs, his brow furrowing and forming deep lines across his forehead.

He looks his age, and it reminds me how much older he is than me and how much more he knows about the world. I feel like I'm riding a rodeo most of the time, gripping the reins, and trying my best not to fall off and land on my ass. Gabe is the mirror opposite, so relaxed and in control of everything.

"People change just as much as their circumstances. Like you changing your mind about me," he says, his lips curling to reveal a small told-you-so smile.

"What makes you say that?"

He pours me a glass of white wine and hands it to me as he speaks.

"Last Saturday, you were coming to tell me that this," he features two fingers between us, "wasn't going to happen."

"And now?" I ask, raising an eyebrow at him playfully.

"Now," he growls, pulling me across his lap, and I'm careful to balance my wine so it doesn't end up all over us. "Now you're here, and there's every chance it might."

"I don't know what I'm ready for," I admit. "This whole thing has caught me completely by surprise."

"That's okay. I wasn't looking for anything either, Evelyn, but I'm bewitched by you. I swear you've put some kind of spell on me. Every time I'm with you I want to freeze time so I never have let you go."

"I hadn't noticed," I tease him.

"Oh, you need me to show you?" he says, tilting me backwards slightly and kissing me harshly on the lips. The sensation of my head being dipped intensifies the sensation of his hot mouth on mine and takes my breath away.

"You don't always have to have all the answers, Evelyn. Sometimes you've got to just go with it."

"I'm trying," I whisper back.

"Don't. Just let go," he instructs as he reaches over and dips his hand into a bowl I hadn't noticed before.

"Take a bite," he whispers, dangling a strawberry over my lips and pushing it in slightly as they part.

He pulls the other half out and runs it over my lips, covering my mouth in sticky strawberry juices. Leaning in, he follows the trail he's left around my mouth with his tongue in a hot, wet lick over my entire mouth.

"Delicious." He grins, taking a sip of his wine.

This time when he kisses me, he lets his mouthful of warm bubbles drip into mine, and I have no choice but to swallow. He pulls back to watch, his pupils dilating, and I melt under his intense gaze. My body tenses in anticipation of what he might do next.

Brushing my hair back from my shoulder, he traces a finger over my collarbone, leaving goose bumps in the wake of his touch.

"You're so fucking beautiful, Evelyn," he growls, narrowing his eyes at me and tilting his glass so the wine spills into the dip between my neck and shoulder.

The warm liquid trickles down my neck towards the edge of my jumper and his tongue catches it, just before it slips underneath. I throw my head back, enjoying the freedom that allowing him to explore my body gives me. Working his way back up towards my neck he plants his strawberry kisses towards my shoulder, biting me softly when he reaches it.

"Your turn," he announces with a dark gleam in his eyes.

Lifting the glass to his lips, he takes a sip before parting his full lips and letting the wine seep down the side of his mouth. Instinctively I catch it with a soft kiss on his chin. His stubble prickles at my lips causing them to burn slightly, matching the scorching heat between my thighs.

Nervously, I trace my lips along his throat, and he lets out a sexy moan that spurs me on. Running my tongue over his Adam's apple, I taste the sharp bite of the wine mixed with the salty taste of him. Inhaling, I breathe him in, and the scent of spices and earth send my senses into overdrive. He may not be a cowboy, but I imagine this is exactly how one would smell.

He spends so much of his time outdoors he looks like a part of it. His hands rough and the lines that form across his forehead when he smiles, a reminder of his undeniable masculinity.

"Fuck, that mouth could drive a man crazy." He gasps, and his eyes shine wildly, allowing me to guess exactly what he is imagining.

Without warning, he spills the remainder of his drink down my chest, the liquid quickly escaping his tongue, and this time makes its way down the inside of my top.

"Gabe," I yell out, my body jumping at the wet sensation of the spillage onto my naked flesh.

He doesn't respond, his licks are hot and teasing against my bare skin until almost all of the liquid is gone. When he's worked his way across my chest, he pauses, tracing his finger along the edge of my jumper. His hand is steady as he draws a neat line from shoulder to shoulder, and I inhale sharply as his fingertip dips slightly below my clothing.

He traces downwards, his fingers barely touching my skin, but the sensation is enough to make be tremble underneath his touch. When I don't attempt to stop him, he embraces my acceptance by following up his touch with tongue. Something tells me he is playing nice, being gentle with me so as not to scare me away.

Fingering the lace at the edge of my bra, I moan in pleasure when he reaches inside and rolls my nipple between his finger and thumb.

"Bite," he demands, pushing another strawberry into my mouth.

This time he pulls my top down further over my shoulder, taking my bra strap with it. With the strawberry between his teeth he spreads its juices over the curve of my tit, his other hand caressing my other one over the top of my bra. After lapping up the sticky red mess, he focuses all of his attention on my nipple, finding it with his tongue first and following it up with a harsh bite that causes me to yell out loud.

"Sorry," he lifts his head up to look at me, eyes full of lust. "Couldn't help myself. Jesus, Evelyn, you're delicious. Let me taste you properly?"

My body stiffens, first in fear at the look in his eyes, as though he's about to lose all self-control, and secondly at the realisation of what he wants to do.

"I can't," I breathe out as his wandering hands roam over my waist, gripping me tightly and he continues to maul my tits with his mouth.

My nipples swell hard under his wet tongue, my damn body defying me and giving the response I really want to give.

"I'm not ready," I whisper, embarrassed to admit that even after all this time, the thought of giving my body to another man fills me with dread.

"Evelyn, it's okay. We'll do this at your pace. I don't care if it takes another fucking ten years, if I get to keep you, then I'll wait for one hundred and ten."

"I don't expect you to do that," I say, tears of frustration springing behind my eyes.

"And I don't *expect* anything from you. Except for you to let me show you some fun."

He lifts his face to mine, tucking my exposed breast back inside my jumper.

"I've never felt like this before, Evelyn. About anyone. You've walked into my life and turned it upside down."

"I didn't mean to," I whisper, the tears escaping and rolling down my cheek.

"But you did. And I can't just ignore the effect you have on me. I think you'd be stupid to ignore your gut feelings on this, too. I know you're scared. I know you're hurting, but I want to make it better for you, Evelyn. Let me be that guy."

"I can't help feeling like I'm doing something wrong."

"But you're not, I promise you. I know how much you must have loved your husband, and I know you might never love anyone again like that. But that doesn't mean that you don't deserve to live your life and have some fun, Evelyn. You're smart and funny, and anyone can see you have the biggest heart. I'm not asking for you to give it all to me. I'd just like you to trust me with a piece of it."

This time it's me who kisses him, gently at first, but as soon as my tongue finds his, the desire that's pent up inside me is unleashed, and in the moment, I take a leap of faith.

"I really want to try, Gabe. I really like you, too."

"Good," he replies, biting at my bottom lip, playfully. "That's settled then, you've got yourself a boyfriend." He smiles a dorky smile, making me chuckle. "And, I got these."

He disappears back inside my top, and I don't resist as his mouth finds my nipples again, and he covers my upper body in a thousand strawberry kisses that tell me how serious he is about waiting one hundred and ten years.

CHAPTER 11

Gabe

Waving her and Marshall off the next day as they drove up the driveway didn't feel right. Even Poppy looked down in the dumps to see them go.

"Hey, Pops, they'll be back, don't you worry."

"I hope they can sleep over again soon, I had so much fun."

"Me too, baby, me too." I squeeze her shoulder, my mind flashing back to Evelyn's perfectly rounded tits covered in strawberry juices last night.

"You know what we have to do now though?"

Her eyes cloud over with disappointment.

"I'm sorry, Pops, but I did tell you we couldn't keep that thing in the house forever."

"Her name's Fluffy, Dad," she scolds me with her usual level of sass.

"Well, whatever her name is, she's got to go back where she belongs. She'll be missing her family anyway, you wouldn't want her to feel sad, would you?"

She looks shell shocked as she processes my statement, and then breaks my heart by saying, "Just because people are away from their family, it doesn't mean they are sad, Dad. That's a dumb thing to say. That's like saying I can't be happy without Mum. Do you think I am sad all the time?"

She screws her face up angrily and glares at me.

"Of course not, I didn't mean people, I was talking about animals."

"It's the same thing." She sulks.

"Sorry, I didn't mean to hurt your feelings, Poppy. I know you aren't unhappy here with me. We got it good, right?"

I playfully lay a soft punch on her arm to coax her out of her mood, and her face lightens a little.

"Yes, we do." She smiles, attempting to punch me back and pretending to get mad at me when I catch her fist in my hand.

"Okay, no more Mr. Nice guy, go and get Fluffy."

"Fine, but just so you know, I'm visiting him e-v-e-r-y-d-a-y," she punches the word out to drive the point home, her sassy disposition restored.

"Got it." I nod and she skips off upstairs to get Fluffy.

Opening the drawer to grab my keys, I see a pile of mail that Poppy must have picked up and shoved there. I hesitate, debating whether to stuff it back in the drawer when I see a solicitor's address on the flipside.

Sighing, I rip it open and a tight knot hits me in the stomach when I read the unexpected.

DEAR MR. HUDSON,

We have been trying to contact you regarding the final will of Mrs. R. Reed.

Please contact us so we can discuss this matter urgently.

Yours sincerely,

Frasier's Solicitors

. . .

R. Reed? My mind races to try to locate a Mrs. Reed, and I grab the back of a dining chair to steady myself. The only Reed I know is my mother, and she's a D, so that rules her out. I wouldn't have thought she'd have had anything to leave me in a will, anyway.

She hadn't even seen me since my dad had moved us away to Liverpool. It must be my mother's family member, perhaps my grandmother.

My dad had always spoken fondly of her when I'd asked about my family, but I'd never been allowed any contact with her. She was too quickly linked to my mother, and that was a risk in my father's eyes. Even though we'd moved hundreds of miles away from Cheshire when I was just a few years old, I think he always lived in fear that she'd come looking for us, or worse still; try to get me back.

Kind of ironic that I'm now in an uncannily similar situation with my baby's mother. The two women had a lot in common, drink, drugs and hurting their kids. Not for the first time, I admit to myself, that my dad and I were also alike. I wouldn't have let him know that, as a teenager I'd put him through hell. We'd butted heads over the years, until Poppy had come along and changed my perspective on just about everything.

"You okay, Dad?" she asks, appearing in the doorway holding the baby goose.

"Yeah, I was just thinking," I reply, letting go of the chair and chucking the letter on the table. I didn't need the money. I'd made plenty at the peak of my photography career, and I'd been sensible with it ever since Poppy arrived. Material things didn't hold any value to me. Angela and I wanted for nothing, but everything that was important was missing, and I learnt the hard way that you can't buy the important things.

Helping Poppy up into the tractor, I decide to call the firm in the morning and let them know I won't be claiming any of the money.

"Don't look so upset, Pops. You can come back with some oats for her before school tomorrow if you get up early enough."

"I'm not stupid, Dad. I know what happens, we did it in science with Miss Heist."

"Did what, love?"

"Meditation."

"What, like yoga?" She looks at me like I've got ten heads and wraps her arms so tight around the gosling, I think she might strangle it.

"No. I mean I know about them flying away for the winter."

"Ohhh, you mean migration?" I stifle a chuckle at the look on her face, realising she got the words mixed up. She's such a goddamn perfectionist. Has been since she was a knee high to a grasshopper. Like most things that were wrong in her little life, I blame her mother.

Angela was all about perfection, it's probably what drove her to drink in the first place. Whenever Poppy was around her, she'd do everything she could to impress Angela, always vying for her attention. It broke my heart time after time when she didn't get it.

That was part of the reason for buying Maple Valley. The farm needed work and Poppy had loved getting stuck in and help with decorating the old house. Seeing her planting strawberries, covered in mud or running through the fields with her hair blowing in the wind turned me to fuckin' mush.

"Stay here, please, I want to do this on my own," she says as we come to a stop near the water's edge.

"Be careful by the water then, Pops. Bye little fella," I say, giving her most prized possession a little stroke for the road. She climbs down and says her goodbyes, carefully placing her furry friend down at the water's edge and waiting until the family swims over to it before she runs back to me.

"You did the right thing, I'm really proud of you, kid," I say on the sombre drive back to the farmhouse. She wears her heavy heart on her face all the way back, and it's doesn't shift until bedtime when I read her favourite pony story. It plants an idea in my head, and as I mull it over for the rest of the evening there's only one person I want to tell.

'Evelyn,' I type into the phone.

No, too formal.

'Hi,'

Fuck sake, I'm overthinking this.
'I miss you' *sad face emoji*

I DON'T HAVE to wait long for her reply.
'What are you both up to?'
'Poppy's asleep and I'm here, thinking about you.'
'I was thinking about you, too.'
'Can I see you tomorrow?"
'I have to work.'
'After work. I'll cook you both tea?'

NO REPLY. I try calling her, but her phone goes straight to voicemail.
Shit. What if somethings wrong? What if I pushed her too hard? She'd been clear that she wasn't ready for a relationship. But then last night...

Evelyn

"SHIT… SHIT… SHIT." I frantically try to stop the leak in the bathroom with every towel I can find, but the water won't cease from spurting out at full pelt. Managing to slow it a little, I make a run for my phone, which is still sitting on the bed from where I chucked it on sight of the gushing water.

Seeing a bunch of messages and missed calls from Gabe, I make a split decision and call him. It's almost midnight, so I'm surprised when he picks up right away.

"What happened?"

"It's my… wait, how do you know something happened."

"You wouldn't just not text back, it's not in your nature. I've been panicking, Evelyn, are you both okay?"

"Yeah, we're okay." I smile, glancing down at my soaked pyjamas. "Do you happen to know anything about water pipes?"

The despair is clearly as evident in my tone as the panic is in his.

"What's happened? I can't come over, Poppy's sleeping, or I'd have come over when you didn't text back."

"I told you, I wasn't ready for a…"

"Evelyn?"

"Hold on, I'm putting you on loudspeaker, I need to swap the towels before I get soaked again."

I juggle the phone in one hand and the last few towels I have in the other, pressing them from the source of the leak.

"Okay, I'm here. It's the toilet, the pipes burst and I can't stop the leak." I know I must sound pathetic, but I don't have much choice given the time. I can't exactly call my dad, he'd wake my mum and then they'd both be over here in the middle of the night. I need to try and deal with this myself. Well, almost by myself.

"You need to try to find the shut off valve, it will be at the back of the toilet, near the floor."

"I can't see it," I say, panicking as the water continues to leak despite the mountain of garments and towels pressed against it.

"It should look like a tap, something you can turn?" His voice is calm, reassuring and the opposite of everything I am feeling right now.

"I see it," I say in a stifled yell, the last thing I need is Marshall waking up.

"Okay, turn it slowly and that should shut the supply off."

I wrap my fingers around the metal knob and begin to twist. It doesn't budge at first, but on a second attempt, it shifts, and the water instantly slows before stopping altogether.

"We did it. It's stopped."

"You did it, Evelyn. Well done, baby."

"Thanks, how the fuck did you know about the shut off valve."

"I'm a guy, I just know stuff," comes his smug reply.

"Ugh." I roll my eyes and place my phone onto the loo seat to enable me to strip off from my soaked clothes.

"So, you're good now?"

Glancing around at the chaos I breathe a sigh of relief before confirming, "Yeah, I'm good. Soaked wet through, but good."

"Now that, I would love to see," he says with a hint of playfulness in his usually gritty tone.

"It's late. How come you're still up?" I ask, quickly diverting the conversation away from my dripping wet semi-naked body that is now tingling from his last comment.

"I was worrying about you, plus I had a few things playing on my mind."

"What things?" I ask, drying myself off and padding over to the bed wrapped in my dressing gown as there are no towels to use.

"The custody battle, mostly. I haven't heard much from Angela, and I hate it when she goes quiet on me, it's usually followed by some kind of game she wants me to play."

"I hate that she has this over you, Gabe. You're such an amazing dad, you don't deserve all of the stress. She should be able to work things out without needing a solicitor."

"Angela's never been much of a communicator. It was always her way or no way."

"That's no good for anyone, especially Poppy."

"I know, now you see why I am still awake, plus I found this letter saying my mum's, Mum has left me something in her will. At least, I'm guessing that's what it's about. I'll find out tomorrow when I ring the solicitor. It's solicitor city for me at the moment."

"I don't envy you. I'm sorry about your grandmother, that must be tough, too."

"Nah, I didn't know her, it's always just been me and my dad. We cut all ties when we moved to London.

"But she must have cared about you to leave you something in her will, even after all that time not seeing you."

"I guess, I never thought of it like that," he reasons.

"All I know is, if Marshall had left a will, I would have been so grateful. It's like a final way a person can share their wishes," I hesitate before adding, "even after they've gone."

"You're right, you know? I wasn't going to bother, but I think I'll meet with the solicitor, and at least see what the will says."

"You should, it could be a letter or something important about your past."

"You're so fucking sensible for your age, Evelyn. Some women are twice your age and don't have their shit together."

I sink back into my pillows resigning to the fact that it's late, and I don't have the energy to deal with the fallout of the burst pipe.

"You think I have my shit together?"

"Sure, you do. Doesn't mean you don't need looking after sometimes."

"By a guy who knows shit, right?" I murmur into the air, my eyes feeling heavy and relaxed.

"An incredible hot guy who knows shit.

I don't argue with him.

"Sleep tight, beautiful."

"Goodnight, Gabe," I whisper into the air, and the faint echo of my hands-free dies when he ends the call.

As I find sleep, I see Marshall's face as clear as day. He's smiling a happy, carefree expression, and his eyes are full of his usual mischievous sparkle. He's wearing his army uniform and links my arm, guiding me down a long red path. I'm holding a bunch of white roses, and as I glance down at them, I realise I'm wearing a wedding dress. Inhaling the familiar smell of Marshall as we make our way down the narrow red carpet, he doesn't take his eyes off me. I blush and shy away from his intense gaze, and when I look forwards again, Gabe is standing at the end of the carpet in a smart grey suit. He's grinning at me and doesn't seem to notice Marshall at my side.

When we reach him, Gabe reaches towards me and Marshall takes my hand, guiding it towards Gabe's. I gasp loudly and jolt upright in bed, hitting the bedside lamp on to wake myself fully. What the fuck just happened? Marshall was giving me away, why would he do that? And why am I dreaming about marrying Gabe? I never want to marry again.

With tears in my eyes, I lie back down and pull the duvet up as tightly as I can around my chin. I knock the light off again, but my eyes are pinned wide open. They fixate on the night sky and the few stars I can see in the distance. For the first time in so long, I feel him around me. My husband. I was used to dreaming of him, but it was usually just his face, not him walking with me and certainly not down an aisle.

Dreaming of Gabe has me shook up for the entire morning, and by lunchtime, Tanya is determined to get to the bottom of my weird mood.

"I want to know everything," she demands over a bowl of Caesar salad. "We both know you weren't sick last week."

I avert her gaze feeling awkward, I'm not about to lie to my best friend.

"What's been going on with you and this cowboy god, then? You must really like him to call in sick."

"I do," I admit. And I'm sorry for being off sick, I guess I just got carried away."

"Don't worry about it, as long as you're around this week we have that engagement party to do."

"I'm on it." I shrug, stuffing a forkful of pasta into my mouth.

"Good. Now back to cowboy god."

"Will you stop calling him that?" I giggle and she rolls her eyes at me, dramatically.

"Okay, Okay. There's not much to tell. He took me on a date, and it just went from there. He's kind of obsessed with me and wants to see me every day."

"You say that like it's a bad thing?"

"No, it's not bad, it's just… I'm not sure if I'm ready for anything, and I don't want to lead him on."

"Isn't he older than you?"

"Yeah, quite a bit older, actually."

"Then he knows exactly what he's getting into, you're not leading him anywhere."

"I guess." I shrug my shoulders and begin to clear lunch away.

"You know what they say about older men?" I don't have to wait for her reply as she narrows her eyes at me and sings, "More experience."

"Oh my god, stop."

"Why? It's good to have a man who knows what he's doing. If I wasn't happy with my man, I'd totally trade him in for an older model."

"You are too much, you know that?"

"I do," she replies, "and you love me."

"I do." I chuckle, throwing my pinny over my head, ready for the afternoon ahead.

Turning towards the door when the bell chimes as someone opens it, I stop dead in my tracks when I'm met with Marshall's mum staring at me. She's clearly as shocked to see me as I am her. Neither of us say anything at all as we take each other in before she comes running towards me.

"Evie, oh my goodness, what are you doing here?"

"I got back a few weeks ago, what are you doing here?"

She throws her arms around me, and we both lose ourselves in a flood of fresh tears, tears that have been saved for this precise moment. I'd gone over it countless times in my head, and now that it's actually here I am completely unprepared for it.

"Just picking up some flowers for my friend."

"No, I mean here in The Cotswolds, I thought you moved away?"

"No, what makes you say that?"

"When I got back, I came over to your place but everything looked different, and I saw a man going inside with his kids. I assumed you'd sold up, I thought you might think there was nothing left here for you anymore." I spit the words out over my sobs and choked up voice box.

"I'd never leave this place, everything is here, Evie. All of my memories... I'd never leave Marshall behind, and now you're here."

"Marshall's home too, I'm so sorry for everything, Joan."

"Guys, would you mind stepping into the kitchen, sorry to be a pain, but just in case we have any customers come in," Tanya interjects, reminding me of my surroundings.

"Of course, sorry, come through, Joan," I say, taking her hand and leading her to the back of the shop.

"I just can't believe you're here, Evie. We never stopped thinking about you, you know? All this time."

"I thought about you both, too. About this day and what I'd say when I saw you both. There's so much to explain, I don't even know where to start."

"I'm hoping you can start by bringing my grandson around to see me? We still live in the same place, it has changed a bit. Candice's man has helped us have all the latest bits and bobs fitted. Stu didn't like it at first, but now he's a dab hand at working all the gadgets."

I smile at the thought of Marshall's dad having new things fitted, he never was one for expensive things.

"So, what's he like then, my grandson?"

She wipes her tears away, and it's as though three years disappear, just like that. All the hurt forgiven. All the sadness put to one side. She's family, and in my grief, I had forgotten our connection. Having it back was like a neatly wrapped present at Christmas time, bringing instant happiness and much needed relief.

"He's just like his dad," I say, honestly, wiping the tears from my own cheeks.

"I can't wait to see him and give him a cuddle. Tell me you're home for good?"

"We are, Greece was lovely, but I wanted Marshall to go to an English-speaking pre-school. It was the right time for us to come home. I wanted him to grow up where his daddy did, I've been showing him all our old hang outs."

Her eyes fill with tears again, and she pulls me in for another cuddle, squeezing me tightly. "I'm proud of you for coming home, it couldn't have been easy."

"It's been a good thing, mostly. Marshall has his own bedroom for the first time, and he's making little friends at pre-school."

"I'm going to go and tell Stu, he's not going to believe you're here. Here's my number..." She pulls out a pen, and I flip a business card over on the counter top for her to scribble it on.

"But, honestly, you're always welcome, sweetheart, you stop by anytime you like, okay. Promise me you'll come."

"Of course, I will. You are one of the reasons we came back. Marshall deserves to have both sets of grandparents in his life, I just couldn't face you both after…"

"Don't, love, no point raking over hot coals. You did what you needed to do to get through, god knows we've all suffered enough. Stuart and I didn't handle the news as well as we should have either. There's no rights or wrongs when it comes to grief, and Marshall was such a special boy."

"He broke my heart," I manage to say, my voice barely a whisper.

"He never meant to, Evie, he would never have done anything to hurt you. My son loved you more than life itself."

"I know. That's why losing him hurt so much," I say quietly, the raw emotions causing my stomach to swirl so much I feel nauseous.

"You two had something special, there's no doubt about that. Some people aren't lucky enough to find that even once in a lifetime."

"I know, and I have Marshall," I say it to reassure myself as much as Joan.

"You're working, I won't keep you, but make sure you come and see me as soon as you can. We really can't wait to spend some time with our grandson."

"I will do, I promise."

She leaves without her flowers, and I grab them from the side and chase after her with them.

"Joan," I shout after her.

"I'd forget my head if it wasn't screwed on. Thanks, love. See you soon, okay."

"See you soon," I reply, passing her the bunch of gerberas and darting back inside where Tanya looks almost as shocked at the unexpected reunion as I feel.

"Well, that got that out of the way then?" She shrugs and her matter-of-fact tone, mixed with my emotions, which are everywhere, causes me to catch the giggles.

"Yeah." I laugh. "I guess it did."

"I finished most of the party flowers while you were talking, but we have a couple of home deliveries, if you want to get on with them?"

"Yes, no problem. If you like, I can deliver them on my way to pick up Marshall, as long as they aren't too far out of the way."

"No, they're local. In fact, you know one of them very well."

I meet her gaze curious to see who it is, as there's a distinctive sense of amusement in her tone.

"A spring sensation, is on its way to a nearby strawberry farm."

"It is? Who would Gabe be buying flowers for? Poppy's birthday wasn't for another couple of weeks, and the gesture is too over the top if it's not a special occasion. "He didn't mention he had anything on."

"Maybe they're for you?"

"Don't be daft, he's not going to have me make up my own flowers. They must be a gift. Poppy's teacher, maybe?"

"Evie, the spring sensation is almost fifty quid, if he's spending that on Poppy's school teacher, I'd be worried."

"I'll make them up anyhow, and let you know when I've dropped them off. That's Gabe for you, I'm learning to expect the unexpected."

"He sounds dreamy."

He's definitely one of a kind," I say as I choose out the prettiest spring stems and begin arranging them into a colourful bunch. By the time I'm finished tweaking and adding bits of gypsophila, the spring sensation is the loveliest arrangement I've done in a while.

Putting another smaller version together, I hang up my pinny and grab the two bunches from the counter top.

"Don't forget to text," Tanya reminds me as I push the door open with my bum.

"See you tomorrow," I say, making my way out and balancing the flowers and my handbag carefully on the way to my car.

A few minutes later I'm eyeing the best rows of maple trees that line the entrance to Maple Valley and wondering exactly what the hell he is playing at.

Knocking at the door, I peek over the top of the huge bouquet like an anxious meerkat looking for its playmate.

When he opens the door, I almost drop the flowers to the floor on sight of his open checked shirt and tight six pack displayed underneath.

"Well, this is unexpected. What, you can't stay away?"

I want to smack that smug smile straight of his face, and I probably would, if it didn't look so damn sexy.

"I'm delivering the flowers you ordered."

"Thanks, do you think my girlfriend will like them?"

My heart sinks straight to my feet, and I can feel the colour rushing from my face as much as he must see it.

"Gotcha." He smiles a charm-the-pants-off-anyone-he-wants smile. "They're for you, obviously."

"You made me deliver flowers to myself?"

"I figured you'd design them how you like them, and it'd get you over here, so I could see you again and make sure you're okay."

"You just saw me all weekend." I sigh with exasperation.

"I know, it was great, wasn't it?"

"Gabe, I have to work, you know?"

"I know, you are working. You're delivering flowers."

"To myself," I throw back, trying to sound more annoyed than I can feel when I'm in his relaxed presence.

"Well, you've seen me now."

"Not for long enough." He steps back, putting his hand to his chin, thoughtfully, and eyeing me up and down, taking every inch of me in.

Evelyn

I'M NOT sure if it was his idea or mine, but staying at Gabe's while the new toilet is fitted had been an obvious choice. It was that or my parents place, and I was enjoying my independence far too much to give it up. Besides, I was having fun getting to know Gabe, and he'd offered to sleep in his guest room, which I thought was very gentlemanly of him.

He's like that, a true English gentleman with good morals and good manners. That was evident in the way he'd raised Poppy, but it was the other side of him that has captured something inside of me. Small glimpses of a man that makes me feel everything that encapsulates being a woman.

Those one liners and alluring comments had drawn attention to a piece of me that I didn't know still existed. The same piece that I'd given away years ago. The more time I spent with him, the more of that piece I found myself wanting to give away.

I'd wriggle my shoulder out of my jumper slightly before he entered the room, or leave my hair loose around him after a shower. Subtle signals that I was ready for whatever this was, and he read every single one like a navy seal reading Morse code.

I am starting to read him too. That's how I know somethings up. I can see it in the lines that have deepened on his forehead and the way his chest muscles flex under his shirt.

"Bad news?" I ask, as he puts his phone down on the coffee table.

"Not bad, just fucking weird."

"Why, what's up?"

"I just got off the phone to this guy, Greyson, says he has been looking for me for weeks."

"Well, he obviously found you if he called… What did he want?"

"Yeah, apparently my old colleague Harry feels it's cool to dish out my details to anyone who asks for them. It wouldn't surprise me if he's given them to my ex as well. I think he still holds a grudge from me packing up and leaving the city."

"Did Greyson say what he wanted?"

"He says I have a sister. Well, half-sister, Sally. Apparently, this Greyson guy is married to her and is ex-army, so he used his connections to do some digging. He says that soon after my dad and I left, my mum had another kid and that she was raised by my grandma."

"The same grandma that left you the money?" I ask, trying to connect the dots.

"Yeah, Rosemary. The weirdest thing is that of all the fucking places in the world, my half-sister, that I never knew anything about, is now living here, in The Cotswolds."

"Wow, Gabe, that's huge!"

"I know. I'm just processing it all. It's Sally's birthday next week, and her husband was calling to see if I would meet her for breakfast. A big surprise type thing because she's been looking for me for a long time."

"Do you want to go?"

"I don't know. I mean, yeah, it's just a lot to take in. First the inheritance from my Grandmother, then a sister I knew nothing about. It was always just me and my dad, you know?"

"I can't imagine never knowing both parents," I murmur as my heart breaks for my son in exactly this position.

"From what Greyson said, it sounds like Sally had a pretty rough time of it, and I can believe it. My dad was always cagey about my mum, but from what he didn't say, I always knew she was a crock of shit."

"Sounds like you and your sister might have a lot to talk about."

"Will you come?" he blurts out, putting me on the spot. Taking in his stressed out features, I really feel for him. He is such a good man, and despite his bravado, it can't have been easy for him, growing up without a mum.

"Of course, I will."

"Thanks, it wouldn't feel right without you. Nothing feels right without you, anymore."

He narrows his eyes at me, his voice becoming a low murmur as he steps towards me.

"I know what you mean, Gabe. We've just kind of snowballed from nothing to this."

He wraps his arms around me, sliding his hands into the back pockets of my jeans and giving my ass a gentle squeeze.

"I like *this*," he growls, making me giggle.

"And this," he whispers, before taking my lips with his own.

"What are we doing? You know I have to go back home at some point?"

"What if you didn't?"

I break our kiss to study his face and check whether he was fooling around or not. Seeing his raised eyebrow and intense amber flecks in his hazel eyes staring straight into mine, I realise he's serious.

"I can't just stay. You know it's not that easy, Gabe."

"It could be. I want this, Evelyn. You and Marshall. This last week has been so fucking good. Having you both here shows me what could be like. I'm a lot older than you, I've done my time screwing around. I know what I want, and if you let it, this could really be somethin' special."

I let out a sigh that's almost as heavy as the weight on my heart. I know he means every word of what he says, and he deserves an honest response, even if it hurts me to give it.

"It's not as easy as that, Gabe. Opening the door to a life with you is like slamming one shut on my ex-husband."

"Damn it, Evelyn, it doesn't have to be. You deserve a life, not just a fucking existence."

"Excuse me? An existence?" I shoot the word at him like a bullet, and it hits him hard because his expression instantly shifts to one of regret.

"I just think you should give this a real shot." He shrugs.

"Why, Gabe, because if I don't, I will have a pitiful existence for the rest of my days? What, I'm incapable of being happy on my own? Because perish the thought that actually what Marshall and I have is way more than an existence. We were doing just fine on our own before you came along with all of your expectations." My voice cracks and my chest tightens as I fight back tears of anger. "You think you are the answer to all my problems, Gabe, but I don't need you to fix me. Marshall died, I can't just stick a plaster of a gaping wound and hope it magically gets better."

"But you can suture, and given time it will heal," he reasons. His words are the truth, and his exasperated tone coveys how much he wants me to believe them.

"Evelyn, I don't want you with me because I think you'll have a shitty life without me. I want you here because I…"

"Because what, Gabe. Spit it out. I'm just dying to know all the reasons why you think Marshall and I can merely exist without you."

"I didn't mean it to come out like that. I want you with me because I love you."

Hot tears of anger are spilling down my cheeks, and this time he shoots the bullet and it hits me right in the gut. *He loves me.* The floor seems to spin underneath me and everything feels distant. Blurry… almost dream like.

"You what?" I gasp, desperate for confirmation that he really did just say that.

He steps towards me, gripping the tops of my arms and staring right into my eyes snapping me out of my dazed trance.

"I love you, Evelyn. I don't know if it's crazy, too soon or whatever. All I know is that I've fallen completely, insanely in love with you, and *that's* why I want you here with me and Poppy.

"You can't just say things like that."

"Too late." He grins sheepishly. "I think that ship just sailed."

"How do you know?"

"How do I… Jesus Christ, are you kidding me?"

"I'm serious. How do you know you love me?"

"Evelyn, look at you. I love everything about you. The way you dote on Marshall, the way you are with Poppy, the way you keep take risks with me that I know you wouldn't take with anyone else, which makes me feel like king of the fucking world."

"That's because I trust you. You make me feel like I can do anything. When I'm with you, it's like I'm *me* again."

Wiping the tears from my eyes I meet his and there's no words left to be spoken. Every wall of steel I've so carefully scaffolded around the broken part of me comes tumbling down in his perfect strawberry kiss. His hands span my waist, and my mouth explores every inch of his.

"Gabe, the kids, I push him off me with both hands against his taut chest before he gets carried away. I have a feeling his willingness to stay in the spare bedroom is wearing thin, and even with the daring streak he brings out in me, the thought of sleeping with him makes me bona fide nervous.

"They'll both be flat out by now," he says in a low rumble.

"We can't just…"

"Enough with what we can't do, I'd rather talk about what we *can*."

His lips curl into a devilishly handsome smile, and his deep hazel eyes trace my chest, as his fingers start to fumble at the top of my jeans. My nipples harden under his lustful gaze, and he palms over my boobs, causing a surge of heat which only makes them swell further. The heat spreads to my cheeks knowing that he can feel the two solid buds through my clothing, and his smile flashes in his eyes at my embarrassment.

"I love these," he moans, cupping each of my curves before pulling at the edge of my top.

I lift my arms in an almost trance link state, allowing him to undress me. My entire body trembling in anticipation at what his next move will be.

It's been so long since I'd been touched by a man, and Gabe was older, more mature. He seems to be much more aware of what my body craves, and the look on his face tells me he knows exactly what havoc he's wreaking.

With the lightest of touches, he traces a line across my chest and around my shoulder, dragging it slowly across my back as he moves around me in a circle. When he's behind me, he breaks the connection and grabs my hips, squeezing them into his groin and pressing his solid erection against me.

"I love this," he whispers into my ear as he grips the curve of my waistline.

His breath is hot, and I lick my lips and swallow hard, trying to regain some composure. Bringing himself back to face me, he drags a thumb along my lower lip and leans into kiss me again.

"I especially love that." He smiles, after kissing me with so much passion that my knees almost buckle underneath me.

I kiss him back as harshly as I can, matching his own level of carnal desire, letting him know that I'm ready, and I want him just as much as he wants me.

"Usually, I like to play, but not this time. This time, I want to show you how crazy I am about you. Will you let me do that?"

"Mmhmm," is all I can manage through the thick fog of my over-loaded senses.

He loves me. I've let someone fall in love with me.

I hadn't even seen it coming, and now it's too late. All I can do is dive in and trust in whatever this new chapter of my life is. I thought I'd never be ready to be held in a man's arms again. But my body is screaming to be held by Gabe.

I flinch as his hands push my bra straps down over my shoulders, recalling the time he'd covered me in strawberry juice. Tonight, was different, Gabe was right. He wasn't playing around. In one easy move, he popped the button from my jeans and slid his hand inside. My core pulsed with a heartbeat of its own and a hunger that could only be satisfied by him.

Pulling my jeans down, taking my French lace boxer shorts with them, I'm left standing in just my bra while he is still fully clothed. In an attempt to even the playing field, I unbutton his shirt, my hands exploring his chest and clawing at his fly in an awkward, frenzied attempt to undress him.

He tosses his shirt to one side but pushes my hands away before lifting me in one swift movement and carrying me over to the side-board. Kissing me as we go, he shoves some bits and pieces out of the way and places me right on the edge.

My legs are closed, but as soon as he traces my inner thigh, they part to allow him entrance, and he presses one finger, then two, deep inside me. I throw my head back as he works my inner walls, taking away just a tiny bit of the throbbing ache inside. I need more of him, and he knows it.

I thought he said he wasn't going to play?"

"I have a feeling I'm going to love this part of you, too, Evelyn."

Then hurry up and take it. Please finish this, I need you.

As if hearing my private plea, he rids himself of his jeans and kneels down in front of me.

Oh shit. I've always felt awkward about oral sex. It was so intimate. Was I ready for this?

"I want to taste you, want to make sure you're ready for me."

"I am ready," I cry out as he continues working my inner walls, stopping only to circle my clit before returning to a steady rhythm of stokes right on my g-spot.

"Almost," he says, before burying his head between my thighs and working every inch of my soaked pussy with his skilful tongue.

I run my fingers through his hair which only spurs him on and intensifies the sensation in my centre. Just as I'm about climax, unable to hold off any longer, the pitter patter of small feet crossed the landing.

"Mummy," comes a sulky cry.

"Shit."

Gabe snaps to his feet, and I run for my jean's, adrenalin flying through my body at the thought of one of them walking in on us. The footsteps tiptoe down the stairs and Gabe shuffles back into his jeans just as Marshall turns the living room door handle. I can't help but let out a small giggle at the look on Gabe's face. He wipes a hand over his mouth and stares at the door like a rabbit caught in headlights.

"Marshall, honey, what's the matter."

"I cawn't sweep, Mummy. My tummy hurts."

"Oh no, you poor thing. Do you want Mummy to come and lie with you?" Gabe rolls his eyes and smiles as I scoop Marshall up and carry him back to bed. My brain has snapped to its senses, but my body still aches to be held by Gabe.

CHAPTER 12

Gabe

$\mathcal{A}$fter waiting hours for her to come back downstairs, I accept that it's not going to happen and decide to give up and try and get some sleep. As I pass the guest room, I sneak a peek at her. She's flat out with an arm over Marshall, and there's no way I could disturb her, not with that angelic, relaxed look on her face. I creep over to the bed and pull the duvet up over them both, planting a gentle kiss on her forehead. She stirs a little, but doesn't wake, and I pull the curtains over, thinking it's strange that she's left them open.

After checking in on Poppy, I hit the sack but don't sleep properly. How can I with a woman like that asleep just down the hallway? Instead, I go over the conversation with Greyson and wonder what my sister will be like.

The next morning after dropping the kids off at school, all my anxieties are put to rest when I meet her. Her husband introduces us, and she instantly puts Evelyn and I at ease. She's obviously just as shocked to meet me as I am her, but it's a good shock.

Sitting around the table sharing breakfast with her and her family, I feel a weird sense of pride watching her as she smiles and chats happily with everyone. The two of us share something in common that bonds us effortlessly, and we share an instant mutual respect for one another.

She knows exactly what it's like to grow up without a mother, in the same way I do. Harsh as fuck when you're a kid, and I only imagine it would be even tougher for a girl. I try to stop drawing comparisons between my new sister, Sally and Poppy. At least Poppy has me in her life. I am far from perfect, but I fucking tried, which is more than our mum ever did and more than Angela ever has.

My chest swells with pride at having Evelyn with me to share this moment, and I notice she doesn't flinch when I introduce her as my girlfriend. It feels like a milestone for us, and even though she hasn't said it, I am beginning to believe this girl could fall in love with me. It doesn't matter how long it takes, I'd wait forever to have her by my side on a hundred more mornings like this one.

"I still can't believe you're here, where do you live?" my sister asks, she hasn't taken her eyes off me since we sat down. It's like she's scared if she blinks, I might disappear. Not a chance.

I've lived with no family for most of my life, having a sister changes everything. Sally filled a huge void, not just for me, but for Poppy, too. I knew she understood because the huge hug she gave me when she realised who I was tells me that she feels the exact same way about me.

"I don't live far from here, I own Maple Valley, it's a Strawberry Farm just outside of Bourton-on-the-Water." Her eyes light up at my response.

"You live here? You hear that, Greyson? My brother lives right next to me."

"I know," her husband smiles, her excitement is infectious.

"I live there with Evelyn, her son, Marshall and my daughter, Poppy," I say, squeezing Evelyn's hand. Okay, so she's not technically living with me yet, but she's as good as doing that now. We can work out the semantics later.

"You have a daughter?" Sally gasps. "Greyson, can you believe this? I'm an... aunty?"

She sounds out the word as though it's a mythical being rather than the title given to a close relative. The concept of family is as alien to her as it is to me.

"If you would like to be. Poppy would love to have you around. I'm sure, she loves being around women, there's only so much time she can spend learning how to drive a tractor."

"I have a niece who drives a tractor. Oh my god, Gabe, I'm so excited to meet her. How old is she. What does she look like?"

"She's six."

"She looks just like her dad," Evelyn chips in.

"You think?"

"She's the image of him, and she is going to be so excited to meet you. She's such a special little girl. We have been planning to have a girly pamper day soon for her birthday, if you'd like to come? I mean, if you're into nails and stuff?"

"Am I into nails?"

My little sister flashes a full set of leopard print fake nails at us, and we all laugh.

"I think we can safely say Sally would be down for a pamper day, she lives for that kinda stuff," Greyson says, taking her hand and kissing her.

I smile at him with nothing but gratitude. He clearly cares about my sister, and he's brought us back together. There are no words to describe how much respect I have for him and every effort he has gone to, to re-unite us.

After breakfast we part ways, swapping phone numbers and promising to stay in touch. I drop Evelyn back at work and offer to pick Marshall up so she can make up the hours she missed from starting late. Truth is, I'm glad to have her out of the way for a few hours, so I can get to work on the secret project I've been working on.

It's not that I want to pressure her into moving in, it's just that I can't bear the thought of her leaving. It didn't make any sense for her to be there on her own and me to be here wishing she was with me.

Even though we'd slept in separate bedrooms or fallen asleep in front of the TV every night, I missed being able to snuggle her up.

After school, we head to the DIY store and Marshall helps me pick out the colour scheme for his new room. I already have an idea of what I'd like to create for him, so I'm glad when he picks out mostly greens. The kids set to work on painting as soon as we get back and the hours pass quickly as we work as a team to get the job done.

Marshall mostly runs around putting handprints on the wall, with Poppy chasing after him and painting over them. I make a mental note to finish the room without the help of my so-called team, I don't think my ears could stand the squealing and giggles for another afternoon.

"Okay, you two, go and play for a minute, while I finish up here, and then it will be time to start the tea. Great work today teamies, come and give me hi five, we smashed it."

They both slap hands with me before running to create chaos elsewhere in the house, no doubt, and I put all the paints away, before locking the room so Evelyn won't see it yet.

The phone rings, and I struggle to hit the answer button with my hands still covered in wet paint.

"Harry?" I ask, balancing the handset between my ear and my shoulder to allow me to wash my hands.

"Yeah, it's me. Gabe you need to hear me out."

"I don't need to do anything for you anymore, Harry. We're not partners, remember."

"I know. But we were, Gabe. We were good partners in the beginning, and that's why I'm calling. I've been seeing Angela."

"So," I hiss into the phone. I always knew Harry was a snake, if he wanted to start a relationship with my bitch of an ex, then it was no skin of my fucking nose.

"So, I wanted to let you know that it's done now. More to warn you really, she's bad news, Gabe."

"No shit. What that woman does is none of my concern anymore, why are you even calling me. You don't owe me anything, Harry."

"Wait," he says, just as I'm about to hang up. "She's MIA."

"What do you mean, MIA?"

"She was using me to get information about you. I didn't realise until it was too late. She's hired a bent solicitor, some ex dealer's wingman. I was there when they were talking… about Poppy."

Every hair on my arms and neck stand at the mention of my daughter's name and my chest tightens. I can hear her playing with Marshall upstairs, the sounds of her footsteps on the creaky old floor-boards reassuring me that she is safe and in no danger. Harry's tone and the essence of the call telling me otherwise.

"What about Poppy. Tell me what was said, Harry. What's she planning?"

"He was giving her advice about the custody battle. He doesn't think he could win it in his usual way. He said if he tried to plant drugs on you it wouldn't be believable and on paper, Angela has no chance of winning."

"She doesn't," I state, the solid knot in my chest easing slightly at the fact.

"He also said that she can't kidnap her own child. Apparently in the eyes of the law there's nothing you could do if she just takes her, as there is no agreement in place."

My thoughts race and I clench my fist in anger, needing to punch something, but having to keep control of myself for the sake of the two kids upstairs.

"She'd have to find her first," I spit into the phone.

"That's why I'm calling. I'm sorry, Gabe, I gave her your new address."

"You have got to be kidding me. Thanks for the call, Harry, now go and fuck yourself. Don't ever fucking contact me again or I swear to god…" The line goes dead as he hangs up, probably the best option given the circumstances.

I pace the kitchen floor, shaking my hands in anger and running through every single possible time when Angela would have an opportunity to take Poppy from me. Would she show up at ballet practice, or when she's at a friend's house? What if she just took her out of school one day, would the school be able to stop her, even if I explain that she's not allowed to collect her?

Angela is well connected. It's how she's as successful as she is. It's how she's able to go undercover and just disappear for months at a time, despite being one of England's biggest celebrities.

Quickly coming up with a variety of solutions that would protect Poppy in almost every eventuality, I'm left with the biggest question of all, the one that fills me with more dread than any of the others. If Angela... *When* Angela shows up. Would Poppy want to go with her?

CHAPTER 13

Evelyn

"Pops, what is it. What's wrong?" She comes hurtling towards me as quickly as she can with fear all over her pretty little face.

"It's Fluffy. She's gone," comes her tearful wail.

"Poppy, that's a good thing. That's nothing to be sad about. That's what geese do. They fly south for the winter, where they can be warm. You know what that means?" I ask, pulling her into my lap and wrapping my arms around her.

"No." She sniffles, and I wipe the tears away from her cheeks.

"It means you did such a good job looking after her that she's been able to go on a great adventure with the rest of her family. She couldn't have done that without all the love and care you gave her when she was little, Poppy. You should be proud and happy, not sad at all."

"Miss Heist told me all about migration, but I still didn't want her to go. I wanted her to stay here with me."

"Well, if you're lucky and very patient, she might just come back to see you next summer."

"Can she do that? Find her way all the way back here?"

"Oh, you'd be surprised, Poppy. Those that are loved always seem to find their way home."

She gazes up at me thoughtfully, and I wipe the last of her tears away, glancing around at the farm from my rocking chair on the porch.

"Is that why you're moving here, because my dad loves you?"

The enormity of her question catches me off guard.

"Yes," I answer honestly. "And, because I care about both of you very much. But I won't move in for good if you're not okay with that, Poppy. It's been just you and your daddy for a long time, and if you want it to stay that way, I understand."

"I like you here, you're really nice." She shrugs, before skipping off into the kitchen.

Gabe steps beside me, handing me a cold glass of lemonade, a frozen strawberry giving it a touch of Maple Valley.

"She thinks the world of you, you know? We both do."

"I think the world of both of you, too," I reply easily, taking a sip of the ice-cold drink.

"Did you contact the solicitor?"

"Which one?" He sighs. "I sorted out the will from my grand-mother, turns out she left me half of an estate she lived on in Cheshire. Sally grew up with her, and she never mentioned me once. Seems weird that she would leave me all that cash without telling Sally anything about me."

"She must have had her reasons," I try to reassure him.

"Yeah, Sally said she kept to herself. Apparently, my mum brought her nothing but shame, and when my dad left for London, he didn't leave a forwarding address. I figure he wanted to get as far away from my mum as possible and was probably worried my grandmother would pass his address on if he gave it to her."

"So, it was just you and your dad ever since?"

"Yeah. I liked it that way. He was great, but there were times when

I felt... different somehow. I used to latch on to my school teachers and pretend they were like a mum to me. Guess I wanted to know what it felt like to have one. Sally said I didn't miss out on much."

"Any mum who could give you up is not a mum in my eyes. It's her loss Gabe. You turned out so amazing in spite of everything."

"I did alright." He shrugs, and I raise an eyebrow at him, making him smile. Looking out at the farm, we both know he's done more than 'alright.'

"I'm glad you sorted out the will, but I meant the solicitor dealing with the custody battle. Did you speak with them, is there anything you can do?"

"Apparently I can apply for a legal injunction, but I have to have good grounds for that."

"Surely Angela's drug use would count as good grounds?"

"Yeah, but I have to be able to prove that she is still using and knowing Angela, she will do everything in her power to prove she isn't. Plus, an injunction stops her having any contact with Poppy, and I'm not sure that's for the best either. Shitty as she is, she's still her mum, and what if she's clean? I don't want to stand in the way of Poppy having a relationship with her mum. It's not as straightforward as it seems."

"It would be easier if you guys could just talk it out. Will she still not take your calls?"

"She's gone missing. No one's seen or heard from her in weeks. Harry, my ex colleague called me to let me know he's given her my address, but that was weeks ago, no one's heard from her since. Her manager and PA are both spinning me some line that she's still in rehab. The press is eating it up, but the truth is, no fucker knows where she is."

"Which means she could just show up, right?"

"Right," he says, through gritted teeth.

My heart aches for him knowing how stressed he must be having the constant threat of Angela looming over him. It seemed so unfair that she called all the shots when it was him who was the one looking after Poppy.

"How about you? You want me to come with you?"

"No, I'll be fine. This is something I need to do on my own."

With the anniversary of Marshall's death looming, it seemed like the perfect time to follow through on my promise and take Marshall to meet his grandparents. Although, it would have been nice to have Gabe with me, if felt wrong to take him over to their house, like I was betraying their son.

* * *

AFTER POPPING into work to help Tanya with some wedding flowers that the bride has changed her mind on, I pick Marshall up from my parents' house and walk along the river to Marshall's parents' place. They are both waiting anxiously at the window when we arrive, and I'm wracked with guilt for what I did to them.

Joan answers the door, bursting onto the path outside and hugging me before pausing to regard Marshall. She looks back at me, her eyes brimming with tears.

"I'm sorry, I wasn't expecting... He looks just like him."

"I know." I sigh, running my fingers through my son's pale blonde hair. "Marshall this is Grandma Joan, and this is your Grandpa Stu."

"Shall we go inside and get some cookies?" Stu asks, speaking for the first time, clearly taken aback from the likeness of his grandson to my husband.

Marshall grabs my leg and doesn't say anything, he's clearly nervous, and Joan crouches down to meet his eye line in an attempt to put him at ease.

"We have been waiting to meet you for a very long time. Your daddy was very special to us, and you are just as special. What do you say you we go inside, get some cookies and see if there's anything fun to do, huh?"

"Okay," Marshall replies, and we follow Joan inside.

Leading us into the lounge I take a seat on the sofa and instantly feel a familiarity at seeing all of the things that used to be here, still in place. Except for a fresh picture of Marshall in a frame and tucked into the corner is the baby photo I sent of my son when he was born.

"Marshall, can I show you something, man to man?" Stu asks him, pushing a huge box into the middle of the floor.

"What is it?" my son asks from the safety of my lap.

"This," says Stu, pulling off the lid, "was your dad's train set. One of the best there is. I've kept it here because he would never let anyone play with it when he was little. It was his favourite thing, but I think he'd let you play with it. I think he'd want you to have it, so I saved it for you."

Marshall peers inside the box.

"Go on," I reassure him, "it's okay, Marshall, you can play with it, if you want to."

Stu smiles at him, and with that he starts pulling all sorts of bits and pieces out of the box. The two boys spend the afternoon building the track and getting the old wind up trains moving, much to Marshall's delight.

Joan quizzes me about everything that's happened since I last saw her, and I share all of Marshall's firsts with her right up until the elephant in the room.

"I wish we could have supported you better, Evie, you were so young. There were times when you were like my own child, I remember your relationship with your parents wasn't always smooth sailing. When you left, it was like I lost both of you. If it wasn't for Candice, I'm not sure I could have kept going."

The mention of my sister-in-law brings back a flood of raw emotion. There was a time when we were as close as could be, and I'm not sure she will be as forgiving at my disappearing act. I'd only seen her once, at the charity gala she held. After that, there'd been no contact at all.

"How is she?"

"Pregnant. She's expecting twins, and already has one little boy, Jenson. He's the cutest little thing." She hands me a photo of Candice with an enormous baby bump. The man I'd seen coming into the house that day is next to her, with his little boy in the photo.

"Wow, she must be so excited. Look how happy she looks, I'm so happy for her. Is that her husband? Where do they live?"

"Just up the river, actually, not far at all. But they are staying in London at the moment. Blake, her husband, is very particular about the care she receives with the twins. They are booked into a private hospital for the kids. I'm heading to the apartment after the birth to stay with her. Blake wants her close after she has the twins, so he can be involved as much as possible, but it's not easy for them. He's just taken over his father's business, and really needs to be in the city."

"Sounds like he's looking after her well."

"She would say too much, but it's sweet, really. He idolises her. Same way Marshall did you. He would want you to be happy, Evie. Has there been, anyone else?" she asks the question in a voice so small it makes me nervous to answer, but she deserves the truth, however painful it's probably going to be.

"Not at first, not for a long time. I'm scared I'll never love anyone the way I loved Marshall," I admit. "But, since I came back to England, there's been someone that makes me want to try. He's patient and kind, and he's great with Marshall."

She takes her time to answer, placing a hand on mine. "I'm glad, Evie. It's what my son would have wanted. He wouldn't want you and Marshall to be alone. You deserve a chance to have the happiness that was stolen from you."

Surprised by her answer, all I can manage is, "Thank you."

Reaching into the sideboard unit next to us, she pulls out a small wooden box with the word 'Son' carved into the lid. I know what's inside before she explains, and my heart plummets to my toes as she hands it to me.

"It didn't seem right to scatter Marshall's ashes without you. I want you to take them with you. Take them some place great, somewhere where Marshall used to smile and be carefree with you. That's where he'd want to be most of all. Rendered speechless and forcing myself to respond to her in any way I can, I hug her tightly.

"I'll take good care of them until the times right," I reassure her.

"I know you will," she murmurs softly, and I squeeze her hand as

Marshall runs towards us and grabs at my leggings, desperate for me to follow him.

"Look, Mummy, look at dis," he yells over to me.

"Wow! Did you get this train working?" I ask as he winds up the train excitedly and sets it off choo-ing around the track.

"He's got a knack for it." Stu winks at him. "He's just like his father."

All three of us adults glance from each other back to Marshall and the train set. We share a moment that will stay with me for as long as I live. Three people bonded by the love for a man who was taken too soon. A man that will forever live on in that love and in our love for my son.

Gabe

"Hey you two, how did it go?"

"Good." She smiles up at me, pushing a dark loose wave behind her ear. "Really good."

"Are you ready for your surprise, Marshall?"

"What surprise," she asks curiously. Marshall's already running towards the stairs, and I scoop him up as I catch up with him.

"Just a little something we've been working on," I say as she follows us upstairs.

Marshall runs straight to the locked guest room, and I shout to Poppy to come and join us.

"Ready, Marshall, count one, two, three."

"Won, too, freeeee," he shouts, and I open the door to his newly decorated space.

"Oh, my goodness, look at this place," Evelyn gasps.

The army theme room looks even better than I'd planned with camouflage curtains and a matching duvet. Marshall runs straight for the main feature, a cabin bed with a slide and army tent over the top.

Pops helps him up the ladder, as I pick up an empty picture frame from the sideboard. The caption reads 'my hero.'

"I thought you could add some pictures of his dad around the room, to really make the place his own."

She throws her arms around me, kissing my cheek then burying her face into my neck. "It's perfect, I can't believe you did all this for him. Thank you so much."

"I just thought, if he's going to be staying here, then he needs his own space. Especially, if he's going to be moving in." I grin at her, kissing her on the mouth and watching Marshall come sliding down the slide with Poppy waiting to catch him at the bottom.

"And look, there's a safety rail. You know what that means?"

"I don't have to worry about him falling out of bed?"

"Exactly. And you don't need to keep checking on him and sleeping next to him." I arch an eyebrow at her, waiting for the penny to drop.

"You did all this just to get me in B.E.D she spells out.

"No." I shrug. "But I'd do it ten times over if it does the trick." I wink at her as she playfully rolls her eyes at me.

"Gabe," she says my name in a way that makes me want to pick her up and march her to my bed right now, but I resist temptation.

"Who's is the handprint?" She asks, tracing a hand across the messy green shape on the wall.

"Mine," Marshall yells with pride before sliding down the slide and running over to prove it by placing his chubby little hand over the splodge.

"Wow, do you think you can do mine?"

"Yeah. I can do evywons," he says matter of factly.

* * *

"I THINK the room was a big hit," Evelyn says, curling up on the sofa.

"I think so too," I reply, handing her a glass of rose wine and raising my own glass towards hers. "Cheers to that, and to officially moving in."

"Cheers." She lifts her glass, parting her lips to take a sip, and I'm on her before she even reaches the glass. We've spent weeks skirting around it, but there's no more hiding the fact that I want her so much it fucking hurts.

"Tell me what you see," I pant out breathless from kissing her.

"My new roommate," she teases.

"And?"

"My boyfriend." Damn, I loved the sound of that.

"What else."

"You, Gabe. I see you."

"And I see you, baby. You're so sexy. Do you see that, Evelyn? Do you see what you do to me?"

"Show me," she whispers, and my fingers tear at her jogging bottoms, desperate to shed the layers of clothing and have her naked. She fumbles with my jeans button, and it spurs me on to cast my own clothes aside until there's nothing in between us.

"Holy shit." She gasps, her eyes glowing amber as they scour every inch of my body. I watch them widen as they fall to my solid cock.

I can't help but laugh. "Sounds about right," I throw back, catching hold of her legs and pulling them so she's lying down. Climbing on top of her, I could easily take her right now. She's tense underneath me, her lips parted, eyes pleading with me to do anything to give her some release. But what would be the fun in that?

Grabbing my t-shirt from the floor, I roll it up and throw it over her face.

"You look beautiful, Evelyn. Every fucking curve is begging me to taste it. Let me play for a while? No peeking, if you see what I'm doing, you'll try and stop me, and believe me, you don't wanna do that."

"No peeking. Got it," she confirms, her voice muffled through the cotton of my t-shirt.

"Try and relax. You don't need to be nervous, I won't hurt you. Not unless you want me to."

Her eyes are wide with intrigue as she pops her head out of hiding to shoot me a warning look.

"Kidding. Just kidding," I reassure her.

One day she'll understand that the pain will be her undoing, but for now, we'll play nice.

Taking her feet, I lift them over my shoulder, shoving a cushion under her ass as it raises slightly. I pause to take in her tanned skin and erect nipples. Pleasuring a woman is second nature to me, after Angela, I'd become the champion of one-night stands.

Pleasuring Evelyn was different. Knowing she's only ever been with one man, a man she shared that much of a connection with, is intimidating.

She's trusted me enough to give herself to me, and I plan to worship every single inch of her in return.

Tracing a finger slowly along from her foot to her thigh, I stop only to pinch her nipple. It's only a gentle squeeze, but she cries out in surprise, and the sound has my cock swelling to the max.

Thanks to the cushion, her pussy is tilted upwards, and I don't know whether to lick it first or fuck it.

Taking her hands, I wrap them around my length, and the sight causes a surge through me that manifests in beads of pre-cum at my tip. I place my hand over hers and begin to pump gently, showing her exactly how I like it before letting go to use my hands on her exactly how I know she'll like it.

My fingers work her hard and fast, while my thumb rolls over her swollen clit in slow circle motions. Her hips buck under my touch, and I let out a low growl when she moans my name.

Pinning her hands above her head, before she makes me climax, I slide my cock between her tits. With my other hand, I squeeze them together and rock my hips backwards and forwards, the sensation almost tips me over.

Kneading her tits as I slide in and out of her cleavage, she writhes around underneath me, hungry for her own pleasure. I give it to her with my mouth, licking and sucking at her centre until she climaxes all over my tongue.

"You can look now," I pant out, before burying my face back inside her, and taking the last of her pleasure with my mouth, as she cries out and grabs my hair.

"I love you," I breathe as I shuffle up and slide my bulging cock inside her. Despite being soaked, she's still tight, and it takes a few gentle thrusts before I'm all the way in.

I slow the pace to a steady rhythm and lock my eyes on hers. She's reluctant to kiss me at first. Shy of her own fucking taste.

"It's okay," I reassure her, pressing my lips against hers. "You taste good."

She parts her lips, and I kiss her harder with every thrust, our lips locked together. Her inner walls clamping down on me so hard that I can barely hold on to my orgasm. I kneel back to delay things, giving her a chance to recover from her last climax before building her next one.

From my new position I can press down on her stomach intensifying the feeling of my solid cock inside her and working her into a frenzy with my fingers, again.

CHAPTER 14

Evelyn

I convulse as he takes my orgasm for his own, along with his. The feeling of his love for me is so intense I can barely breathe. Shaking, he collapses on top of me, and I wrap my arms around him, a tear streaming down my face. I never thought I'd have another moment like this. Gabe had been so willing to give himself to me in every way he could, but I hadn't expected that I'd ever be ready to do the same.

To put myself completely out there. Vulnerable. My heart unlocked and wide open to be stomped all over if that was what fate decided.

Yet here I am.

"Gabe," I whisper. He lifts his face to mine

"What do you see?" I ask him.

"I see the woman I love."

"What else?" I smile.

"A woman who is scared but brave all at the same time."

"And?" I raise an eyebrow, pressing him the same way he pressed me.

"A woman who loves me back?" he says quietly, as if not daring to speak his thoughts out loud.

I nod my head and lean forward to kiss him. "Yes," I say, kissing him again. "I do. I love you."

"I love you, too, Evelyn. So fucking much, baby."

"I know. You don't go easy on me, do you?"

"Did you want me to? Truthfully?"

I shake my head, and he grins, jumping up off the sofa and handing me a box of tissues.

"Good, because that was just the warm up. Let's clean up, and then I want you in my bed."

I let out a sulky groan, and he chuckles, wiping himself clean and grabbing our clothes off the floor. We tiptoe past the kid's rooms like two naughty teenagers, and I don't even set foot inside the door before he throws me onto his bed.

He wasn't kidding about just warming up, and I wake up the next morning with an aching, burning sensation between my thighs. It stays there for the entire school run and makes me blush when Tanya asks about Gabe at work.

"You've been quiet lately," she remarks as we sit down for a quick lunch break.

"Have I?" I answer, trying to sound nonchalant.

"Yep, which means you broke up with cowboy god. Or you slept with him."

I say nothing, but the warmth in my cheeks betrays me.

"Oh my god, you slept with him, Evie, that's amazing. Was it good? Is he a keeper?"

"I hope he's a keeper cos' I've fallen in love with him."

"You've what! Oh my god, Evie, that's crazy. Come here, I'm so happy for you."

"Thanks, I can't quite believe it. It's all happened so fast, but it just feels right."

"That's all you can go on. There are no guarantees with any relationship, you know that better than anyone."

"I never thought it was possible to fall in love twice."

"Girl, look at Jlo, she's fallen for a dozen guys and is still looking. Just be thankful you didn't have to kiss too many frogs before you found your guy."

I chuckle at her comparison and finish the last few bites of my sandwich before we get to work on some seasonal designs.

"That's gorgeous," I say, checking out Tanya's red and yellow design.

"Thanks, it's called:

"Fucked-by-a-cowboy-god."

She parts the air above her head with her hands as though revealing a golden plaque with the absurd name written across it.

"Don't you dare write that on the signage," I argue, and we both laugh.

"That's pretty," she offers, pointing at the green and white arrangement I'm just finishing.

"Thanks, it's called, Frog-Kisser."

"We'd probably sell more of these with that name, than we do if we use the usual 'autumnal arrangement'."

"Ha, we probably would," I agree.

"Have you two moved in together? I noticed the lights were off at your place when I walked past the other day."

"I'll bet you did, Sherlock."

"A girls gotta get her gossip somehow," she's says, rolling her eyes.

"I would have told you, we just didn't want to make it official too soon, we've not known each other that long."

"You know I don't give a shit about that, Evie. So, is it official now?"

"Mmmhmm, he decorated Marshall his own bedroom."

"That's too cute, sweet and sexy, hey."

"Shhh," I press my finger to my lips as a customer walks in and heads straight for the 'Fucked-by-a-cowboy-god.' We both suppress our laughter when she asks for the price.

The rest of the afternoon is spent the same way, and by the time we leave we've got a 'Screw-My-Ex', 'Fuck-Monday's' and 'Adulting-Sucks' collection neatly displayed in the window.

When I arrive to pick Marshall up from preschool, I'm a few minutes late, and the teacher is waiting for me outside.

"I'm really sorry, I got caught up at work and…"

"It's no problem, Ms. Embers, you're only a few minutes late. I wanted to speak to you about something, have you got time to pop into the classroom for a minute?"

She's smiling at me, but it's the first time she's needed to speak to me about anything outside of parents evening, so I'm running through a whole heap of things that could be wrong. I follow her inside where Marshall is piecing together a jigsaw puzzle and runs instantly over on sight of me.

"Hi, baby, have you had fun?"

"Yeah, I pwayed football with Casey."

"You did, that's so cool, Marshall. Do you want to finish that jigsaw while I speak to your teacher, and then we will go home?"

"Okay. Come and see it in a minute."

"Of course I will," I say, turning my attention back to his teacher.

"We just wanted to say how pleased we are with Marshall. He's such a bright little boy, and he's come on leaps and bounds in a short space of time. His fine motor skills are what we would expect to see from a child of six, even seven years old. I didn't realise he was such a talented artist."

"He's been painting with his…" I pause to consider what Poppy is to Marshall. They'd become so close, and I had dropped the ball a little when it came to creative activities, it has been Poppy that's been painting and drawing with him most evenings.

"Friend." I finish the sentence as she picks up a stack of papers all with his scrawl on them.

"This is just some of the drawings he's done in the past week, the detail on this one is really quite something."

I take the page from her, my body feeling a little numb, and my mouth rendered speechless as I study the painting. It's mostly blobs of paint, but you can clearly make out a girl, boy, two grownups and half a dozen strawberries blobbed around the edge of the page in red splodges.

I know exactly who the people in the picture are, and it touches the deepest part of my heart that he's drawn it. The feelings we had all developed for one another were new, and in a lot of ways unexplainable, but this drawing right here is a palpable summary of the life we were quickly creating. I hadn't realised, until seeing it drawn out by my son, that this was so much more than a relationship. We were becoming a family. A blended, unusual one with a shit ton of things to be figured out, but all four faces were smiling in the picture. Glancing from the page to my boy and back again, a sense of pride swells thick in my gut, Marshall was right. We were happy. All four of us had found happiness together, and it's so much more than I ever expected would be possible after losing Marshall.

Regaining my composure, I turn my attention back the teacher.

"Thank you for showing me these and for your kind words, I'm so proud of how well Marshall is doing. As long as he is happy then I am."

"Please, take your time to look through them, it's not often we see such an accelerated rate of development here in pre-school. Whatever you are doing, keep doing it, it's obviously working."

"Do you mind if I take these with me?"

"Of course, believe me we, have plenty more paintings here." She gestures around the room full of mish mash, hodge podge paintings on the wall that have been completed by the kids.

Walking over to Marshall, I help him to put the last few pieces in the jigsaw before presenting him with the picture.

"Did you draw this?"

"Yep. I did it for you."

"Thank you, it's very good. Is this me?"

He nods his head. "And is this Gabe and Poppy?"

"And that's all shrawberries," he exclaims, throwing his arms in the air, and I pull his little body into mine, squeezing him tight.

"It's my favourite picture. Shall we take it home and put it up on the fridge?"

"Okay," he replies and we head back to Maple Valley listening to his favourite nursery rhyme CD in the car.

As soon as we get back, I sense something, as usually either Poppy or Gabe would run out to meet us, depending who saw us first.

My fears are confirmed when I find Gabe in the kitchen with his head in his hands.

It instantly dampens my own spirits to see him looking all stressed and tense, he's always so relaxed and care-free.

"Everything okay? Marshall do you want to watch some Sponge-Bob? I walk into the lounge and flick it on for him, knowing it will buy me five minutes to get to the bottom of whatever's going on with Gabe.

No sooner than I've set foot back in the kitchen it comes spilling out of him, his voice a mix of anger and despair.

"She turned up at school."

"Who did?" Knowing instinctively who he is talking about.

"Angela, I don't know what game she's playing this time, but Poppy's really upset. She said she saw her watching her through the fence at lunch time. She doesn't understand why she wouldn't speak to her if she was right there at the school, and you know what, neither do I. What am I supposed to say to that? She's right, it doesn't make any sense, it's like she's playing a sick, fucking twisted game, and Poppy's just a pawn in it."

"Have you heard from her at all? Has she made any contact with you?"

"Nothing. She's obviously biding her time. This is Angela. It's what she does, fucks with people. Poppy's freaking out over it, and there's not a damn thing I can do about it."

His jaw is flexed and fist clenched tight. He's clearly pissed and I hate seeing him so riled up.

"Why don't you go and get some fresh air, take a load off, and I'll see if I can talk to Poppy," I offer, not entirely sure what I could say to her that would make things any better.

"You don't mind?"

"Of course not. Maybe she just needs a girl talk."

"Okay, I'll be back in five. Thanks, Evelyn. Even if you can get her to come out from under the duvet, that would be a start."

"I'll see what I can do," I say, forcing a smile and hoping it looks easier than I feel.

"Marshall, I call into the living room, I'm just going to speak to Poppy for a minute, so come upstairs if you need me, okay?"

"Okay," he mumbles with his eyes glued to the screen.

Climbing the stairs with the pictures still in my hand, I knock on her door and gently call out her name.

There's no reply.

"Poppy," I say it a little louder this time, knowing full well she heard me the first time.

When she doesn't answer, I open the door and pop my head around to see a giant shaking lump of duvet on the bed. Running over to her, I sit on the edge and place a hand over the wobbling bedsheets.

"Aw, Poppy, don't be upset. Whatever it is, I'm sure your mum and dad both wouldn't want you to be sad."

The shaking slows a bit, and I hear her fighting to catch her breath between sobs.

"Why don't you come on out from under there, and we can talk things through?"

No response.

"I actually have something that might make you feel better. I'm going to put it up by your pillow. It's something Marshall made at school, his teacher was really proud of him today and said someone has been teaching him lots of new art skills. You've really helped him to learn, Poppy, that's such a clever and kind thing for you to do."

I fold the page neatly in half and shuffle it in underneath her duvet, edging it forward to persuade her to take it from me.

A few minutes later, a tearful Poppy appears from her safe haven.

"Did he draw this?"

"Yeah, it's us. He's even added the strawberries around the edges."

"He's drawn it like we're a family, but we're not. You're not my mum, I like you, but you're not... it's just not the same."

"Oh, Poppy." She breaks down in a fit of tears again, and I'm unsure whether to cuddle her up or not. "Poppy, I'm not trying to be your mum. You already have a mum, and I would never try to replace her. I know this has all happened quickly, and it's okay if you're not okay with that. You should know that I really care about you and your dad, and I want what's best for you both. I know what it's like to not have the one person you want with you, it's really hard. It's okay to be upset about that."

"She was right there at the fence, and then she just disappeared. What if she never comes back?" She snuffles, spent of tears and exhausted by the overwhelming emotions.

"Poppy, she'd be crazy not to come back."

"What if she is crazy, I heard my dad on the phone saying she's crazy, but I didn't think he was telling the truth. What if he was?"

I sigh heavily before answering with trepidation. "Sometimes grownups say things they don't mean. All you need to remember is that your mum and dad love you very much. It's not always easy for them to show it, but that doesn't make the love any less real. Know what I mean?"

She nods, indicating that even at her tender age she has an understanding of how complicated adult relationships can be. The disappointment in her mum has made her unfairly wise beyond her years.

"Shall we go and find Marshall and put his picture up on the fridge?"

"Okay." She smiles up at me, putting a brave face on but seems, at least, a teensy bit more relaxed. We walk downstairs together, she doesn't hold my hand or anything, but I sense that she appreciates the solidarity.

Gabe

"Poppy, you're up. Are you feeling any better?"

"A bit." She shrugs, helping herself to a shortbread from the cockerel shaped cookie jar.

"Good. I hate seeing you upset, Pops."

"Sorry."

"Don't say sorry. You don't have to be sorry, it just sucks. I want to cheer you up, but I can't, and it drives me crazy," I say the last part in a scary monster voice, earning a small giggle from her.

"You know there is one thing you could do to cheer me up."

"Anything," I reply.

"We could go to that special place for tea. The one with the fish tank."

"Would that cheer you up?"

She nods, already looking happier at the prospect of a night out together.

"Would you like just the two of us to go, or invite Evelyn and Marshall? It's completely up to you."

"Let's all go, Marshall will love it there."

"Okay, you go and change out of your uniform, I'll call ahead and book us a table.

* * *

Luckily everyone likes Chinese food, and by the time we're on our fourth course at the restaurant, Poppy's in much better spirits. Stuffed full of just about every dish on the menu, we drive back home. As soon as I pull up, I get a sinking feeling when a black limo comes into view.

"Evelyn, take the kids straight inside, and I'll catch up with you in a minute."

"What's wrong, Dad. Who's in the car?" Poppy asks, the better spirits already quashed and replaced with anxiety.

"I'm not sure, I'll let you know if it's anyone important." I turn to face her and force a smile. "Don't worry, Pops, it won't be anything to worry about. You go inside, and I'll be in, in a minute."

As soon as we step outside the car, Angela's high pitched, theatrical tone pierced the air.

"Poppy! It's me, princess, oh my god, look at you," she shrieks, running towards a shocked looking Poppy.

Fuck, I thought she would have at least let us have a few minutes to talk things through before descending on her like a vulture attacking its prey.

I move forward in one heavy step that creates a solid wall between the two of them. This will be on my daughters' terms, and I shoot Angela a death stare that lets her know that.

Evelyn speaks first. "I'll be inside," she mumbles, eyeing me to check if I want her to take Poppy with her. I simply nod my head, and she scoops Marshall up, carrying him indoors.

Bending down to Poppy, I say quietly and as calmly as I can, "Do you want to say hi to your mum? You don't have to, it's up to you?"

"It's okay, Dad, I'll talk to her."

Reluctantly stepping out of the way to allow Angela access to our daughter, I fight the urge to punch something.

"Oh, honey, you're growing so fast, and I'm missing it all. I'm so sorry I haven't been in touch, Mummy's been sick, but I'm better now."

Sick. That's one word to describe it.

Poppy doesn't say anything, but she doesn't pull back from Angela's tight embrace either. The sight of her little arms clinging on to her mum, as though she may disappear into a puff of smoke any minute if she lets go, has my heart aching.

"It's so good to see you, my darling. And you're so beautiful."

"Thank you, Evelyn always says that too."

"She does?" I receive a cold glare over Poppy's head as Angela continues to cuddle her.

"Well, that's because it's the truth. You know, you look just like me when I was a little girl. Except, your clothes, obviously."

Poppy looks bruised and asks, "What's wrong with my clothes?"

She pulls at the edge of her loose yellow sweater. She'd chosen it because it's her favourite colour, and she wore it with matching trainers and a pair of skinny jeans.

"Nothing. It's just… Well, I bought you some new ones, anyway. Let me grab them from the car. I think you'll love them, they're so much more suited to the city."

"Mum?"

"Yes, darling."

"I'm glad you came to see me, but I really don't need any new clothes. I don't spend much time in the city. I am fine in these clothes, here with my Dad."

"For now, yes, but when I take you…"

"Shall we step inside?" I grab Poppy's hand, and in a show of insecurity, Angela grabs the other one. She won't be taking my daughter anywhere without discussing it with me first. Poppy's only just settled into life in The Cotswolds, there's not a chance I'm going to have it disrupted all over again.

The sound of the limo door opening causes me to glance back and a skinny, tall man dressed all in black steps out and nods at Angela. She's brought her bodyguard to visit her kid? Is this woman for real? Poppy spots him too and looks more than a little intimidated.

"Tell him he won't be needed," I demand through gritted teeth.

She hesitates, but glancing back down at Poppy's worried little frown, she shouts back, "Wait here, Damian."

He looks royally pissed off, which can only mean they've fucked at some point or are planning on it. Giving her a look that lets her know that I'm fully aware of her dirty little secret, I turn my attention back to my daughter.

"Poppy, why don't you go inside and see what Evelyn and Marshall are doing while I talk to your mum for a while?"

"No," she answers firmly as I guide Angela through my kitchen and into my lounge. If feels so alien seeing her in my space. The home that Poppy and I have created together, and I had a sickening feeling she was about to try and tear it down. That's what my ex does. Destroys and demolishes. She's a walking, talking wrecking ball, and I feel like the wall standing in her way, about to take the brunt as she bulldozes straight through our daughter's life.

"If it's about me, I want to hear it."

"She's right, Gabe, I've come to talk to Poppy."

"Okay," I say, through gritted teeth. "Let's all sit down and talk things through, it's been a long time since you last saw your mum. Angela, we are happy that you're here, especially Poppy. She has really missed you."

Angela sits opposite us in her overpriced skin-tight pencil dress and ridiculously pointy high heels. Her look screams expensive and celebrity. If you could choose an outfit to look as little like a parent as possible, that would be it. The black dress is like a symbol of the different paths are lives have taken and how little we have in common anymore.

"I've missed you too, Poppy. That's why I've come back. I wasn't well, but I'm much better now and able to take care of you. I've been offered a new role in a huge TV series. A reality show, actually. 'Celebrities on the Loose.' It's set in Australia, we get to live there for a year while we film. Isn't that amazing? They want you to be part of the show, baby. Imagine that! You would be famous, just like me. We will be on TV together and get to spend all our time together. Can you believe it? Isn't it the best news?"

"I… I would be on TV?"

"We both would. It's a chance to properly get to know each other, we've never had that before. I know I haven't been the best mum, but I do love you. I've always loved you, you're the reason I've been able to get better. Everything I've done is for you, Poppy."

"You can't be fucking serious," I yell, unable to maintain my cool any longer. "How fucking dare you come here and put ideas in her head like this. After everything you have put her through. Get out. Get the fuck out of my house and don't ever come back."

"No, Dad. Please stop. Please don't send her away." Poppy begins to sob uncontrollably and darts past me, through to the kitchen.

"Poppy, wait," I shout, turning to follow her.

"Look what you've done, as fucking usual. Shown up and create a shit storm. I meant what I said, stay the fuck away from both of us, and get a lawyer, I'll see you in court."

Evelyn appears, having overheard the commotion. "Don't be too hasty, Gabe, think about what Poppy wants. What she needs. You two have to find a way to work together, do what's best for your daughter. I'll go and talk to her, give you two time to talk things through.

"Tell her I'm sorry. I'll be out in just a sec."

Angela's hands are shaking when I look back at her, a tell-tale sign that she's desperate for a drink, which only pisses me off even more. Evelyn's right, I messed this up, no one else. It doesn't matter what my feelings are toward Angela, she's still Poppy's mum, and I need to deal with it like a man not some angry kid.

"I'm sorry, Gabe. I didn't mean to cause any of this I just wanted to see my daughter."

"See her and destroy her life all over again, you mean. Jesus, Angela. Have you any idea how much she misses you. How much she needs you. She's spent her whole life trying to fit into your world, maybe it's time you tried stepping into hers."

Evelyn steps back into the room with a panicked look troubling her features.

"She's gone. Poppy's gone, Gabe."

"Have you checked upstairs?"

"I'll check again, but the back doors open, did you leave it like that?"

"Fuuuuck," I shout, dragging my fingers through my hair and running straight for the fields.

"Gabe, wait, you'll need a torch. It's pitch black out there," Evelyn shouts after me.

"No time, stay here with Marshall in case she comes back," I instruct her, already running towards the lake.

It's where she goes when she's upset, or happy, or when she's had a rough day at school. She knows I follow her, but I often let her get far enough ahead that she feels like she's on her own. I think the sense of freedom helps her put things right for herself, but that's in the day time. Now it's dark and no place for an almost seven-year-old to be running around. What if I'm too late? How long had we been talking before realising she was gone? Fuck, I couldn't take it if anything ever happened to her.

"Poppy… Pops."

I call out her name as loud as I can, my voice echoing across the wide-open space. It's met with silence and the sound of wind whistling through the branches of the maple trees surrounding us. My chest feels tight, and I'm struggling to see anything, but there's no way I'll give up, not until I find her.

Reaching the edge of the lake, I stop on sight of the light hitting the water.

"Poppy," I call out again.

"Go away," she shouts back, and my heart almost leaps out of my chest at the sound of her voice.

"Poppy, it's not safe out here, sweetheart. I need you to come to me, and we can work things out."

"Leave me alone."

I follow the sound of her voice and try to keep her talking, so I can locate her.

"I'm sorry, Pops. Please, let's talk things through."

"I just want to be on my own." She sniffles, and I finally catch sight of her. She's sitting on a fallen log, hugging her knees and balling her eyes out. God, what have I done, she's never seen me lose my cool like that before. I must have terrified her?

"Poppy, listen to me," I say, pulling off my jacket and wrapping it around her along with my arms. She crumples into me, sobbing wet tears into my t-shirt.

"I shouldn't have shouted like that. I didn't mean to upset you, I just felt really, really angry. But I know that's not an excuse, and I promise you Dad will never shout like that again. I know you're upset, but everything will be okay, we can sort this out together."

"I don't want to go, Dad. I don't even know where Austraga is."

"Australia. It's the other side of the world, and you don't have to do anything you don't want to do."

"But if I don't go, I'll never see my mum again."

"That's not true, your mum's work comes and goes. She might have a different job offer next year that's closer to home. She doesn't have to take this one." It's tempting to add 'the selfish bitch,' but I quash the urge and focus on my girl.

"The main thing is that we talk about this like grownups, and I know that's hard because you're still so little, but sometimes even little people have to be grown up. It's not fair, but it's just the way the world is."

Her tears seem to settle, and her shoulders are shaking less. I notice she's hugging me back now as oppose to just leaning into me.

"Come on," I say, pulling her up and carrying her back towards the house.

CHAPTER 15

Evelyn

"*D*o you think I should go after them?"

I glance down at her shoes and don't need to say anything, she's not going anywhere in those god-awful spiky things.

I can't help thinking how I'd be if that was my son out there all alone in the dark. It's worrying enough that Poppy's out there, but Gabe knows his daughter. I don't doubt for a second, he'll find her, I just won't be able to stop panicking until he does.

"I could ask Damien to help, if that's any use?"

"Damien?"

"My bodyguard," she explains.

"Oh Jesus, no. That's really not a good idea, she doesn't need a stranger trying to reason with her. She will have been upset enough hearing all the… hearing you and Gabe talking."

She blows the air in frustration, the same way a moody horse would. "I wouldn't call it talking. Gabe was getting all heated the way he always does when things don't go his way."

"His way?" I ask, trying not to get caught up in an argument that really isn't any of my business.

"That's Gabe for you." She shrugs and heads back onto our lounge, flopping into the sofa and crossing her legs over. "He decides to walk out on me, then he decides to move to the middle of nowhere, and now he thinks he can dictate where and how my daughter grows up."

She sounds genuinely pissed off. She can't seriously believe that Gabe has just waltzed around making all these decisions, with her playing no part in them.

"Surely, what happens with Poppy is down to do what both of you decide. Maybe you should try to give her a say in things too, you know, listen to what she wants."

"And who are you? Mary-fucking-Poppins?"

"Excuse me?"

"You heard me. Why are you even still here, don't tell me you and Gabe are going steady? Please. That man has never been able to commit to anything except his camera and his kid."

"For Poppy's sake, I'm going to overlook that little dig and ask that you don't make anymore. I'm here because I live here and that it's any of your business, but Gabe and I have been serious about each other for a while.

"Yeah right. He was serious about me, until he wasn't. Don't say I didn't warn you when it all goes to shit."

"Look, Angela. I don't know you, and quite frankly, I have no inclination to get to know you, but I do know your daughter. She needs you to put her first. What goes on between myself and Gabe is not your concern."

"Oh, I see. You want to do the whole step mum thing. Well, that's cute. Except it won't be happening. Gabe has had his time with Poppy here on this…"

She pulls a face that I think translates to the word farm, though she's clearly to disgusted by her surroundings to define them.

"I'm better now, and when Gabe has calmed down, he will see

sense and chill about the whole thing. It's literally a year, he can come with us if he's that bothered," she adds, flippantly.

The thought of it sends my heart racing. There's no way Gabe would give up everything he has worked so hard to achieve to follow Angela's career around again. I'm confident he wouldn't leave me, and the suggestion that he might has me seething. It takes a lot to wind me up, but this woman has managed it in just a few throw away comments. Everything seems so disposable to her, like she could take it or leave it... including her daughter.

"It's a huge deal. Look around you, Angela. You need to wake up to what is going on here. Gabe has worked his ass off to make this place what it is, and he's done it all with Poppy at his side. Those two are like rhubarb and custard, you just don't separate that stuff. He dotes on that girl, he'd do anything for her. Taking her away from all that support..." My voice cracks as I reach the brink of tears, but I force myself to continue. "...All that love, it would be unfair to both of them, but mostly to your daughter."

"So, what's you alternative? I crawl back into the woodwork, and you live here like a bunch of hillbillies pretending I don't exist?" She spits her words out venomously, and any inch of empathy I had for her and her situation dissolves like butter in a hot frying pan.

"I really don't think you're in a position to judge anyone, do you?" I snap at her.

"What the fuck does that mean?" she hisses at me.

"You're a mess, Angela. Gabe told me everything. How he tried to make things work for Poppy's sake, how you trapped him by getting pregnant in the first place and then proceeded to use your daughter as a tool for getting what you wanted. You have put them both through hell, and I won't allow you to do that to them anymore. Even if Gabe chooses to let Poppy go with you, we will fight tooth and nail to make sure he gets to have regular contact with her, and I don't just mean over the phone."

"We?" She smiles a calculating snarl at me, and I cross my arms to create a barrier between us.

"Yes, we. Gabe and I are a team, I think you need to understand that when you fuck with him you fuck with me too, and I don't take kindly to being fucked with."

She appears dumbfounded by my sudden change in temperament and doesn't reply, only giving me more gumption to continue.

"Now, if you don't mind, I have my own child to see to, so I'm going to go upstairs, and if you know what's best for you, you're going to sit the fuck down and wait for Gabe and Poppy to get back. Then, if she's willing to listen, you're going to apologise for springing something like that on her and hug her. Tell her your glad she's okay and that you can see how happy she is here and that if she wants to stay, she can. Walking away from her will be tough on both of you, but tearing her away from her dad, the only consistent adult she's had in her life would be cruel."

She looks at me like her minds been overloaded with too much information to take in. Her eyes are swimming with tears and her perfect features devoid of any expression.

"Are you hearing what I'm saying, Angela. You gotta do what's best for Poppy, not what's best for yourself. She has a home here with Gabe. A life that she is happy with."

Wiping the tears from her eyes, she fixes her skirt, regaining composure and says calmly, "Much as I hate to say this, and I do really hate to say it, you're right. I want to take her to Australia to be in my show and keep me company. I thought it was a good opportunity for us to get to know one another. I hadn't really thought about what she would want, she's just six. I hadn't expected her to be so…"

"Independent?" I smile, thanking god that the penny may finally have dropped. She passes me an almost smile. "Maybe you and your daughter are more alike than you think," I add, before leaving her alone with her thoughts and heading upstairs to bathe Marshall and get him ready for bed.

It's not long before the door clicks open, and I hear them coming in. Poppy is giggling, and Gabe sounds cheery. A wave of relief washes over me, knowing that they are both okay.

Once I've settled Marshall, who is a little clingier than usual, like he senses something is wrong, I make my way back downstairs.

Standing on the kitchen side of the living room door, I'm surprised when there's only two voices I hear. Sitting at the dining table, I mindlessly flick through the pages of my girly magazine. I don't want to intrude on them.

After a few minutes, Gabe pops through to the kitchen to get a drink, passing me an apologetic look.

"I'm sorry, Evelyn. I lost it, and that's not cool. It won't happen again. Where did she go?"

"I told her to wait here until you got back so you could talk."

"Typical, Angela. Didn't get her own way so she's done a runner again." He grimaces and pours Poppy a cup of milk.

"How is she?" I ask.

"Come and sit with us, I think she's okay. I just freaked her out by kicking off like that."

"Did she run far?"

"She was all the way down by the lake," he replies with wide eyes letting me know he'd gotten a fright, too.

I follow him into the living room and sit next to Poppy on the sofa. I don't say anything, not wanting to force her to communicate if she doesn't want to. She just snuggles into me, and I stroke her hair quietly as I watch Gabe try to convince her that her mum will come back and hasn't gone again for good.

It breaks my heart to know that she is so upset by her mum's sudden appearance and equally abrupt disappearance.

She's not the same girl for the next couple of weeks leading up to her birthday, she's quiet, subdued and can't seem to get excited about anything.

We don't hear from Angela, which Gabe says is unsurprising, but her showing up takes its toll on all of us. We're both weary of when, and if, she will reappear, and what trouble she will bring when she does.

"Maybe, she's gone to Australia to start filming the show," I suggest one night over a glass of white wine.

"Nah, she wouldn't have given up that easily. She'll just be biding her time, and probably working out how to get hold of a passport for Poppy."

"Do you have one for her?"

"Yeah, it was always me she travelled with, I've still got it upstairs."

"She could easily get a copy though, Gabe. You need to make another appointment with the solicitor and get some more legal advice."

"I know, I'm seeing him again on Wednesday."

"We should get some sleep, is everything set for tomorrow?" I ask, glancing around the room at a sea of pink balloons and a stack of neatly wrapped gift boxes all ready for the birthday girl.

"She's going to be so excited, I'm hoping it'll take her mind of everything. She's been stressing out recently."

"I've noticed that, too. She's not had her usual spark. It must be so hard for her. She wants to stay home, but she wants to get to know her mum, too."

Gabe

I WAKE at the crack of dawn, the sunlight flooding in through that window, as Evelyn insists on leaving the curtains open at night. Poppy clambers up into bed with us, closely followed by Marshall.

"Wow, everyone's so awake this morning, anyone would think it was Christmas," I remark, hiding my head under the pillow.

Pops tries to wrestle it back off me shouting, "It is a special day."

"Evelyn? Do you know anything about a special day?"

"Um, no, I know it's Tuesday, but I don't think there's anything out of the ordinary planned," she teases, pretending to wrack her brain for any special occasions until Poppy almost explodes.

"It's my birthday," she shrieks loudly, and I pull a shocked expression before attacking her fiercely with kisses all over her head. "Oh, it is? Totally slipped my mind."

"I know you're lying, Dad. You are the worst liar. I could tell from your face the whole time."

"No, you couldn't."

"Yes, I could. We could tell, couldn't we, Marshall?"

He nods shyly in agreement with her.

"Well, if it's your birthday, you would have presents, and I don't see any presents?"

"Want to come and help me find my presents, Marshall?" she asks, holding a hand out to him, which he takes without a word. The silent partner in crime.

Kissing Evelyn gently on the forehead, I threaten to cover her head in kisses, too. She wrestles me off and jumps out of bed, throwing on a hoodie. We follow the squeals of excitement downstairs to find Poppy jumping up and down in suspense.

"Can I open them; can I open them now?"

"Of course you can. What are you waiting for? Get stuck in."

She tears the paper off and falls to pieces over her new pony book collection and opens the rest of the presents at lightning speed.

Throwing her arms around me, she thanks me a dozen times before I tell her about the last present.

"Poppy, once you get changed, there's one more present, but it's not wrapped up."

"That's okay, I don't care about the wrapping," she gushes.

Her eyes search the room for the extra gift.

"It's not here, run up and get changed, and I'll take you to where it is," I instruct.

"Come on, Marshall, come and get dressed. Ready for another present?"

Marshall obliges, and the two of them go upstairs to change.

"You think she's excited?" I joke with Evelyn.

"Maybe just a little." She giggles.

"I fuckin' love this, you know? Us. Here. Like this."

"It's pretty special, right?"

"*You're* pretty special, Evelyn." As usual, she blushes at my compliment, and her eyes dart away from mine to avoid making contact.

Ignoring her coyness, I step forward and grab her ass cheeks, squeezing them tightly as I pull her close and kiss her.

Her sweet mouth has my cock immediately twitching in my sweatpants. She must sense it press against her groin as she mischievously runs a hand over my swelling and whispers, "Later."

The single word loaded with so much intent that I'm inclined to bend her over the dresser and teach her a lesson for being such a cocktease.

Instead, I tense up in frustration. "Jesus, Evelyn. You'll pay for that."

She passes me a look that tells me she's dying to, and it doesn't help my raging hard on situation whatsoever.

Made worse by the fact that she smirks at me as I shuffle to find room in my pants upon hearing the kids running downstairs.

"Slow down, you two," I call up to them.

"You know what I say about running down the stairs."

"Sorry, Dad," Poppy offers. "We're just so excited."

"And so you should be," I confirm, causing her to let out a loud squeaky sound that I think is aimed to convey her excitement to me.

I crouch down as Marshall carefully reaches the bottom stair.

"Wanna ride?" I ask.

"Yeah, pwease," he replies, already trying to climb onto my shoulders.

"Let's go," I proclaim, heading outside and towards the wooded area at the back of the strawberry fields.

Evelyn grabs Poppy's hand, and I grab hold of Marshall's feet to keep him steady, his little hands grabbing at my head as we go.

When we reach the clearing, Poppy gasps when she sees the treehouse in the distance. She takes it in as we walk closer, bringing her birthday present into view.

"Is that a tree house, Dad?"

"Not just any treehouse, Pops, it's your birthday treehouse. I built it just for you, for those times when you need to be on your own, or have secret adventures... or have your friends' round for tea. I thought you'd enjoy having a girly place to yourself."

She stopped listening no sooner than I'd gotten the first few words out of my mouth and stops to squeeze me tightly.

"It's perfect," she exclaims, before running ahead at maximum speed, trying to reach her new hide-out as quickly as she can.

When she's way ahead of us in the distance she remembers her manners and shouts back, "Thank you," at the top of her little voice.

"I told you she'd love it," Evelyn squeezes my hand, and we speed up our pace to catch up to Poppy.

She's already shimmying up the ladder when we catch up with her.

"Be careful," I shout up, placing Marshall onto the ladder and helping him climb up.

"I love it, I love it so much," Pops shouts, throwing her hands in the air and twirling around exactly how I imagined she would.

CHAPTER 16

Evelyn

The tree house makes me a little anxious having the kids up here with us is a very different vibe from when Gabe and I first spent time here. It makes me smile to see the netting that surrounds us and is clearly visible in daylight. He's thought of everything and the smile on Poppy's face has definitely made all his hard work, worthwhile.

After she explores every inch of the space and discovers the art supplies that he's organised into plastic rainbow-coloured drawers for her, I have an idea.

"How about we eat breakfast al fresco today?"

"What's ow frewsco," Marshall asks curiously.

"It means we eat our breakfast right here in the forest," I explain.

"Mummy, can I have omelettes pwease? With ham and cheese?"

"Of course you can, anyone else for omelettes?"

"Me," Gabe and Poppy shout in unison, and I can't help but smile from ear to ear at the sight of their matching cheeky grins. They are both so alike, with their dark features and full pouty lips.

The sight of him playing with the kids and fooling around with them both has my heart exploding like a cannon in my chest. I hesitate for a moment to drink him in, this beautiful man that has been so patient with me. So willing to wait and nurture my fractured heart, and piece by piece put it back together again. It's in this moment of hesitation that I realise that I'm not that broken-hearted girl anymore. Yes, I'm still hurting, but I'm slowly accepting that pain is just one part of me. Not every part of me is defined by what happened.

"You okay, babe?" Gabe shouts over to me, knee-deep in felt tip pens and scrap paper as the kids make pictures to put up in the treehouse.

"I'm good. I'm really good," I call back, my emotions threatening to overwhelm me. I didn't ever expect to feel so complete again. It was a simple moment, and it wasn't even about Gabe and me. It was about more than that. Something bigger than any of us individually. The thing that touched a deep place in my heart more than anything was the realisation that we are a family.

Gabe narrows his eyes at me, sensing something is wrong.

"Omelettes," I announce, not wanting to interrupt what he's doing with the kids. Before he has time to respond, I carefully step over the edge of the tree house decking and find my footing on the ladder.

The walk back to the house is relaxing with the fresh air filling my lungs with energy and life. There's something about Maple Valley that makes you feel on top of the world, and when no one's looking, I throw my arms out to the side and spin around as I go. A huge smile spreads across my face at my newfound sense of freedom. Or belonging. Whichever way you look at it, it makes me happy. I guess it's through belonging to someone again, that I've found my freedom.

The thought causes my mouth to settle in a small smug smile that I keep for myself, and it quickly fades when I reach the house. The long black limo with blacked-out windows can only mean one thing.

Angela.

Her tall, skinny frame comes into view as I get closer, and I watch her knock on the door. I'm in two minds about whether to turn back around and pretend I haven't seen her. This was nothing to do with me, and I don't like to meddle in Gabe's life. The life he had before me.

I'm not naive, he's a thirty-five-year-old man with a past. I knew that when I met him. If it were any other situation, I would never dream of intervening, but I love Poppy. I know how much this is hurting her, so as Angela turns to walk back to her flashy limo, I chase after her shouting her name.

"Angela," she turns around, halting in her heels and staring at me blankly.

I speed up, trying to catch up with her before she changes her mind and decides that talking to me is a waste of time.

"Wait, we're not in," I blurt out, hating myself for feeling suddenly inferior to THE Angela Farrow. And it's true what they say, the TV adds pounds. This woman is a long, lean package of perfection, and even stood in the mud of Maple Valley, she looks every inch the movie star that she is.

It's funny how to the world, she's a brand, a cash cow and a household name, but I remind myself that to me, she's just Poppy's shit mum. The thought gives me zero satisfaction but snaps me out of my bewitched state that I'll bet most people fall into when they are in the presence of someone like Angela.

"I mean, we're in, but Gabe's taken the kids into the woods. He's built Poppy a tree house for her birthday. I know you two got off on the wrong foot the other day, but I'm sure Poppy would love to show you around if you want to come and see it."

She doesn't budge, tucking a flyaway hair behind her ear and calmly replying, "I was just dropping a gift off for *my* daughter. I wasn't planning on staying."

"Nevertheless, I'm sure Poppy would love to see you. Why don't you wait here, and I'll run back and get her. Then you can give it to her yourself."

She scowls at me with red pouty lips and shakes her head. "I don't want to upset Poppy, especially on her birthday. I am sure you have plenty of nice things planned for her, you seem like a real good kid."

Her comment kicks me in the gut the exact same way she intends it too.

"We do, but you're her mum. Gabe mentioned you haven't had many birthdays together, so I thought it might be important… to you both."

"Oh, it is. That's why I will be going ahead with the custody application after all. It cuts out all of the bullshit in between. I don't have time to waste spending weekends fussing and fighting with my ex over who Poppy should spend time with. I have waited this long to be a mum, Gabe's had his turn, now it's mine."

I reel at the information that she delivers with a Tyson Fury style punch. Almost as though she enjoys it, revelling in the knowledge that this is going to destroy Gabe. Could she really be *that* cold?

Chilled blood pumps through my veins as I panic, knowing I need to say something to stop her, to convince her that this is a bad idea, but I'm stumbling over the words.

"Angela," I start, tentatively. "I really think you should think about this, before making any rash decisions. Why don't you talk to Poppy about what she wants, come around for dinner one night this week and spend some time working things out? I think it's really important that she has both of you in her life."

"Excuse me for coming off a little…" She fumbles for the right word before placing a confident hand on her jutting hip bone. "Harsh," she continues. "But what *you* think really has no importance to me whatsoever. I can see that you like Gabe and are enjoying this whole little situation you have going on, but I'd really appreciate you staying out of this."

"What about your daughter?" I fight back. "Does she get a say in any of this? You can't just pick kids up like a book at the library, returning them every time the mood takes you and expecting them to just sit and wait around until you decide to return. Children aren't like that, Angela. Life isn't fucking like that.

And, yeah, maybe you're right, maybe I should stay out of this, but maybe I can't. My kid has no dad. He doesn't have the option to sit down and work things through. To make choices and decisions. He has nothing and you," I swing my arm forward, gesturing towards this insolent bitch, "you do have that option, and you don't care. You don't bother to ask your daughter what she wants because you're scared of the answer. You're scared that when it comes to it, she won't choose you. Jesus, Angela, it doesn't have to be this way. You could both love Poppy and be in her life, why can't you see that's exactly what she needs."

I fight back a lump in my throat at the mention of everything my boy has lost and hope that it's enough to make her see how important it is that she works this out with Gabe.

Instead, she scowls at my feet, looking me up and down with a face like she's just sucked on a lemon and replies calmly, "I think this is all getting a bit heated. Please pass my gift onto my daughter, and tell her I will be coming to see her again soon. You can tell her father that the custody battle will be going ahead and that I am not backing down on this. Poppy is just a child, she doesn't know what's best for her, but any judge in the land will see that the life I can give my daughter is far more sufficient than this…" She glances around at the farm surrounding us before whipping her hair over her shoulder the exact way I'd seen her do on an American TV series a few years ago, and disappears back into her blacked-out limo.

* * *

I MAKE THE OMELETTES, but my mind is elsewhere and I burn myself in the side of the pan.

"Aaaagh," I yell out loud, tossing the pan back into the hob and running the cold tap over my hand to soothe the small red patch of skin.

When it eventually numbs, I grab some plates and cutlery, pack them into a bag and toss in a jar of chocolate spread for good measure.

Far from the calm stroll, I'd had towards the house, I paced the field angrily back across it. I didn't want to let Angela get the better of me or spoil Poppy's day, but she had managed it all the same.

The most frustrating thing of all, is feeling so helpless in the situation. Usually, I can always come up with a solution, but there are no obvious answers for Gabe or for Poppy and dreadful as she appears to be. She is still her mother when all is said and done.

"You're back," Gabe shouts down from the treehouse on sight of me, he has Marshall in his arms, and they both wave at me. The sight instantly lifts my dark mood, and I quicken my step to reach them as fast as I can, craving the happiness they bring.

"Careful," Gabe calls down, as I climb the ladder, juggling the bag full of our breakfast. "You need a hand?"

"No, I'm good," I say as I almost reach the top where my cowboy god is waiting for me with a sweet kiss.

"Thanks, I needed that," I say quietly, walking over to where the kids are still busy colouring and begin to dish out the omelettes.

"Everything okay?" he asks, sensing something is wrong.

I shake my head slightly, not enough for the little ones to notice, but enough to let him know we need to talk.

"Poppy, would you mind sharing out the omelettes while I help Evelyn with something?"

"Sure, Dad. Thanks for making them, Evelyn, and for bringing the chocolate spread. It's my favourite." She smiles, pulling the jar out of the bag.

"You have to have your favourite on your birthday, right?"

Gabe, squeezes the top of my arm, jerking his head to one side, and I follow him out onto the platform surrounding the main treehouse.

"Angela was here," I whisper.

"What, at the farm?"

"Yeah, I just saw her. She was dropping off this for Poppy's birthday," I explain, fumbling in the pocket of my hoody and passing him the small gift box she left behind.

"Well, did she say anything? Did you invite her to stay?"

"Of course, I did."

"And?"

I shake my head, lowering my gaze from his. "She said she didn't want to stay and that she's still planning to go for custody."

His eyes burn with anger, and he runs his fingers through his hair, the veins in his forearms bulging as the rage floods through every fibre of his being.

"I can't believe she's still going ahead with this, I had hoped she'd seen sense and decided to call things off. I haven't heard anything from a lawyer or anything since she sent me a letter about it, but that was weeks ago."

"Did you speak with a lawyer?"

"Briefly, but only to discuss my options. I didn't give them the go ahead for anything further, as I didn't think I'd need to."

"Well, you need to. But it is Poppy's birthday, so let's put this to one side and fire some emails off tonight, once she's settled. A day isn't going to make any difference."

His gaze roams the line where the treetops reach the sky, and I wonder whether he's hearing anything I am saying.

"Gabe," I step closer to him, wrapping my arm around his, "whatever happens we will fight this. You're not on your own, and I have got your back one million percent."

"You didn't sign up for this, you deserve someone who is…"

"Someone who is you, Gabe. I love you. Every part of you, and Poppy. I love you both. So, let's go over there, eat our breakfast and enjoy our day together like we planned."

"I love you, too, Evelyn. More than you know."

My lips curl into a small secret smile that passes between us before we head back over to the kids and have breakfast in the treetops.

It's so peaceful up here, with the sound of the birds filling the air and mixing with the sound of laughter, as Gabe pretends to be a jungle monkey, and the kids impersonate him.

When he introduces them to the zipline, a short while later, I almost have a heart attack.

"They will be okay, you know?" Poppy attempts to reassure me as Gabe sails through the air with Marshall locked in his arms and wedged in his lap.

"I don't think I can watch," I murmur through my hands which are covering my entire face apart from the v-shaped gap I've left to peep out of.

"Mummy, wook!" Marshall shouts to me, and I force myself to smile and wave. Gabe's grinning back at me, knowing exactly what I'm thinking.

"He loves it, look at that smile," he shouts back before they disappear through the clearing in the trees.

"Has your dad always been such a daredevil?" I ask Poppy who is gearing up for her turn in the zipline.

"Yep," she grins the same mischievous grin that Gabe wears, with a matching set of sparkly white teeth and full lips.

"Let me guess, that's where you get it from, then?"

"Yeah, and Marshall. It's in genetics, we did it in science. You get some bits from your mum and some things from your dad, that's right isn't it? I think that's what Miss Heist said."

"That's exactly right, Poppy, well remembered," is all I can say.

She thinks of Gabe as Marshall's dad. I had never thought of it that way, Gabe and I had moved so quickly that neither of us had stopped to think about their perception of us. I wonder if Marshall thinks of it that way, too. They both seem to have accepted the situation and adapted while we grownups are left playing catch up.

I can't get what she said out of my head and later that afternoon as we make our way around the aquarium, I keep looking at Gabe in a whole new light. I hadn't realised that maybe my son needed a father. Maybe he needed Gabe just as much as I did. He rounds the corner hand in hand with Marshall, who has an enormous dolphin balloon in his other hand. They both look so happy together. Marshall has a daddy, and I will never let anyone let him forget that, but that doesn't take away from the fact that a man in his life, especially a man like Gabe, could be a good thing.

Poppy and I pass them each an ice cream cone and we find an empty gap on the front row at the sting ray show. Poppy's eyes are wide in awe the entire time and every time I glance at Gabe, he's watching his daughter, delighting in her enjoyment. He knows how much she loves animals, so this is the perfect birthday treat for her. I wonder how I got so lucky to find such a kind and caring man who looks *that* good.

Gabe

EVERY TIME I glance up at Evelyn, she's watching me, and I wonder what the fuck I did to deserve her. Her dark waves are swept back in a simple ponytail that reveals the line of her collar bone and I follow all the way down to her cleavage. Her simple grey vest top is loose and cut low enough to reveal the swollen peak of her rounded tits and the sight makes me want to motorboat the shit out of them. She catches me staring and smiles her beautiful fucking smile at me. Wide and uninhibited, making her eyes dance like they've got stars in them. Nothing like the sad smile she used to wear.

I smile back at her, wanting her to know that whatever she's feeling for me, is reciprocated. Times twenty.

"Sexy," I mouth at her over the top of the kid's heads, nodding towards her perfect tits and causing her cheeks to flush pink.

She widens her eyes at me, giving me a not-now-the-kids-are-here look, and I carry on staring as though I don't care.

We get to bottle feed the rays and stroke the turtles, which Poppy thinks is the best thing ever. Marshall falls in love with a frog, then almost kills it by squeezing it too tightly and then dropping it, which the rest of us fall apart laughing at. Once we know the frog is going to survive the ordeal, of course. We argue all the way home about the million reasons why we can't have a pet terrapin, and I finish the day with Poppy's favourite pony story.

I put her to bed, just the two of us, and she wraps her arms around me real tight.

"Night, Dad. Thanks for my birthday, it was my best birthday ever."

"You're so welcome, baby. I'm just glad you had a good time."

"I loved the aquarium, and I really would like a baby terrapin," she says sleepily.

"We'll see," I can't help saying as she snuggles down. Tell me how anyone is supposed to say no to this tiny bundle of beauty? Her hair spread around the pillow, her eyes close, succumbing to her tiredness and I lean forward, kissing her head one last time before tiptoeing downstairs.

"Did she settle okay?" Evelyn asks, already curled up on the sofa in her pyjama bottoms.

"Yeah, did Marshall?"

"Flat out," she replies.

"So, you thought you'd put those on?" I raise an eyebrow at the fleecy, baggy pants she's slipped into. "Are you trying to send me some kind of message?"

"Like what?" she asks, pretending to be completely unaware of exactly how unattractive those things really are.

"Like, I'm on my period, don't come near me?"

She falls apart laughing. "What? I thought they were cute." She chuckles.

"Yeah, for a five-year-olds slumber party maybe."

"Oh, so you don't want me because of my pants?"

"Wait, I never said that."

"Are you saying you don't find me attractive in these babies?"

She pouts sulkily, her full lips swelling and awakening my cock in spite of her ugly ass pants.

"I'm saying I'd prefer you without them," I reason, walking over to the sofa and grabbing at the cuffs. I pull her feet hard, knocking her backwards and yanking at the bottoms. She squeals and wriggles playfully as I tear off the pants to reveal her smooth naked flesh.

"You can't just grab someone's pants off them."

"You can when their ass belongs to you."

"You think you own my ass?"

"I'm about to show you that I own your ass."

"Are you threatening me, Mr. Hudson?"

"Fuck, there's something so sexy about the way you say that," I growl.

"You like that whole porn vibe, babe?" She giggles, laying back on the couch and looking up at me. Parting her knees and reaching between her legs, stroking over the thin piece of black lace that covers her centre.

"I'm ready for you now, Mr. Hudson," she moans out, her voice low and sultry before she throws her head back and laughs. The care-free sound mixed with the sight of her fingers touching her own pussy has me almost ready to explode.

"Oh, I see, my baby's been watchin' a little dirty porn. I had no idea that's what you're into," I tease. Reaching for the remote, I flick on the tv and punch in the code that lifts the parental controls.

"I do not watch porn," she exclaims, putting on a horrified voice and whispering the last word like she's too shy to say it out loud.

"Well, we better fix that," I tell her, unbuttoning my pants and lowering myself onto the sofa.

"Wait, what is that? Oh my god, turn it off."

"Why, don't you like it?" I ask, ready to switch off the tv and devour my girl. Her eyes are wide and staring at the screen as the guy manoeuvres himself into the perfect position for a sixty-nine.

"It's not that, it's just… look I'm not that experienced and…"

"Evelyn, you don't need experience to be with me. What they're doing, the sixty-nine, it's real easy, and I think you'll enjoy it. Watch, if you don't like it, just slap me, and I'll stop, okay?"

"Okay," she says, giving me, the green light, and I jump up, ridding myself of my jeans before displaying my bare cock right in front of her face.

I don't need to explain anything further; her natural instincts take over, and she licks my swollen tip before parting her lips to take me fully in her mouth.

"Remember, you don't like this, you let me know."

"Hmmm," she moans, the end of my solid erection filling her mouth as she licks and sucks, waiting for me to thrust in deeper.

Tearing her underwear from her curvy ass, I dive right in, burying my head between her thighs sucking on her swollen nub. I support myself with one arm and stroke her soaked inner walls with my fingers.

Only when she's pushing her hips forward, begging me to let her find release do I give her what she wants. What we both want.

"Gabe," she moans, against my cock, and I lower into her mouth. She takes me all the way down to her throat. She wants to please me for no other reason than the fact that she's convulsing underneath my lips, in a state of ecstasy of her own. I love that she wants to make me feel every second of her enjoyment, and she matches me expertly. It's like we're locked into a pleasure war in a battle of who can make each other cum quickest.

The sensation of her swallowing my cock only spurs me on to pleasure her further. I want to make my mark on her. Take her selfishly, until all she can think of is me.

The sound of the on-screen couple finding their release plays in the background and only encourages Evelyn to be louder than ever before.

I lose control of my pace, and she takes the lead, pulling her head away only when she needs to breathe before taking me back fully into her mouth. Changing arms, I use my hand to circle her clit and bring us to our climax.

She moans out my name in a breathless whimper, and I push myself to my feet, struggling to stand.

"Fuck, baby, wait there I'll grab you a tissue," I say, trying to gain control of my jelly legs enough to be able to stand and notice her mouth is still full of my orgasm.

She gulps hard before grinning at me.

"Shit, Evelyn. I didn't expect you to swallow, are you sure you're not a secret porn star?"

"I'm sure." She giggles, taking the tissue from me and cleaning herself up. "That was…"

I cut her off. "Hot as fuck. Get over here," I say, crashing onto the sofa next to her once I've got my boxers back on.

We snuggle up and she flicks on The Bachelor, which I secretly love watching with her. What? It's a bunch of hot chicks in bikinis, don't judge.

THE NEXT MORNING, she calls in and lets Tanya know she's running late. I told her not to, but she insisted on coming with me.

"We do this together," she says. "We're a team now, remember. You got my back, now let me have yours."

"Okay," I accept, squeezing her hand, as we walk into the solicitor's office together.

"Take a seat please, Mr. Hudson. Mr. Bunchell will be with you shortly."

CHAPTER 17

Gabe

For the next five months I put the term 'having my back' to the test. The custody battle brought ups and downs, highs and lows, and the pressure of a wrecking ball landing on a grasshopper. Crushing and suffocating, as though there is no hope of any way out. Evelyn had proven that she is there for me every step of the way, and I fucking love her wholeheartedly for it. By my side through every solicitor's appointment, every night pacing the lounge too riled up to attempt sleep. She even offered to attend the mediation sessions Angela and I had been offered, but there was a limit to what I was willing to put her through.

I knew the bitch would pull some dirty tricks and all those character references from well-respected celebrities are surely going to swing it for her. I hadn't anticipated that her drugs counsellor would show up to support her, and even though I hated to admit it to myself, I am secretly happy that she is doing this for the right reasons. Do I think that means I believe that being with Angela full time is what's best for Poppy? Fuck, no. But I'm sad that we couldn't have worked something out between, us as it seems like she is serious about wanting to be in our daughter's life this time.

It has been one hell of a journey, but there's no chance I could have gotten through it without Evelyn and dealing with endless stress and drama had solidified our bond so tight that nothing in the world could break us. It feels surreal that we are finally at the point of no return, and in just a few minutes the judge will call us back in and seal our fate. Every sleepless night spent tossing and turning, mulling every possible outcome over in my head, until I almost drove myself crazy, boiled down to this moment.

My knee is bobbing up and down uncontrollably. Hands balled into tight fists, and every few minutes I'm up and about, pacing the corridor outside the courtroom like a lion stalks its prey. I catch eyes with her across the hallway. Angela's dressed in her usual skin-tight black dress and killer heels. She quickly looks away, avoiding my gaze as though looking at me would reveal the truth. Like she'd be able to see all of the hurt she was causing me by trying to take my daughter away. I continue to stare her down, willing her to look back in my direction because I want her to see it. I want her to know exactly how much pain she's causing me, in some tiny hope that she might change her mind, call this whole thing off, and we could go back to the way things were. Shifting my gaze to my shoes, I try to steady my bouncing knee, fully aware that that's never going to happen.

"Mr. Hudson, please return to courtroom four," comes a snooty voice over the tannoy.

"Remember, whatever happens, you'll always be Poppy's dad, and she will always know just how much you love her," Evelyn's gentle voice would usually soothe me, but nothing can calm me today.

I walk into the courtroom feeling as though I could fucking vomit any minute. I can only imagine this is what it would feels like to face a life sentence for murder or some other heinous crime. Except, the only thing I have done is fight for my daughter. None of this made any sense, and it was a complete 360 from where this all started.

I recall the day that Angela told me she was pregnant. I'd had a similar sickly feeling then. The smug smile she'd gave me, knowing that she'd well and truly trapped me in a situation I did not want to be in. She knew damn well I'd never walk away from my daughter, she'd known it then, and she sure as hell knows it now. It doesn't stop her passing me that same smug smile across the room though, as we take our positions next to our solicitors. The battle is over, weapons placed on the ground, every ugly lie she'd thrown at me during the two-hour hearing, sailing around the air around us and making the room feel stifling. I shuffle my tie to try to avoid the sensation that I am suffocating and clear my throat.

The judge enters and summarises his findings from the hearing and the reports that have been prepared. I listen to the legal jargon, trying to pay attention but willing him to hurry through it and get to the verdict.

"I am awarding shared custody of Poppy Sky Hudson, to both of you. You will share parenting responsibilities of her equally. A fifty percent split."

My thoughts race and I glance over to Angela, knowing she wasn't expecting this either. How the fuck would that work, it's not as though Poppy can spend half the week in Australia and jet back for her half a week with me. Evelyn must sense I'm struggling as she squeezes my wrist, willing me to unclench my balled fist and relax, at least a little.

The judge frowns at Angela over the top of her glasses and shuffles her papers before continuing.

"I am granting Mr. Hudson a residency order meaning that Poppy will reside with her father on a full-time basis, and I am awarding Miss Farrow weekend overnight visits once per week. Every Saturday, Poppy will stay with her Mother, and, Miss Farrow, you will return her to her home address no later than 4pm every Sunday."

"But… my job," Angela shouts out, and the judge only scowls at her even harder this time.

"Miss Farrow, you will do to remember that we are here to determine what is best for Poppy, *not* what is best for your career."

She nods to the usher, who responds by abruptly announcing, "Stand please."

The judge walks out of the room, leaving us to wonder what exactly just happened. I've never even heard of a residency order, I thought that shared custody meant the kid going back and forth between both parents.

"This is good news," Evelyn reassures me as I walk out into the hallway and let the news sink in.

I'm not sure if it's the shock of the outcome or the relief of knowing I'm not losing her. But my eyes well up, and I swear a tear rolls down my fucking cheek. Wiping it away I turn to Evelyn who looks as relieved as I feel.

Angela marches past us with her bodyguard in toe and can't help herself from hissing, "I hope you're fucking happy," as she passes us and storms out of the court.

"Why don't you sit for a minute, Gabe? You're looking a little bit pale." Evelyn manipulates me into a sitting position, but I honestly feel as though I'm not really here. Like none of this is real, and the room is spinning at such a pace that I feel dizzy and slightly nauseous.

"I thought I was going to lose her."

"I know you did, but you didn't. Everything is as it should be, no judge in their right mind would have taken Poppy away from you. Anyone can see how much you love her, and that's what kids need more than anything else in the world. Angela could be a multi-billion-aire, and the outcome would have still been the same."

"I don't even know how this is going to work. The woman despises me, plus she's moving to the other side of the world. I don't see how it's practical."

"I don't think you need to worry about all that for now, let's just go and pick up Poppy, explain everything as best we can and enjoy the evening with her. You can only control what you do in this situation and hope that Angela meant it when she said she has Poppy's best interests at heart.

"You're right, Evelyn. I honestly don't know what I would have done without you these last few weeks."

"You've been there for me too, Gabe. You may not have realised exactly how, but trust me, you have. Now, let's go and get your baby and spend some time together, hey?"

"It wasn't true, you know?" I explain, needing to reassure her.

"Which part?"

"Most of it. I never cheated. However tough times got between us, I wouldn't have. It's just not me, and you know the violence didn't happen. You know me, Evelyn, I'd never hurt a woman."

"I know," she soothes. "I wouldn't be here if I didn't..."

"I knew she'd try and drag my name through the mud, but I never thought she'd blame me for her drug habit."

"She definitely pulled all the stops out."

"I'm just glad the judge saw straight through her."

"Me too. I guess the truth always wins out, right?" I lift my head, bringing our eyes into alignment and notice, for the first time, the strain the custody battle has placed on her. It showed in the dark circles around her exquisite eyes and the way her forehead was tense, creating lines that weren't usually prominent. I averted my gaze, not wanting to see the overbearing burden I'd placed upon her shoulders. I was supposed to be the fun guy, the one who made her forget about the gaping wound in her oversized heart. It was me who desperately wanted to fix it, to repair it and replace all the hurt it contained with love.

Instead, I'd taken and taken from her, absorbing every bit of the heart she wore so willingly on her sleeve. Absorbed it like a sponge drinking in water, and I hadn't even been careful to make sure I didn't wring her dry. It wasn't Evelyn's style to ever show how much this last few months has taken out of her, but it was written all over her face, and I've been so consumed with my own emotions, I hadn't stopped to consider hers.

Evelyn

It breaks my heart to see my man hurting like that, and I don't blame him for being pissed. All the accusations she'd thrown at him were so personal, and he'd just stood there. Taking bullet after bullet without even flinching. Despite his anger, he'd appeared nothing but calm and collected throughout the entire hearing. For that, he has my admiration, and for fighting for his daughter, he has my respect. For the way he looks in a suit, he had my whole heart, and I let him know it by landing a soft kiss on his lips as we reach the car. He kisses me back but isn't himself, and he's subdued on the way to collect Poppy, quiet and lost in his own thoughts. I don't try to snap him out of it, deciding to give him his headspace and just let him be.

"Mind if we pop home first, I just want to change out of my suit, I don't want Poppy worrying."

"Sure, but I really don't think she'll care what you're wearing."

"She will, I always used to wear suits for work, and she hated me working. It's one of the reasons I gave up photography."

"Do you miss it?"

"Taking pictures, yeah, but being a pap? No way. It was a cutthroat game full of fake ass nobody's trying to prove themselves. And I hated the look on Poppy's face whenever I had to leave her to go to work."

"It's definitely not like that anymore." I smile. "Poppy works just as hard on the farm as you do, or at least she thinks she does."

"Oh, she thinks she runs the place," he says with a lighter note to his tone. Pride evident every time anyone mentions her name, and it's easy to see why, it would be difficult for anyone not to fall in love with Poppy, she is such a special little girl.

"I could do with changing into something comfier if we are going out for tea. I'll throw some jeans on."

"Don't be slipping out of that dress around me, we'll never make it out of the door."

I laugh, Tanya's dress, which I'd lent for the occasion, was definitely more risqué than I'd usually wear, especially during the daytime. With my high heels and neat ponytail, I didn't feel like myself at all.

We pull up into Maple Valley emotionally drained from the day, and the level of relief screams out in the silence between us.

"You've got to be fucking kidding me," Gabe exclaims and my eyes immediately look up to see what's got him all riled up.

Angela.

SAT on the step outside our front door, her smart jacket exchanged for a huge knitted cardigan and her caked-on mascara now smeared down her cheeks.

Gabe storms over towards her, shouting ahead, "Go fuck yourself, Angela."

I wince at the situation, I've always hated confrontation. What could she possibly want from him now anyway? Would she ever tire of trying to ruin his life?

"Gabe. I just want to talk to you, please. For Poppy's sake?" she snuggles through her tears, desperation in her tone.

Gabe hesitates, sighing heavily before opening the door. "You've got five minutes."

"I'll leave you two to talk," I say, suddenly feeling like an intruder in my own home.

"No, she can say whatever she has to say to us both. God knows she's dragged you through almost as much hell as me these last few weeks."

I take a seat at the kitchen table and Angela does the same.

"I'm sorry, Gabe, I want to tell you that I'm sorry."

"For what, lying in court or trying to take my daughter?"

"Everything. I'm sorry that I trapped you by getting pregnant in the first place. I could see that you were a good man, probably one of the only people I could trust back then, and I was scared of losing you."

My eyes widen at her honesty. Gabe's face remains deadpan, his full lips pulled in a tight line.

"I never meant for things to go as far as they did, with the drinking, I'm not blaming you…,"

"You just did, Angela. You just blamed me in a court, knowing that if word gets out, that'll be splashed all over the press."

"I'm trying to apologise. Things just went too far with my solicitor, I was scared. I didn't want to lose my daughter, just the same way you don't. I told the solicitor to use every dirty trick he had. Wouldn't you have done the same, if you thought you were going to lose her?"

Gabe's expression shifts to blind range, and his jaw is clenched so tight it looks almost painful.

"No, Angela. No, I would not do the fucking same," he hisses at her.

"That's only because you wouldn't need to," She screams at him, completely losing it now. You're here with your perfect house and perfect life. You get everything so right all the time, you always did. I'm a fucking mess, as your girlfriend quite rightly pointed out. Or at least I was."

"Why are you here? Haven't you done enough damage for one day?"

"I wanted to apologise, face to face and show you that I'm serious about being involved in Poppy's life. For the right reasons. I know my flaws, all the mistakes I've made. Most of them are splashed all over the papers, so it would be difficult to hide from them, which is what I've been doing for so long. I really did go to rehab this time, Gabe, and I stuck at it. You should know that even though I've gone about this all the wrong way, I am ready to be a mum to Poppy. Like a proper mum."

The revelation appears to give her courage of conviction, and her tears dry, the lines on her forehead giving away the stress that the court case has brought to her life, too. I don't want to pity her, but just like Gabe, I found myself compelled to listen to what she has to say.

"When I first came here, after I got clean, I had this idea in my head that we'd be a family again." Gabe visibly recoils, and my blood turns to ice in my veins as anger begins to bubble under my skin.

"Then I saw everything you have created, the life you have... It's so different from everything we had, but I'm not stupid, Gabe, I know that's what you probably love about it. I don't blame you. Anyway, I guess what I am trying to say is that when I saw you here with her, I was jealous. Crazy jealous. I did some things I'm not proud of, but I am really trying. I hope you can find a way to forgive me so that Poppy can have both of us in her life. I didn't take the reality show offer. I'm moving back to London and taking a break for a while."

My head is spinning, Angela Farrow taking a break. The woman is a powerhouse. Powerhouses don't just take breaks, and they certainly don't get jealous of women like me. But she just confirmed both. I can tell Gabe is as shocked at the news as I am.

"You actually told them you are not taking the Australia show?" he asks, his tone quiet and full of disbelief.

She smiles. Not that shitty smug smile, or the sultry one that says she wants him back. It's a sad smile that shows the toll the celebrity lifestyle has taken on her, and you'd have to be made of stone not to accept her apology.

"It's been a long day. I'm not sure what you're expecting, but I always have Poppy's best interests at heart, and I know how much she would love you to be in her life. Why don't you swing by on Saturday and spend a few hours with her, maybe take her out for lunch or something. I'd suggest taking things slowly, give her a chance to get to know you."

"Oh, Gabe, I'd love to. Do you think she'd want to come?"

"I'm sure she'd love to," I chip in, proud of my man for accepting her apology. Proving again there's nothing he wouldn't do for his daughter.

Angela stands, wiping the smudged mascara from her eyes and turns to me saying, "Maybe you could come with us, Evelyn. I can see that you have developed a relationship with my daughter and that she trusts you. Perhaps she would like it if we went together."

Christ, I wasn't expecting that.

Gabe's eyes widen at me, letting me know that I don't have to accept.

"Sure," I found myself saying, "why not."

"I'll see you about twelve," she says formally adding, "if that is okay with you?" in a softer voice. Her inner coach reminding her to think about other people, probably something she's not had to do very often since she became a huge star. I appreciate the sentiment and accept her offer before she wraps her cardigan around herself, whipping her hair over her shoulder all movie star like.

"I won't let you down this time, Gabe, I'm in this for the long run."

"You let Poppy down, and it'll be your name that's dragged through the mud next time," he growls. It is a threat that all three of us know he is serious about carrying out, and I can't blame him.

CHAPTER 18

Evelyn

*I*n the days after the custody battle things settled down, but everything was that little bit sweeter knowing that Poppy could stay with us. The air felt lighter, fresher somehow, and all four of us were more relaxed than we had been in months.

Work had been manic, and there has been so much going on that I hadn't even thought about the anniversary. Now it's here, all the same feelings hit me just as hard as last year. In fact, just as hard as the day I lost him.

"Are you sure I'm okay to take these?" I ask, signalling to the pretty bunch of red roses on the counter top.

"Of course, are you sure you don't want me to come with you?"

"No, Gabe said he wants to do it. I think he just wants to support me, you know?"

"He's such a great guy, Evelyn, I'm so happy for you both."

"I'm happy too, Tanya, we all are."

"Are you still okay to open up tomorrow?"

"Yes, no probs," I reply, hanging up my apron and grabbing the roses on my way out.

"I'll see you just after lunch," she shouts after me, and I throw her a casual wave to let her know I've heard her.

When I reach my old place, Gabe is already waiting for me, leaning in my doorway and smiling that sweet smile he always saves for me.

"Remember the first time I walked you home?"

"You kissed me," I accuse him, my thoughts recalling the way his kiss had taken me by surprise and all the feelings it had stirred within me.

"And you fucking loved it," he smugly points out. He arches an eyebrow at me, daring me to say otherwise. Instead, I put the key in the door, and this time, he follows me inside.

It is instantly weird having him in my space, despite my efforts to redecorate, the fact remains that this was my first home with Marshall, and having another man here just doesn't feel right.

Feeling equally as awkward as I obviously do, Gabe offers to wait outside, but I don't feel comfortable here either. Like the hundreds of other things, it's a trigger. The kitchen makes me think of all the meals I would have cooked in here for Marshall, all the bottles of wine we'd have drank together. The memories of what had once been my hope for the future caused that unsettling, sickly feeling in the pit of my stomach that I spent so long trying to fight off.

"Are you sure you're ready to do this?" Gabe asks, interrupting my thoughts. It's okay if you're not ready. There's no set timeline on these things."

"No, I'm ready. I want to do this. I've been thinking about it for a while," I reassure myself as much as him.

Grabbing the small wooden box off the bookshelf, I place it carefully at the bottom of my nude leather handbag. It's as though the contents are too heavy for me to carry, despite weighing barely anything at all. It perfectly replicates the pain I carry in my heart from losing him.

Swallowing hard, I step outside, and with Gabe at my side, make my way along the river back to the spot where it all began. My feet know the route so well that my body walks itself there, my thoughts roaming uncontrollably elsewhere. It was a perfect day to say good-bye. Not like the funeral, nothing had been perfect about that. This feels different. *I* feel different. I'm ready to let go of the pain, and being back in The Cotswolds has allowed some of my memories to come back to me. Now, when I think of my husband, I don't think of heart-break, my thoughts are full of happiness and laughter. Long summer days and sweet first kisses, somehow, they had begun to take over the dark thoughts that had plagued me for so long after losing him.

"Okay, this is the spot. This is where we used to come all the time. After school or during summer breaks, we'd come here and just be, just the two of us.

"It's a real pretty spot," Gabe offers, glancing around.

No one could deny that, especially under the clear bright blue sky.

"Come on, I'll show you our secret place."

"You don't have to," he hesitates.

"I want to. I want to share every part of me with you," I say easily, tugging his hand inside of the church yard. We follow the winding path until our tree comes into view.

"This is it, this is our place," I almost whisper, unable to find my voice on sight of the place that held so many secrets and memories of my life with Marshall.

"Would you mind just giving me a minute?"

"Take as long as you need, Evelyn."

Squeezing his hand as a silent thanks, I step forward and part the branches of the willow tree, bending down to fit underneath the way I used to. The light falls between the branches, causing lines on the ground that break up the shadows.

"I'm here," I whisper, placing a hand on the damp grass below my feet.

Closing my eyes for a moment, I inhale deeply and don't attempt to fight back the tears that pool in my eyes and spill down my cheeks. Taking the box from my bag, I open the lid and see the ashes inside, I snap it shut again, unable to face them.

Forcing my eyes to look around, needing to ground myself again, a million flashes of Marshall come back to me like dandelion seeds in the wind. They are out of sync and disorganised, but they all bring a little bit of him back to me and a brief moment to be in love with him again. It gives me the strength to re-open the box and scoop a handful of his ashes into my hand.

Rather than throwing them to the ground, I hold my hand out flat and let the breeze take them. When it does, my heart stops beating for a minute, and my tears run dry. Taking the rest of the ashes and doing the same, I let a piece of my heart go with the last of them. I let the cool air snatch the piece of me that belonged to Marshall and carry it away.

Snapping my hand shut, I pull it into a tight fist and bring it to my mouth, keeping it there for just a minute. The ashes mostly disappear into the grass, but some of them sit and almost glisten in the light between the shadows. It feels so right to leave him here, in his safe and happy place, hidden away from the rest of the world.

Emerging from my hiding place, I notice Gabe sitting on the grass, waiting for me, and he immediately jumps to his feet to check that I am okay. Wiping the tears from my eyes, our eyes collide as he makes his way towards me.

"I don't know what to say to make things any better," he mumbles, pulling me into his arms and hugging me tightly.

"Just you being here make things better. I know it can't be easy for you, and you didn't have to come."

"Like I said, this is part of what makes you who you are. I'm glad I came. Glad I got to see this part of you that no one else has, I like it here…." He pauses, checking out our surroundings. "In fact," he continues, "I think Marshall and I would have had a lot in common." He brings his gaze back to me, eyes full of lust. His flirty comment lightens the mood, and I smile a small smile.

"I think you would have too," I agree. "But in other ways, you are completely different. I'm so lucky to have found two incredible men who love me the way both of you have loved me."

"It's us who are the lucky ones, Evelyn. Especially me, I still get to," he points out.

"Oh fuck, I was going to do this later, but something just feels right. If I'm way off the mark and completely out of line then just say, Evelyn, but I..." Kneeling down on one knee in front of me, I'm unable to prevent the tears from spilling down my cheeks.

For a second time today, I swear I miss a heartbeat at the sight of him on the ground before me, my strong man kneeling with a look of sheer vulnerability in his eyes as he searches mine.

"Evelyn, since the moment I first danced with you, I have known that you are the only woman I will ever feel this way about. I love you so much it fucking hurts sometimes. The thought of losing you causes me physical pain. I know how important what you had with Marshall was, and I would never try to take away from that, or replace it. But, I do want to have you by my side for the rest of forever. Will you marry me, Evelyn? Will you be my wife?"

It doesn't add up for a minute. The sight of him kneeling not ten feet from my tangled spider web of history with Marshall was already a lot to take in, but his words...

My head is reeling and spinning, making me slightly dizzy and unable to offer anything other than a glazed, blank expression on my face.

Gabe's appears is unperturbed by my state of shock, and he holds a ring box up in front of me containing the most stunning clear diamond ring I have ever seen. I can hardly speak through the thick lump in my throat that's swollen and stopping any sound from passing my lips.

I stare past the exquisite jewel, searching Gabe's face for something real. His eyes are wild, all the nerves and emotion revealed in the flecks of amber that glimmer in anticipation of my answer. My inside voice yells at me to say something.

Anything.

I part my lips, licking them to try to encourage some moisture and movement, but my mouth is as dry as the Sahara Desert. His eyes are pleading with mine, and I notice his fingers are trembling slightly around the edge of the ring box he is still holding out towards me. Unable to coordinate my brain to my mouth enough to get a single sound out, I nod my head and throw my arms around him.

"Yes?" he asks, desperate for me to say the word he so wants to hear. Breathing in, I force it out, wanting to give it to him. Wanting to give myself to him. Ready to give myself to him. Completely.

"Yes!" I sob. He wipes my tears away from my cheeks with his thumbs, cupping my face and bringing his lips to mine. His kiss is gentle but demanding all at the same time, and it spins my world on its axle, making me lose my bearings. In this moment he is the only thing that exists, and he picks me up, spinning me around in excitement and places me back down on the ground again.

I pant, catching my breath, and I am suddenly overcome with an overwhelming feeling of peace. The breeze sails through the leaves of the willow tree, making the branches dance as though they are alive. Gabe holds my hand, squeezing it tightly and understanding my need for a moment to take this all in.

My hands tremble as he slides the ring onto my ring finger, and I look down at my feet in disbelief that right here, this very spot is where Marshall and I shared one of our very first kisses. Tilting my hand up to look at the ring Gabe just put there, the sunlight catches the diamond and makes it twinkle and shine. It's almost as though Marshall is sending a message to me in the only way he can, and I somehow know that he is okay with this. He is ready to let me go.

"Are you okay?" he asks, knowing something is wrong.

"I'm so okay." I smile, "Let's go home, Gabe."

Gabe

IT WAS THE WRONG TIME, wrong place and wrong way to go about it. I have been planning to ask her for weeks and trying to think up some over the top way of proposing, but the words had flown out of my mouth without a thought in my head. I wanted to be the one to love her. It isn't easy seeing your woman grieve so hard for another man, but I could tell from the look on her face when she walked out from underneath their sacred place, she was ready to let go. Her eyes were wide, and her expression resembled a lost puppy. She looked scared and alone, despite me being right there with her, and I fucking hated it. There was no way I was going to let her feel like that for a second longer than she had to.

Even though I went about it all wrong, it didn't stop her from saying yes. This gorgeous, hot, fucking perfect woman said yes to marrying me. As I drive us back home, it doesn't seem real. I thought my second chance at life was complete, I had the farm and Poppy. Meeting someone had not been in the plan, but Evelyn had given me so much more than I ever thought I wanted. She had given me her whole heart, it didn't matter that it was smashed to pieces, I would spend the rest of forever trying to put them back together for her.

As I listen to her chatting with Poppy in the kitchen, I start to formulate a plan to surprise her and celebrate our engagement properly. Even though I know she will hate anyone making a fuss of her, it's what she deserves. I want to show her that even though it might seem as if I rushed the proposal, I have been thinking about marrying Evelyn for a lot longer than she has any idea about. I make some calls and fire off some emails, putting plans into place before joining all three of them in the kitchen. Four, if you include the hedgehog that Poppy has rescued and is keeping in a box on the kitchen table for an indefinite period.

"Something smells good," I say, sniffing the air as I walk towards them and take time to look into each of their mixing bowls.

"We're baking, Dad," Marshall throws at me, stopping me dead in my tracks. He says the word in the exact same tone that Poppy uses, mimicking her perfectly. It sounded strange coming from his cute, high pitched little voice that, under normal circumstances, would surely say something like, 'Daddy' or 'DaDa.'

Evelyn's dark eyes widen at me over the top of his head, as though the word will somehow land Marshall in trouble. I pause, giving her chance to explain that I'm not his daddy, that he has a different daddy. But she doesn't. Instead, she places a hand over her chest and swallows hard, looking to me for the answers.

Marshall looks up at me too, annoyed that I haven't shown an interest in the concoction he is stirring up. He's wearing half of it on his face after repeatedly licking the sticky mixture from the spoon. I've never seen a cuter little boy in my life.

Marshall would always be his daddy in the stars, but without realising it, I'd become his dad here and now, and it made my heart swell like a fucking helium balloon in my chest.

"Wow, you're doing a great job," I praise him, putting my hands on his shoulders, peering into the bowl and then across to his mum.

"What's with all the mixing? Exactly how many cakes are you making?"

"One," Poppy chips in. "But it's going to be *three* tiers high." She uses her hands to replicate her excitement about the prospect.

"Three tiers? Someone must be celebrating something." I shrug, dipping my finger into her mixing bowl and sucking off the gooey sample.

"Dad." She swats my arm in annoyance. "No tasting, we want it to be a surprise."

"Yeah, no tasting," Marshall agrees, using the same annoyed tone, and I arch an eyebrow at him, silently highlighting the fact that he's already eaten half the contents. Everyone giggles, and the fun atmosphere bounces around in the air surrounding us, the way it always did when the four of us were together.

"Marshall, shall we leave your mum and Pops to finish off the cake, we could go and pick some strawberries for the top, if you like?"

"Strawberries," he plays with the word thoughtfully, deliberating over his predicament. Come outside and eat strawberries, or stay inside and eat more cake mix. I empathize with his dilemma.

"What did you just say?" Evelyn stops whisking and holds her wooden spin in the air, her eyes pinned on Marshall, though he is blissfully unaware.

"Strawberries," he repeats for her, without hesitation.

"Oh, my goodness! That's it, baby. You said it, you said straw-berries."

He looked at her as though she was speaking an entirely different language or was from an alternate universe, but I understood perfectly.

I'm not sure when his language had improved so much that he was able to say words like strawberry properly, but my chest swelled. This time with pride rather than raw emotion. The same pride I felt when Poppy brought her school work home covered in smiley faces and 'well done' stickers, and when she was May Queen in the parade. He is growing up and learning new things all the time, and it makes me feel good to know that however small, I am part of the reason why.

Deciding that he will probably puke if he licks another dollop off the spoon, Evelyn ushers him out of the door with me, and I spend at least an hour with him out in the fields. When we return, the perfectly sculpted three tier cake is smothered in buttercream and waiting for us on the dining table. Poppy is beaming a proud, accomplished grin as she carefully sets some plates out for us.

"Now that's a cake," I declare, steading the chair for Marshall to climb up onto.

"Does anyone know *why* we've baked such a special cake?" Evelyn asks, eyeing the kids with curiosity, waiting for their ideas on what the special occasion might be.

"Is it your birthday?" Poppy asks, her eyes wide with intrigue.

"Nope. Marshall, why do you think we made this great big cake?"

"Is it 'cos we can all eat it, and then we don't need to have any tea?" Marshall suggests, inquisitively.

"Not quite, little man, but nice try," I say, ruffling his hair.

"Okay, you can stop guessing. Your dad and I have some really important news to share with you, and we think it's something to celebrate."

There it is again.

'Dad.'

The single word, and her casual use of it, melting me on the spot. I squeeze her hand from across the table as she continues, "If it's okay with both of you, we are getting married. Do you both know what that means?"

Poppy lets out a huge squeal that slightly resembles, "Oh my God," and leaps up from her chair, throwing her arms around Evelyn before running towards me for a bear hug. When I finally peel her arms from my neck to take a look at her, I realise she's crying.

"Are you okay, Pops? You can say if you're not, there's no rush."

"I'm just so happy," she blubs out, and the sweet declaration almost has me crying along with her.

Evelyn's dabbing her eyes and cuddling Marshall whose only response is, "Does this mean we can eat cake now?" His bluntness has us all laughing, and Poppy grins through her tears. Nobody bothers sticking the strawberries we've collected on, instead we dip them into the buttercream and enjoy the fruits of our labour.

By the time we are done, there's cake crumbs, buttercream and the remnants of strawberries all over the table, and I place my hands behind my head, leaning back and scanning the scene. Poppy's sucking her fingers clean, Marshall's pretending to feed his toy train some of the leftovers and Evelyn starts to clear away the mess.

Her dark waves are tumbling loose over her shoulders, her expression is relaxed, and more than anything, I notice how blissfully happy she looks. I smirk to myself knowing that it's me who put that sexy as hell smile on her face, the one that meets her eyes every time she flashes it at me. I know because I feel equally as fucking happy as she looks, knowing that the gorgeous woman in front of me, is mine for keeps. I make a mental note to remind her of that delicious fact tonight, when I have her in my arms.

CHAPTER 19

Evelyn

"Come on, we're going to be late.

"We're coming, we're coming," Gabe shouts back. Running towards the car looking ludicrously sexy in rugged boots, ripped jeans and his usual checked shirt. He'd thrown a white t-shirt underneath to smarten the look a little, but on sight of him, my mind wandered straight to the six pack underneath. The same one I was running my fingertips down last night, tracing a pattern over his tight abs that lead all the way down to his groin. I recall the way he'd groaned so sexily underneath my touch, and the memory causes a blush to my cheeks that settles as tingles between my thighs. He doesn't miss it, narrowing his eyes at me over the top of the car after we fasten the kids in.

"What are you thinkin' about there?"

"Nothing particular," I lie, unable to take my eyes off his stubbled jawline. I shiver, reminded of how it felt, scratching me as his face was buried in my most sensitive spot.

"Good times, huh." He grins, running a hand over my bare thigh, and causing me to shudder under his touch, as it triggers a visual flashback of last night.

I shake my head at him, and he just laughs at me. Completely, unashamed and aware of the effect he has on me.

As we drive out of Maple Valley and head over to Sally's, we laugh and chat with the kids in the back of the car. When we pull up, everyone is gathered on the porch outside, and I feel a little nervous. Aside from Sally, we won't really know anyone at the baby shower, but I know how important it is to Gabe that we are here for his sister.

Gabe opens the door for the kids, and I jump out, grabbing Marshall's hand as we walk over to greet everyone. Glancing up, my gaze crashes straight into a familiar face staring back at me.

Candice? What in the world is my sister-in-law doing here? She looks just as shocked to see me as I am to see her.

"Evelyn, what are you doing here?"

"Candice," I say her name out loud letting the shock of seeing her settle in. "Candice, it's so good to see you, meet my son, Marshall."

"Gather up everyone," Sally's husband hurries everyone along, making sure they shout cheese as he takes our picture. My lips move but no sound comes out, instead I'm staring at Candice, and her eyes are fixed on Marshall.

As soon as the flash goes off, she's hugging me tightly. "Oh my god, Evelyn, I've missed you so much. Mum said you were back. I've been dying to see you. How are you?"

"I'm good, I'm really good," I say, nodding in excitement. I forgot exactly how close Candice and I were, and now she's here, it is like seeing my old best friend again after far too long.

"Mum showed me the picture, when you had the baby. I couldn't believe it."

"Neither could I. Candice, this is Gabe," I say, looking up at my man.

"Nice to meet you, Gabe. Sally's told me lots about you and Poppy. Evelyn, shall we find somewhere to talk, there is so much to catch up on."

"I just can't believe you're here," I say quietly.

"Sally is my best friend. She did say her brother had a girlfriend, but I had no idea."

A dark-haired man in an expensive-looking polo shirt interrupts. I recognise him from my first visit to Marshall's parents' house, it is the same guy who was there that day.

"Candy, let's go and take a seat, Angel. You look as though you've seen a ghost," he says, putting an arm around his wife and brushing a flyaway hair away from her face.

"I feel as though I have," she says, glancing back at Marshall, unable to take her eyes off him. As I follow her inside, she clings to my side as if we are going to disappear again any minute.

"He looks so like my brother," she whispers.

"I know. He is just like your brother in so many ways. He's just as headstrong, for a start."

"He's beautiful." She smiles, her voice full of emotion that reflects my own as we fight back the tears together. "All the time you were gone, Evelyn. You should have reached out. I would have been there for you. I was so angry at you for shutting me out. I know you were hurting, but it's like you thought you had the monopoly on pain and as though your pain was somehow worse than ours."

"It wasn't that, Candice. I just could face you, any of you. The more I ran away from everything, the harder it became to reach out, and before I knew it, years had gone by."

"I don't want to waste any more time, I think we both know how precious it is," she points out, her frown settling into a milder expression.

"I am truly sorry for shutting you out. Now that I'm here, I don't know what I was thinking. Back then, it seemed like the only option.

"It was like we lost you both. You were my best friend." She sighs deeply as pain flashes in her eyes, and I wince knowing that it's me who put it there.

"You still are mine," I share with her.

"Marshall," I say, placing him on the floor beside me. "This is your Aunty Candice, baby. Say hi."

He stares at her awkwardly before burying his face shyly into my yellow sundress.

"Oh, you are not shy," I chastise him, playfully. "And who are these two lovely girls?" I ask, turning my attention to the two brunettes who are identical, aside from their curls. One has tight ringlets, while the other has loose waves that are slightly lighter than the other.

"These two bundles of love are your nieces. This is Annie..." She reaches over to squeeze Annie's little chubby hand as her husband balances her expertly on his hip. "And this here is Aimee," she says, jiggling the twin with the tighter curls on her knee and making her giggle.

"My nieces," I repeat, loving the sound of the words on my lips. She still thought of me as a sister, after all this time. It was over-whelming to see how happy she is, knowing the amount of pain losing her brother caused her. We were the only two people in the room who understood it, and we shared a look that acknowledged our under-standing.

But this was not a day to dwell on our losses, we had done enough grieving to last a lifetime. This was Sally's baby shower, a day for new beginnings and a time to make some new memories.

Poppy and Gabe join us, and I wrap an arm around Poppy. "And this, is my best friend, Poppy," I say.

Candice holds out a hand for her to shake, saying, "Well, aren't you just the sweetest little lady. I love that dress. You think you could get that in my size?" she asks, instantly putting Poppy at ease.

Sally bursts over in a frenzy of excitement, shouting at her husband, "Are you getting all of this, Greyson. Keep taking pictures!"

"Yes, boss." Greyson raises an eyebrow at Candice's husband with a look that says, don't-fuck-with-me, and the two men laugh together as he pulls out the camera and begins snapping shots of us all.

"What's happening?" Sally asks, squeezing onto the sofa next to me and looking to her best friend for answers. "I take it you girls know each other?"

"That's Evelyn," Candice explains, waiting for the penny to drop and sighing when it doesn't. "Marshall's Evelyn."

"You're Candice's brothers' girlfriend? Oh my god, I do remember you mentioning an Evie."

"Marshall was my husband," I clarify.

She stares between the three of us, her expression shifting from confusion to sheer delight.

"So, you are basically my best friends' sister, and my brother's girlfriend, at the same time? I can't believe this! You girls are going to send me into an early labour." She sighs, and we all giggle.

"It's crazy, Candice is my sister-in-law, and I don't know if we are supposed to be sharing this yet, but you might be my sister-in-law soon, too." I hold up my engagement ring for them to see.

"You're getting married." They both gasp in unison, and I nod happily, trying to gauge Candice's reaction.

"Family," Sally announces. We can all be one huge, crazy family."

"Family," Candice confirms, smiling at me, and a look passes between us that seals our sisterhood. A look is all we can manage, as none of us can clink beers or hug when our laps are full of children, but I wouldn't have it any other way.

Gabe

I'D BEEN WORRIED Evelyn would have no one to talk to, but I haven't seen her since we got here. Instead, she's fussing over Candice's twins, and I can't quite believe that she is best friends with Sally's best friend. It was all kinds of small world crazy, but the sight of my woman surrounded by love has my heart pounding so heavy in my chest it feels like it might burst.

"It's a D850," I say, manoeuvring Greyson's camera around to check the model. "You'd probably have to change the lens up if you wanted clearer shots, but it's a decent kit to start with."

"Thanks, Sally got it for me, she's obsessed with taking pictures, and she's put me in charge of taking the first shots when she has the baby. I just don't wanna fuck it up, you know?"

"I'll send you some lenses, I might even have some in my old equipment that may fit."

"You're into taking pictures?"

"I used to be a pap." I shrug.

"Jesus, don't say the P word around Blake, he'll have his size tens up your ass and kicking you out before you realise."

I glance over at his friend, who's rubbing his nose against the tiny nose of his baby daughter's nose and making her giggle uncontrollably, and arch an eyebrow at Greyson.

"Yeah, he might look like a pussy cat, but he's ex-army. He's tough as they come, not that you'd think of it when his Mrs. is in the room."

"Why would he be so bothered that I'm a…"

He cuts me off, looking slightly pissed that I'm about the say the word again. "Blake runs Laine Corporations now, just took over from his dad. His only sanctuary from the paps," he mouths the last word, avoiding saying out loud, "is living in The Cotswolds. It's a far cry from London, and he likes it that way."

"I knew he looked familiar," I say, looking back over at the guy in a whole new light. Behind his relaxed designer polo shirt was the playboy I used to chase around town with his new bit of skirt. Funny, how things work out. I would never have recognised him, and he won't have a clue who I am, yet we'd probably crossed paths a dozen times in the city.

"Beer?" Greyson asks, cracking open a bottle of bud and handing it over to me.

"Cheers," I reply, taking it from him and tilting it towards his before sipping back the cool drink.

"Looks like the chicks are heading outside, let's go and rescue Blake." He smirks. I follow him out onto the lawn where an older guy is flipping burgers over on a burning barbecue.

There're bubble guns for the kids, and I see that Poppy has taken over babysitting duties, showing Marshall how to work it and blowing bubbles over the twins who are clapping and laughing in their buggy. Evelyn catches my eye as soon as I step out onto the patio, waving at me to come over, and I walk over to where they have blankets laid out on the lawn.

"You've come at a good time," Candice comments as I reach them.

"Candy is getting married," Evelyn explains, she was just telling me that she still hasn't booked a photographer."

"Um, maybe I should leave you, girls, to talk weddings," I say, getting ready to stand and head back over to where Greyson and Blake are casually sipping their beers.

"I was wondering whether you could do it, Gabe?" Candice asks. "I really don't want it to turn into a media circus, and I'm hoping everyone there is family or a close friend. I want to keep it as intimate as possible."

I nearly spit my fucking beer out at the idea. "You want me to shoot your wedding? Where are you getting married? You haven't even seen my work," I challenge.

"The Dorchester." She shrugs.

"The Dorchester?" I repeat in shock. "You want a quiet, intimate affair at the most prestigious hotel in London?"

"Yeah. Do you think you can do it? I have everything else sorted, it's really only the photographer I need," she pouts.

"I haven't taken any photos in years, you'll need a professional for a wedding at The Dorchester."

"Evie said you are a professional?" she fires back.

"How about you meet me there next week? Evie, Sally, are you up for a trip to London, girls? I'll get Blake to sort us a limo so we can travel together. I have been meaning to go and sample the menu, it would be so much more fun if we could go together."

"It has been ages since we had a girl's day." Sally sighs, smoothing a palm over her neat baby bump.

"Oh my god, Evie, you can be my other bridesmaid. This is perfect!" Her blue eyes widen as the idea dawns on her before she continues, excitement bursting out of her like fireworks. "Both my best friends at my side on my wedding day. Oh, this has made my whole year. Evie, you've no idea how much I missed you."

"I've missed you too," my girl replies.

They all turn to me, three pairs of lashes fluttering in my direction. Glancing around, I see Greyson and Blake still swigging back their beers without a care in the world. They lift them in the air, gesturing to me, and I look back to see the girls all still staring at me, waiting for an answer.

"Okay, I'll come with you and take some test shots, that is all I'm promising," I say, jumping up and making my escape before I'm roped into any more girly chat.

"Nice one for that," I joke with the lads as they get to work organising the food for everyone.

"What, you thought we'd come over and spend some quality time together?" Greyson jokes. "Don't forget Sally and Candice have known each other for years. We've served our time, figured you could take some girl talk for the team," he adds.

"I'll remember that," I warn, grabbing the sauces from the side and joining in arranging the buffet.

CHAPTER 20

Evelyn

Organising three get-well-soon bouquets, I try to catch Tanya up to speed.

"Okay, I think I got it. So, Sally is Gabe's sister, who's married to Greyson. Greyson served in the army with Blake who is Candice's husband?"

"Exactly, see, you do listen when you need to."

"So, Sally will be your sister-in-law, once you marry Gabe, and Candice still wants to be your sister-in-law too?"

"Basically, yeah."

"This is like something from one of those small-town rom coms you used to make me watch," she teases.

"I know, it was surreal for me, too. I just stepped out of the car, and there everyone was. Candy has twin girls now, as well. They are the cutest thing I've ever seen."

"Awww, do they look like her?"

"A little, they've got her husband's dark hair but her and Marshall's blue eyes."

"What's she like with them?"

"She just dotes on them, and Jenson. She's really taken to being a mum."

"I can picture her like that. We will have to all go out for drinks, sounds like I've missed way too much," Tanya announces.

"Yeah, we can definitely plan something, cocktails maybe? I could invite Sally too. I think you'll like her; she reminds me of you a little bit. I'll ask her when I see them next week. We're going to see Candice's wedding venue together. She's asked me to be her bridesmaid."

"That's sweet of her, oh my god, you just reminded me…. Speaking of weddings," she says, pulling out her huge book of mood boards from under the counter. "We've got that London wedding coming up, and I need to go through the details with you. The brides wedding planner phoned again this morning, she said she trusts us to do what-ever we want. God, I hate it when they say that." She rolls her eyes and throws the book open onto the countertop, looking exasperated.

"Why?" I chuckle.

"It just leaves the choices so open. It's like, 'I don't know what is perfect for my wedding, but I expect you to know.' So much pressure." She grimaces.

"We will be fine, it's just a wedding, right? Like any other wedding you've done. You are so much more talented than you think, Tan, just go with what feels right."

A slow smile spreads across her lips. "I was hoping you would say that." She flashes me with a secretive grin. "Because, I have a few ideas I would like to try. It's risky, but I think the risk will pay off."

"See, you've got this," I encourage her.

"*We've* got this," she argues. "I'm going to need your help if I want to pull this off. It's a pastel, rainbow theme, like this." She begins pulling flowers from the buckets and gathering them together excit-edly, to give me an idea of what she's aiming for.

"When's the wedding?" I ask.

"October 1st, so it's going to be cool, and we need to bear that in mind, but The Dorchester is really accommodating. They have a side room where we can store everything, and they've said they can adjust the heat for us in there, if we need them to."

Much to Tanya's confusion, I begin laughing. "The wedding is at The Dorchester?"

"Yeah," she snaps, annoyed at my reaction.

"On the first of October?"

"What, you think I'm punching above my weight offering to do it. The bride requested **us, re**member. She saw my work at a bridal fair and specifically asked me to do it, I know it's not what we'd usua…"

"It's Candice's wedding," I explain. The Dorchester wouldn't double book a wedding date, and she definitely said October first was her date."

"Oh my god." Tanya's eyes widen. She pulls up her emails on her phone, checking for any clues she had missed.

"I can't believe it, everything was arranged through her wedding planner, I would never have known."

"I'll help as much as I can, but you might need to get an assistant, as I'm her bridesmaid, don't forget. I won't be able to help much on that day."

"Shit," Tanya exclaims, I never even thought about that. I just can't believe we finally get a big break, and it's Candice who has given it to us."

"We will have to call her and let her know, she's not going to believe it. I think she'll love your ideas, though, she loves pastel colours. She likes things simple and understated but a little quirky at the same time, so the rainbow theme will be perfect."

"Do you know what her budget is?" Tanya asks, interestedly.

"No idea." I shrug.

"She doesn't have one. No fucking budget, can you imagine getting married and not setting a budget?"

Tanya's excited tone makes me smile, I hadn't even thought about

Candice being rich now, but there was no denying she was. It hadn't changed her at all, but the dress she was wearing at Sally's baby shower was obviously expensive, and I noticed her simple but classy diamond earrings too.

"I guess my sister is a badass." I giggle.

"Don't be going all fancy on me with these new sisters you have," she warns.

"Candice isn't exactly new, and anyway, are you saying I'm not fancy, Tanya?" I joke, pretending to be shocked.

"Well, you do live on a farm now. That's pretty fancy, Evie."

"I guess, but Maple Valley isn't really like that. It just feels like home to me."

"What are you going to do with your house?" she asks, as we continue flipping through her mood board pages for inspiration.

"I have been thinking about selling, but I don't think I can do it. I like the thought of keeping it for Marshall, in case he's ever struggling and in need of his own place. I want him to always have somewhere to call home. I have played with the idea of renting it out, that way seems like the best of both worlds.

"That's a good idea, that way you can build up some savings and still have the house for when Marshall is older."

"I figure he can decide what to do with it then."

"What about you, Tanya, everyone's getting their happy endings, when is yours coming?"

"Well, if you asked me last week I would have said never." She sighs. "But, I did meet up with the lawyer again last Saturday. It was only drinks, but...." She smiles at me with a look in her eye that screams mischief.

"Oh my god, look at you! You like him."

"Maybe just a little. Like I said, it was just drinks."

"And when are you 'just drinking' again?" I ask.

"Friday night," she replies, throwing her hair over her shoulder all sexy like.

"I've got to dash, Gabe's planned something for tonight, but I want to know more tomorrow. I want details!" I shout from the kitchen, hanging up my pinafore and grabbing my bag.

She's quiet as I pass back through the shop, and I call out to her as I open the door, "Tomorrow."

I drive home thinking about Gabe's surprise and what it might be. I love the way he is always surprising me and keeping me guessing. I never know what is coming next with him, and that's the best part. His commitment to filling my days with cute gestures to show me how much he loves me gives me so much to look forward to. Before Gabe, all of my happy moments, aside from Marshall, were memories. Now I can see that there are still so many fun moments ahead of us, and it fills my heart with hope.

Gabe.

GROWING impatient I check my watch again and glance out of the kitchen window, all three of them should be here soon, and I can hardly wait to see their faces when I show them the surprise I have planned. I messed up the proposal, but hopefully tonight will make up for it.

Seeing Evelyn's car pull to a stop, I watch her get out. She's saying something to Poppy, which makes them both laugh as she helps Marshall jump to the ground. She's dressed in her usual sports leggings and hoodie but still manages to look hot as fuck as she grabs the kids' stuff, and they walk inside.

"You're late, guys, come on." I hurry them along. "Kids, go and grab your wellies, there's someone very special coming to see you."

"Is it Grandad?"

"No, what makes you say that," I ask my daughter, mouthing, "hi," to Evelyn as she tidies away the kids' bags.

"I heard you on the phone," Poppy shrugs.

"Well, Grandad might be coming over later, but that's not the surprise. Hurry and change your shoes, so I can show you."

"What's got you so excited?" Evelyn asks as the kids rummage around the shoe box to find their wellies and put them on.

"You'll see." I smile, loving the curiosity in her expression.

"It's nothing like the zipline, is it?" she asks, her eyes widening in terror, making me chuckle.

"No, it's nothing like that. Okay, kids, you ready?"

"They both run to the kitchen door, desperate to reveal the surprise."

"Is it a treehouse?" Marshall asks.

"Nope. No more guesses, you'll see soon enough."

I lead them around to the back of the house where I've been working on building the stables for the last few weeks, every time Evelyn has been at work.

All of their jaws drop to the floor on sight of the completed stables with all four ponies tacked up outside and ready to ride.

Poppy breaks down into tears and runs over to me, throwing her arms around me. "Dad, are these ours, like really ours?"

"They sure are. There's one for each of us, so we can ride together. It's just like I promised you, remember?"

"I remember, but I didn't think it would come true. They are just so perfect, I love them all."

"Ponies!" Marshall shouts, staring up at them in awe.

"Gabe, how did you… When did you?"

"I have been planning it for a while. When we rode together at the equestrian centre, I saw how much you enjoyed it and stopped by the next day to get some advice from the owner. It started as one small pony and then kind of escalated."

"You don't say." She grins at me. "And the stables, you built all this?"

"I did. I'm quite the cowboy now, you know? So, who's up for coming for a ride with me?"

"ME!" everyone shouts in giddy unison, and I grab the helmets I bought, helping the kids put theirs on.

"Marshall, you'll ride this lucky fella," I say, patting the side of the smallest of the ponies.

"Are you sure this is safe, he's still so little."

"I'll walk with him, until you find your feet, Marshall. Do you think you can ride this one like a big boy?" I ask. He nods, and I lift him on. Glancing back, I see Poppy stroking over the mane of the white pony I chose especially for her. When she was little, she used to dream about living on a farm one day, and the dream always included a white pony. She looks completely spellbound by the reality of her dream coming true.

"Are you going to ride that thing, or just stand there stroking it?" I ask, lightening the mood.

"Ride it." She grins through gappy teeth, and I grin back at her, knowing how happy she is.

Holding the rein of Marshall's pony, we set off at a slow pace, across the fields. I stay by Marshall's side to stop him from wobbling off, and Evie rides side by side with Pops. No one speaks at first, everyone silently concentrating on what they are doing. Aside from Marshall, who keeps yelling giddy up, I swear the kids an adrenaline junkie.

After a few minutes, everyone relaxes into the slow rhythm of the horse's movements, and we laugh at some of the name suggestions Marshall has for the horses. Poppy already has hers picked out, of course. She's dreamt of owning a horse called 'Sparkle' since forever.

We ride up towards the tree house where the real surprise is waiting.

"Surprise!" everyone shouts from the marquee I set up earlier.

"Gabe!" Evelyn yells accusingly, her eyes reading the huge 'Happy Engagement' poster in front of us.

"We couldn't get engaged without celebrating." I shrug, lifting Marshall down from his pony, so he can run to his mum's side.

"Grandad!" Poppy calls out to my dad in excitement. "I knew you were coming over, I just knew it."

"Am I dreaming?" he asks, rubbing his eyes and taking a second look at Poppy, who sits tall and beams at him.

"Nope, I really have my own pony, Grandad. What do you think?"

"Best looking pony I've ever seen." Dad smiles, first at Poppy, then at me.

"Dad, this is Evelyn."

Evelyn climbs down from her pony and offers my dad a hand-shake, which he ignores, pulling her in for a tight Hudson hug.

"It's so good to meet you."

"Finally get to see where my lad gets his good looks from, hey?" I roll my eyes, I thought he would have gotten bored of trying to embarrass me after thirty-five years. Apparently not.

"And his charm too." Evelyn giggles, looking around to see everyone who's here. I take the horses and tie them around a tree, out of the way for a while. Poppy follows Sparkle closely, telling my dad every detail about her plans with him over the weekend.

Marshall takes up his usual position on Evelyn's hip, and I wave over to the barbecue that Greyson and Blake are stood sharing a beer at. It's simple hot dogs and beers with a huge cake to keep the kids happy, but the look on Evelyn's face tells me she's happy.

I watch her chat with Candice and Tanya, she looks relaxed and carefree. It suits her.

"This is such a great party, Gabe. I'm so glad you invited us," Sally says, looking up at me.

"It wouldn't have been the same without you, sis." I smile, and she squeezes my arm. "I love that we are part of each other's life now. I never want to miss a single thing. You have to invite me to everything, okay?"

"Only if you do the same."

Stepping in closer and lowering her voice, she says quietly, "You didn't miss out, you know, Gabe. On Mum, I mean. You have done so well for yourself, what you have here is really special. I know this might sound weird because we only just found each other, and I'm younger than you, but I'm really proud of you."

"Thanks, it doesn't sound weird at all. I feel exactly the same, Greyson seems like a great guy, and you have your baby on the way.

Good to see we're representing team normal and not passing a shit ton of issues into the next generation."

"Cheers to that and to us living our best life." She smiles, tipping her glass of fruit juice towards my bottle of Bud.

"Cheers." I chink my bottle against hers, and we both take a swig of our drinks.

CHAPTER 21

Evelyn

*F*or the next couple of months, we spend as much time together as we can, but it's not easy. Betty's is crazily busy, and I work longer hours that I mean to, but it's hard to say no when your best friend is your boss. The warmer weather brings strawberries by the bucket load, and Gabe works his ass off to get the business off the ground. The toilets finally arrive, and the kids design some flyers, that we post all over the village.

It doesn't take long for word to spread, and the farm is filled with strawberry pickers most days. Poppy adopts a cat, which is pregnant, so it ends up being four cats, and Marshall spends most of his time chasing after the kittens and trying to catch them.

Angela keeps to her word and sees Poppy most weekends. She still spends a silly amount of money on items that are far beyond things she needs or should have at her age, but she takes it all in her stride and sticks most of them under her bed for safe keeping.

There's still tension when she comes to collect her, but Gabe does his best to bite his tongue, for Poppy's sake.

With all the best intentions in the world it's been almost impossible to coordinate a time when Sally, Candice, her friend, Rainy and I are all free at the same time. So, it feels good to all be standing in the same room, and I take a long sip of my glass of bubbles, savouring the moment.

"Are you sure about the hair?" Candice asks me for what must be at least the tenth time.

"Candice, you look…"

"Like a fucking goddess," Sally shrieks on sight of Candy all dressed in white.

"Literally," Rainy beams.

"Your hair is perfect, everything is perfect, you are the perfect bride," I finish, fixing the bow on her backless dress.

"Blake is going to freak out, I never thought I would be able to wear lace again."

"Is it uncomfortable anywhere?" I ask, worrying it might be digging in to her scars.

"Nope, with the under layer, it feels gorgeous, I can't believe I'm really doing this.

"Are you ready to see yourself?" I ask, smoothing down the pale blue chiffon of my floor length gown.

"Ready as I'll ever be."

"One… Two… Three!" Sally and I shout, and I spin her around on three to face herself in the huge ornate mirror of The Dorchester Hotel penthouse suite.

I watch her draw a sharp intake of breath on sight of herself in the flowy, lace gown. Tears prick her eyes, and Sally and I also tear up at her next words.

"I'm beautiful."

"Of course, you are," Sally reassures her. "You're a total babe. I told you you'd make a badass bride." She shrugs, pretending to be nonchalant but dabbing under her eyes so as not to ruin her makeup.

"One more thing," I say, grabbing the pastel bouquet full of baby blue peonies. "Your something blue."

"It's stunning, thank you so much, Evie." Breathing out slowly, she regains composure. "Okay." She smiles. "I can do this."

"Of course you can," Rainy reassures her. "You were born to be Blake's wife, Candy. He's a lucky man."

"If I can pull off this pale blue dress, then you can go out there and marry him," Sally exclaims.

"Do you hate it?" Candice asks, sounding worried.

"Not now that I've added my own little twist," Sally smirks, sticking out her foot to reveal a pair of leopard print stilettos.

"Sally," we both cry out in panic.

"Kidding, just kidding." She laughs, kicking them off and replacing them with the same matching suede court shoes as the ones that I'm wearing.

"Not funny." Candice laughs waving her bouquet in Rainy's direction.

"He's a lucky guy," I say, as Joan and Stuart appear with the kids. Marshall is dressed in a smart pale blue sailor suit with his blonde locks in a neat comb-over that looks too old for him in the cutest way. Poppy is dressed in a similar blue dress to mine and has been given the job of flower girl, which I thought was really sweet of Candice to include her.

The twins steal the show and look like two blue fairies from the front of a Christmas card. Their tutu-style dresses are full of blue flower petals with their curls clipped to one side, and Candice begins to tear up again.

The ceremony is lavish, and the flowers look so good my heart could burst with pride for Tanya. The walls are covered in flowers and fairy lights, and there's pastel rainbows framing every mirror in the lavish room. There are diamond chandeliers, specially laid pastel blue carpets, white chairs with blue sashes, every single detail has been planned to perfection. It was easy to see there was no expense spared for their wedding, but aside from the body guards manning the doors, there was no one in the room who wasn't one of Candice's family or friends. I have no idea how she's pulled it off, but her dream of a small, intimate wedding was fulfilled.

As we make our way up the aisle, there is barely a dry eye in the room as everyone glimpse**s** Candice in her wedding dress. Blake doesn't take his eyes off her, and as we walk towards him, it feels like they are the only two people in the room. I take my seat next to Gabe, with Poppy and Marshall at our side, and watch on as my sister marries the man of her dreams. It takes me back to my own wedding, and I wish with all my heart that Marshall was here to see Candice say her vows. I feel like I'm watching for the both of us, and it makes me happy and sad all at the same time.

After the service, the room is transformed into a champagne reception, and the best man's speech is announced.

"Ladies and gentleman, thank you for being here today to witness this grand event. I'm not talking about the wedding of course, I'm talking about Blake, finally admitting that I'm the best man."

I've known this guy since we were skinny, spotty teenagers. Oh wait, one of us still looks like that." Blake throws Greyson a death stare, and we all laugh.

"But seriously, we've known each other for a long time, and although I'd never usually get all mushy, I do want to say that he's like a brother to me. He's got me through some dark times, and I've saved his ass more times than I can count. I better say he's saved mine too, or he'll start kicking it after this speech is done.

When he met Candice, I knew they were made for each other. She doesn't take any nonsense. I learnt that back when I made a pass at her on a plane out to South Sudan," he jokes. "On a more serious note, I'm sure we all know there's someone who isn't here today."

My heart skips a beat as I realise who he's referring to. "So, I'd like to give a special mention to Candice's brother, as without him, she would never have gotten her hands dirty volunteering in South Sudan, and she would never have fallen for my best mate." I swallow down the thick lump in my throat. Today was a day for celebration, Marshall wouldn't have wanted anything less than happiness for his little sister.

Greyson continues, "So, cheers to Marshall, and cheers to this amazing woman. I know you are all looking forward to being a part of their lives for many years to come, so please, can you all raise your glasses to Mr. and Mrs. Laine, the bride and groom."

"The bride and groom," the room repeats, holding their glasses in the air.

The rest of the night is spent dancing to live music, and the grandparents take the little ones upstairs early so that we can continue to celebrate until the early hours of the morning. Gabe and I make the most of the opportunity, drinking a little too much champagne and booty dancing like no one is watching.

When he finally takes me to bed, it's not to sleep. It's to cover me in those sweet, strawberry kisses that I've come to adore so much. His lips sending a direct message to my centre every time he lands one on me.

"Gabe," I moan out as he licks and sucks all the way along my inner thigh. His contact is slow, and deliberated, not because he isn't desperate to devour me, but because he is more interested in pushing my boundaries. He relishes in the torturous pleasure of making me wait until I can barely breathe and every fibre of my being is pleading for him to make love to me. When his tongue finally makes contact with my centre, it's hot and relentless, lashing over my most sensitive spot over and over again but always taking his delectable mouth away right before the pinnacle moment.

He lowers his focus, licking measured, calculated licks all the way through my parting and using his fingers to work me back up into a panting frenzied mess. Only when I beg for him to make me his own, does he give in and let me have all of him. Every bewitching inch.

* * *

IN THE MORNING, everyone has breakfast together before waving Blake and Candice to send them off on their mini honeymoon. Candice thinks they are staying in London for the night, but it's our best kept secret that Blake is flying her to Paris in the company helicopter.

Gabe and I make the most of our night in London by taking the kids to see all the tourist hot spots. We drink afternoon tea in Harrods, and Poppy spends her birthday money on an overpriced sparkly collar for her adopted cat. Marshall poses next to the guards at Buckingham Palace, and we feed the pigeons at Trafalgar Square. By the time we are back at home, everyone is exhausted, and on Monday morning, Maple Valley is full of moody faces. I have to prac-tically drag Poppy and Marshall out of bed, and even Gabe skips his usual morning workout.

Glancing in the rear-view mirror as we set off on the school run, I can't help laughing to myself.

"You will both be home again later, and I'm sure you'll enjoy it when you get there," I reassure them, trying to coax them out of their sulky disposition.

After dropping them off, I stop by the church yard on the way to work. It's a beautiful morning, with the colours on the leaves all changing and the air so crisp and fresh. There's a low autumn sun, but it's bitter cold, and I pull the collar of my coat up a bit, to try and keep warm.

There's no one around, which is always the case early in the morn-ing, it's when I like to visit. It's quiet and calm, and by the time I've reached our place I've usually always gathered my thoughts. I had hoped that would be the case today, but as I pace the winding paths, my thoughts whirl around my head so fast that I can't keep up with them. We'd been so careful, there was only the one time that we hadn't used protection, but then, I guess, all it takes is one time. I have no idea how Gabe's going to take it, that's why I've come here, to get my own head around things first.

I stand and stare at our tree, willing it to give me answers or some sort of sign, but there's nothing. I don't feel him around me anymore, and it pisses me off. Annoyed, I sit on the bench nearby and try to figure out how I feel about having a baby. Gabe's baby. One minute I'm happy, then I'm overwhelmed, then I'm all emotional, it's just a lot to take in. Glancing down at my tan Chelsea boots, I notice a robin dancing in my path. I hadn't seen it land, and it only stayed for a few seconds before flying away again, but somehow it made me feel better. I'm not sure if I believe in things like signs, but seeing the robin comforts me, and I leave the graveyard ready for another new chapter to begin.

They say when one door closes another one opens, but for me, it hadn't been that easy. My door was not ready to be opened. After losing Marshall I'd slammed the door shut, locked it up and planned never to open it again. Gabe had been patient, he hadn't expected anything from me, and he'd allowed me to keep my broken heart bolted up safe until, piece by piece, it had begun to mend. I don't know when or how it became whole again, but I do know that I'm alive. Gabe bought me back to life. Back to myself, and I intend to live and be present in every single moment with the man I love because I know just how precious the gift of life truly is.

The End

EPILOGUE

Eight months later.

"What are we going to call her, Mummy?" Marshall asks, peeking inside the rocking crib and staring at our baby girl for the first time.

"I'm not sure, what would you like to call her?" I reply.

"I'm just so happy that she's a girl." Poppy sighs dreamily, reaching over and placing a hand on her tummy.

"She's a very lucky little girl to have you two looking after her."

"How about Daisy?"

"What made you think of that, Poppy?"

"Well, when I was riding Sparkle the other day, Dad took me up to the lake, and it was covered in Daisies. They were everywhere, and it looked so pretty. I think she looks as pretty as a Daisy."

"Daisy," Marshall says out loud, as though he is toying with the idea.

"I like it," Gabe chips in.

"Okay, all in favour of Daisy, raise your hand."

All three of them do, and I smile down at my daughter and gently stroke her rosy cheek. "Daisy you are then," I say, lifting her out of the crib and into my arms. She wriggles around and settles in to a cosy position between my arm and chest, and I stare down in awe of her. She has a full head of Gabe's dark curls, and she has his full lips, too, with the same cute button nose that Marshall and I have. She is perfection wrapped in a soft pink blanket, and I couldn't be anymore besotted with her than I am.

It was so different this time around, having someone to share it with, and we have so much to look forward to. Gabe has been amazing through the entire pregnancy, which took him completely by surprise. I'd caught him off guard with the news one day when he'd been out working on the farm. He'd came home filthy, tired and sweaty, to find the kids wearing matching T-shirts. Poppy's said, 'I'm going to be a big sister, and Marshall's had the same message except replaced with the word 'brother.'

His jaw had almost dropped to the floor when he saw them, and I'd positioned myself perfectly to catch it all on camera, including a selfie of us kissing straight afterwards. He'd treated me like a princess for the entire nine months, even learning massage techniques to ease my lower back pain in the last couple of weeks. At first it was a little over-whelming, and I had to adjust to letting someone help and not doing everything on my own, but a few weeks in, and we found our way. We included Poppy and Marshall in everything that we could do, to ensure they were part of this new adventure. I think coming with us to the scans helped them to understand what was happening a lot more and each of them had drawn pictures of what they think the baby will look like.

"Are you sure it's not too much having everyone over? I can always call and cancel, I'm sure they won't mind waiting a couple of days."

"It's already been more than a couple of days," I reply in frustra-tion. The emergency C Section had taken its toll on me and Daisy. Since she arrived, everything has been such a whirlwind, which is why we are only just getting around to the fun things, like naming her.

"Well, if you start to get tired, I'm sending everyone home, and that's, that," he warns.

"I feel fine, I can't wait for everyone to meet her, especially now that she has her name."

"Drink this and put your feet up for a bit, I'll take the kids out to run off some steam before everyone gets here."

"Yes, boss," I tease, taking the mug of tea from him and rolling my eyes, even though I love the idea of a few minutes peace before the chaos begins.

I sigh and let my body relax into the sofa once they've gone. The painkillers are helping, but I've quickly learnt that there's no comfortable position after a C section. It's more trying to divert your thoughts away from the pain, and what better way to do that, than cuddles with your new daughter.

"Daisy," I whisper her name out loud, and she looks up at me with wide eyes through tiny dark lashes. She's like a doll and is easily one of the best things to ever happen to me.

I eventually bring myself to part with her and place her back into her crib, tucking her in neatly and rocking her slightly. It doesn't seem like two minutes before I'm jolted from my semi nap by the shrieking of Poppy and the loud shushes from Gabe, following closely behind her. Noticing that Daisy has dozed off, I join in with the shushing.

"Sorry," she whispers. "It's just, you're not going to believe this."

"What is it, come and tell me," I reply, gesturing for her to come closer so she can tell me what's got her so worked up.

"It's Fluffy!" she whispers in the loudest whisper possible, and I try not to laugh, so I don't pull any of my stitches. "She came back! Dad said we could take the horses up to the lake to pick some daisies for the party, and she was just right there. She noticed me straight away. She's huge now," she gushes.

"That's amazing," I say quietly.

"Shhh, don't wake Daisy up," Marshall scolds me, looking annoyed.

"I won't, we can talk when Daisy is sleeping, we just can't shout."

"Is it 'cos we might scare her?" he asks with fear in his eyes.

"A little bit, yes. But she will get used to noise as she gets older, and then she can shout along with you."

I turn my attention back to Poppy. "I knew she would come back, remember what I told you?"

"No." She looks confused.

"I said, those that are loved always find their way home," I remind her.

Gabe smiles at the three of us, and the raw emotion of us all being together as a family is apparent in his soft expression.

The doorbell goes off right before Sally lets herself in and bursts through it, closely followed by Greyson who is carrying my nephew, Noah, in his arms. His long dirty blonde locks make him look so much like his dad, but there is no denying he has Sally's dark chocolate eyes.

"Oh, my goodness, look at you. No one looks that good after giving birth, that's just not fair," Sally exclaims as she rushes over to hug me but realises she can't. Well, not properly, anyway. Her eyes light up on sight of Daisy, who has woken up at the sound of our visitors. "Can I pick her up?"

"Of course, you can. You don't have to ask, you're her aunty," I remind her.

Sally scoops her up, takes one look at her and glances towards Greyson, whose eyes widen upon reading her thoughts.

"Oh no, not happening," he warns her.

"I'm not saying right now, but look at this face," she says, wandering towards him to introduce him to Daisy.

Throwing her best puppy eyes at him, she manages to squeeze a "we'll see," out of him that has everybody laughing. I wince at the pain in my stomach as it tenses up and warn them all not to be so funny, as it's not fair to me.

Poppy shows the kids to the table where Gabe has set some crafts up for them and hands Noah one of her toy elephants from bath time to play with. She's so good with other kids that I'm almost certain she'll be a teacher one day.

Candice and Blake arrive soon after with Annie and Aimee dressed in matching pink jog suits. If it wasn't for their hair, no one would be able to tell them apart, and we spend the whole afternoon together. Jenson is his usual excitable self, running around the place and getting as many of the kids toys out as possible, without ever really playing with any of them. He's at that age where he is into every single thing and more, running around like a little torpedo, which Blake finds hilarious and Candice not so hilarious.

Tanya saves the day by arriving with a huge box of cupcakes for everyone to share, and I gush over the ridiculously oversized bouquet of blue flowers she's designed for me.

"They're gorgeous! Thank you so much." I squeeze her hand.

"You look amazing, tired but amazing. How are things?"

"A little crazy, but I've never been happier," I answer honestly. "How are things at Betty's?" I ask, wondering how she's been getting on without me.

"Manic. I'm coping, but I've got three potential new girls lined up to interview next week. After Candice's wedding, the calls haven't stopped coming in, and… Gabe, come here a sec, you should probably hear this," she says, waving a hand at him to come over.

"Hear what?"

"I was just saying to Evie that since Candice's wedding, the calls have been coming in non-stop from some huge clients, who we would never have dreamt of working with before. It's not just the flowers they want, Gabe, it's the photos. People are crazy for them, and they're willing to pay big money. Let me know when things settle down at home and you're ready to get to work because I'm not takin' no for an answer," she gushes, taking us both by surprise.

He agrees to think about it, but I can tell by the look in his eyes and the way he spends the rest of the afternoon taking snaps of everybody that he has found his passion for photography again.

"I can't believe it, Tanya, I'm so happy for you. You're finally getting the recognition you deserve."

"Oh, I'm getting recognition all right." She winks at me playfully, and I grin.

"The lawyer?"

"The lawyer needs his own flower arrangement design when you're back on your feet."

I can't help giggling even though the pain is excruciating, and Gabe appears by my side with Daisy in his arms. "She's getting niggly, is she due a feed?"

"She will be soon," I confirm, glancing at the time.

Gabe politely lets everybody know that it's time for them to go, we only have a few hours to rest before our parents arrive.

* * *

MY PARENTS ARE ALREADY in love with Daisy, and I'm so relieved they like the name we have chosen for her. They spend most of the time letting Marshall and Poppy show them around the stables, as it's the first time Gabe's dad has seen Daisy, so they let him have some quiet time to get to know her.

When they return, Mum heats a cottage pie that she's cooked for everyone, and even though I'm not hungry, I'm grateful for the gesture. At least until she starts going on and on about Gabe and I having a Greek wedding at the Island Restaurant. It had been a sore point ever since Dad found out about me being pregnant. He has made it more than clear that he's not happy about me having a baby out of wedlock. But I've learnt my lesson, and I'm doing things my own way, at my own pace. He seems to respect my wishes a little bit more this time around. Maybe we are both learning something.

* * *

HAVING everyone here has been lovely, but I'm not going to lie, so was having them all go home again and leave us to be just us. Gabe settles Marshall and Poppy, leaving me to rest with Daisy in the crib next to me. By the time he comes back downstairs to us, he looks as shattered as I feel.

"You okay, baby?" he asks, his voice tired but full of concern.

"I'm more than okay, Gabe," I answer, dreamily.

"Tell me what you see?" he asks, taking me by surprise with his familiar question.

"I see my world," I reply, and his lips curl into one of his small, secret smiles, the type that makes him look ultra-kissable and ultra-mine.

That night before getting into bed, I close the curtains. Not because I don't want to see the stars, but because I don't need to. I know Marshall is always with me, I carry him in my heart and always will. The same heart that is completely filled with love for Gabe. That's the thing with hearts, if there's love there to begin with, then it doesn't matter how many times they are broken, they'll always find a way to become whole again.

The End.

ACKNOWLEDGMENTS

First and foremost, thank you to my husband for always encouraging me to follow my dreams and be the best version of myself I can be. You are my happy ever after and I love you. Always. Thanks to my daughters who are the loves of my life and my reason for everything.

Huge love to my kindred spirit, Tasha for being my best friend and ride or die, always.

Pam Gonzales! Without you there would be no books. Your indie author tool box organises my creative chaos into something that resembles a real-life author and I appreciate it more than you could ever know. I can't wait to see where this journey takes us, to hug you in real life and to be friends for life. Love you!

Angela and Karen, my official street team, this one's for you babes! My biggest cheerleaders and dear friends, I am so lucky to have found you and appreciate everything you do. From listening to me moan and rant, talking me off the ledge when I feel like giving up on my stories and putting life on hold to read anything I send you. You girls are the best and I love you lots.

To my gorgeous Hannah's Honey's, you babes are the best bunch of girls, I could ever wish to have by my side throughout my writing adventures. I love getting to know you on a personal level and without you there would be no Hot Hero's. You all inspire me to keep writing, keep reading and keep believing in love by sharing glimpses of your real-life stories with me.

Shout out to my book babes for life and RtM ladies for keeping me sane and smiling come rain or shine, I know that I can weather the storm with you boss babes at my side.

LJ Evans, you sprinkle your magic over all of my books with your beta reading skills and I love you for always keeping it real and for being my friend.

Claire Westbrook, thank you for letting everyone know my books exist! You always share everything I post and I am super thankful for all your support in spreading the word about my little corner of the book world.

Mostly I want to thank YOU for reading my book and taking a chance on a new author. It means the world to me and every time you leave a review or reach out to share your thoughts on my stories, I cry. Happy tears. This is my dream and by reading my book, you are helping to make it come true. Here's to sharing many more stories together, love and kisses xoxo

BEFORE YOU GO

If you enjoyed this story, I'd love you to leave an honest review. Reviews are what keep indie authors like me going and help other reader's decide whether or not to take a chance on my words. Even a few words would be hugely appreciated xoxo

STAY IN TOUCH

I love nothing more than hearing from you, so please do keep in touch? The best way to keep up to date with all things Hannah Blake is to sign up for my newsletter, **Hannah's Hello.** I promise to send teasers, sneak peeks and cover reveals little enough not to annoy you but often enough that you'll be in the know! Also, when you sign up, you'll receive a **FREE** romance read as a welcome treat.

Hannah's Hello Sign Up

Website

Facebook Reader Group

Facebook

Bookbub

Goodreads

Instagram

Tiktok

Twitter

Pinterest

BOOKS BY HANNAH

Hot Hero Series
Loving A Hero
Healing A Hero
Losing A Hero
Series Box Set

Cockpit Series
Cockpit Series (Series Prequel)
Take Me Away
Take Me Anywhere
Take Me Completely
Take Me Now
Take Me Forever
Take Me Home

Lani Bay Series
Innocent Hearts (Series Prequel)
Hopeful Hearts

ABOUT THE AUTHOR

Hannah Blake writes sexy and sweet contemporary romance with emotionally compelling characters that stay with you long after you turn the last page. Readers adore Hannah's fun, heart-warming, and deliciously sexy, Cockpit Series where her Parker brother's will fly you around the world in a whirlwind of adventure while they learn that sometimes you have to take a chance and choose heart over head.

Hannah Blake's emotional journeys always celebrate flaws and imperfections. Her books are perfect beach reads for contemporary romance lovers who enjoy reading about fiercely loyal every day hero's and smart, sassy heroines with complex and relatable issues.

Printed in Great Britain
by Amazon

26389004R00145